Books by B. V. Larson:

STAR FORCE SERIES
Swarm
Extinction
Rebellion

IMPERIUM SERIES
Mech
Mech 2

HAVEN SERIES
Amber Magic
Sky Magic
Shadow Magic
Dragon Magic
Blood Magic
Death Magic

Other Books by B. V. Larson
Velocity
Shifting

Visit BVLarson.com for more information.

ISBN-13: 978-1460953136
ISBN-10: 1460953134
BISAC: Fiction / Science Fiction / Adventure

SWARM

(Star Force Series #1)

by

B. V. Larson

STAR FORCE SERIES
Swarm
Extinction
Rebellion

The night before the invasion, the whole sky looked *wrong* somehow. It was the color of it, I think. The sky was purple, rather than blue or black. It was as if the sun never completely went down that night, but instead turned a dark umber and lurked beneath the bottom rim of the world, lighting up the heavens ever so slightly. Only a few shreds of cloud moved along the horizon, over the Sierra Nevadas to the east. Each strip of cloud was tinged a deep red, the color of wet rust or dried blood.

Other than the strangely hued sky, it felt like a typical Central California night in late spring. It wasn't stormy, but a cool breeze came down from the foothills as the evening deepened. In the fields around my farmhouse, a thousand stalks of ripe corn rippled.

Jake, my oldest, performed his usual shrug when I asked him if he had completed his list of chores. His short, black hair was as shiny as a crow's feathers. His eyes were blue and piercing. He looked so much like me his sister sometimes called him my evil twin.

When I took my son out to the stable to *prove* he hadn't shoveled the stalls, the horses were uneasy, shuffling about and sidestepping. They showed the whites of each big eyeball and tossed their heads, but didn't shy when I reached up to stroke them. Frowning, I joined Jake and we finished the shoveling. He looked at me, surprised to get help with a chore he loathed. I pretended nothing was wrong. Truthfully, I didn't want to leave him alone out there.

Afterward, we came out of the stable to find the moon was rising. The fields were rustling and the smell of ripe corn and fresh-cut alfalfa hung thickly in the air. I kept looking over my shoulder, up at that

1

strange sky. We'd bought this place, my wife Donna and I, as part of a back-to-the-country dream. My colleagues called me the "gentleman farmer" and theorized I must be commuting through cow herds each morning to the university. I loved it out here and even after Donna died I refused to move back to the city. But in all my years out here, I'd never seen a sky like this one.

Jake ignored everything that was wrong with the night and headed upstairs. He would spend the evening surfing the web, twiddling with his headphones and pretending to do homework. My second child, Kristine, knew the moment she saw me that something was different tonight. She'd always been more intuitive.

"What's wrong, Dad?" she asked, looking up from her algebra paper. She was thirteen, and this year her body had a new shape I found upsetting. She looked like her mother—except she was skinny and wore braces. To me, she was perfect.

I shook my head as I tapped her algebra book. "Nothing, Kris. Don't get distracted."

Kristine went back to her homework, and I went back to gazing out at the strange purple sky. Nothing changed, so I headed for the computer in my study. I had a lot of grading to do, but fortunately most of that was online. I logged into the university website for the last time and began answering emails and grading lab projects.

Teaching online wasn't as easy as it sounded. Computer science students asked hard questions of their professors and typing in comments was often more work than simply discussing things in person. Sometimes I missed the simplicity of a pen and paper. Even scribbling notes in the margins of printouts was better than typing everything. Red-penned circles and Xs were wonders of communication that we'd lost somehow, over the years.

Some hours later I chased the kids to bed and fell asleep myself. I dreamt of my wife Donna, who had died nearly a decade ago in a car accident. We'd hit a chain link fence and gone right through it. The steel posts had whipped around the car as the chain link wrapped us up like a net. One of the posts had come through the back window and impaled Donna.

She looked at me from the passenger seat. I saw her eyes in my sleep. Her lips moved, trying to tell me something, but her staring eyes were the eyes of the dead.

It was the eyes that woke me up. I sat up in bed, gasping.

2

I'll always wonder what it was Donna had been trying to tell me. If I had stayed asleep one minute longer, could I have heard her voice? Maybe everything would have gone differently...if I had.

-2-

The second night—the bad night—started off good. Both my kids were in a fine mood. It was only Tuesday, but school was out next week for summer, and the excitement of the coming vacation had caught up with them. We went to bed late, after watching movies over the net and eating popcorn. It was one benefit of growing up without a mom: there was no one around to tell Dad it was a school night.

The ship came to loom over my little farm sometime after midnight. It caught Jake first. I don't know why—perhaps because his room was on the eastern side of the house. I heard later they had come from the east, following the darkness around the world in a wave.

I was asleep at the time of the ship's arrival. The walls shook, and my TV fell off the top of the armoire. That's probably what woke me up. The TV crashed and I threw myself out of bed, believing we were in an earthquake. I shouted for the kids, ordering them out of the house. This quake seemed like a bad one.

In movies, when they come for you, there are always lights in the sky beaming brightly into your windows. There were no bright lights at my house. In fact, the entire farm was bathed in deep shadow. This only made sense—I realized as I passed the window at the end of the hall in my tee-shirt and underwear—because there was a huge ship looming over us. It blotted out that strange, purple sky. I saw it hanging up there without a sound. It was maybe a hundred yards long and half as wide. It was completely dark, with no lights or visible engines. As black as pitch at the bottom of a well, my grandmother would have said. I paused and stared in amazement for several seconds.

4

I heard another crash, in Jake's room. I ran down the hall, calling his name. There was no answer. When I reached his room, the bed was empty. His window had been smashed inward. Shards of glass and a torn out black screen lay on the floor. Jake hadn't even screamed, as far as I could recall. Then I looked out the broken window and my brain froze over for a second or two.

Jake hadn't been taken away by some kind of magic beam. Instead, a thick, cable-like, multi-segmented arm had reached down and plucked my boy out of his bed. It resembled the body of a two-foot thick snake—long, sleek, and black. Was there someone up there in the ship working a joystick and collecting specimens? That was my first stunned impression. I got the feeling that to them, we were things that crawled under rocks at the bottom of the sea. They were the scientists who had come down to our world to poke about and disturb our tiny existence.

When I'd gotten over my shock enough to move, I ran outside. Kristine joined me on the porch. She stared up with me at the ship with the snake-like arm. Jake was in the grip of the hand. He still wasn't screaming, but he was squirming, so it hadn't killed him yet. As we watched, he disappeared with the arm up into the ship's belly.

Kris' mouth hung open, full of braces. Her eyes blinked in horror. "What do we do, Dad?"

"Get in the car," I ordered.

"What about Jake?"

"I'll get him," I said. I had no idea how to perform such a miracle, but I was determined to try. I raced back into the house and snatched up my keys and my Remington 12-gauge with a box of shells. I was going to blow off that snake-arm, or at least blast away at the ship. What else could I do?

I ran back outside. The screen door had latched itself shut. I straight-armed it and the flimsy aluminum thing snapped off the frame with the sound of ripping wood. Kristine sat inside the car looking out the passenger window, terrified. I thought to myself, in a disconnected moment, that Jake would be angry when he found out she had taken the front seat. He was the oldest, and since time immemorial in our family, the oldest kid had always gotten to ride up front with Dad.

I loaded the Remington and trotted out into the gravel driveway, craning my neck to look up. Jake and the arm had vanished, but I kept loading. The ship hadn't moved, so maybe they could be convinced to give Jake back. It was the only thing I could think of.

When I raised the gun to my shoulder, I saw a darker spot open up on the bottom of the ship. It was then that Jake fell back down to earth, plummeting out of the ship. He landed in the horse trough…or rather half-in and half-out of it. That broke his spine, I think, but he was probably dead before they'd dropped him. I ran to him, making choking sounds. Kristine was screaming inside the car, her high-pitched cries muffled by the closed windows and doors.

There was my boy…dead, with his face looking up at me from underwater. The rest of him was bent at an impossible angle, limp and draped over the steel edge of the trough. There was blood everywhere. He had been gutted, then dropped.

I fired a shell at the ship. It probably wasn't a smart thing to do, but I no longer cared. I left Jake and half-ran, half-staggered—still in shock—toward the car. It was time to run for it.

That's when I saw the snake-arm clearly for the first time. It had slid silently down again while I had stared helplessly into my dead boy's eyes. It punched through the passenger side window of my car and grabbed my daughter, who was struggling to escape. She had managed to get the driver's door open. She crawled over the seats and tried to run, but the snake-arm had a loop around her mid-section. The arm dragged her backward.

I raised my shotgun and fired a second shell, at the snake-arm this time. I saw a tiny cluster of orange sparks, as if I'd hit metal. There was no other visible effect. I kept running to my daughter, but I didn't make it.

Kristine held onto the steering wheel with grim determination, but that didn't last more than a second. She was ripped screaming from the car, dragged through the broken window and hauled up into the ship.

I could see a darker spot up there, where she had disappeared. I circled under the ship, all around the farmhouse, raving. I thought about firing up at it, but feared I might hit Kristine somehow. I suppose I could have driven off in the car, or ran out into cornfield to escape, but I didn't even think of these things.

It didn't matter. Kristine's body fell, flopping, out of an opening that yawned in ship's dark belly. She crashed down onto the roof of the house. I could tell right away she was broken, but I climbed up there anyway. I got on top of the garbage cans, then onto the rickety fence which my wife Donna had told me to fix until the day she died, but I'd never gotten around to. From the fence, I managed to scramble up onto the shingles and run to where Kristine lay. My face was wet, either from tears or blood, I'm not sure. I'd been clawing at my own face by that time and it was difficult to see, so it could have been either.

Her eyes were open, and there was terror imprinted forever on her brow. I've never forgotten that look. The memory has hardened my mind like nothing else in my existence.

The snake-arm got me next. Coming up from behind, it plucked me off the peak of the roof. I no longer cared if the arm took me. In fact, my only thought was to hang onto my Remington, which I somehow managed. I had lost the box of shells, probably back when I found Jake.

I held my gun, and I held my fire. My only hope was that I would get the chance to blow a hole in something. Something softer than steel.

I was deposited in a quiet chamber. It wasn't big, maybe the size of a bedroom—or an examination room. I wasn't thinking too well at that point, so I just kept turning around, aiming my gun at the walls. I didn't try to find a way out. Right then, I didn't care about escape. I was no longer trying to run away. Everyone I cared about was dead, and all I wanted now was revenge. I wouldn't say I was calm—far from it—but I was *cold* inside.

Looking back, my unusual behavior saved my life. Part of the wall opened, dissolving away to nothing. A being took a half-step forward.

This being was an alien. There had never been anything like it on Earth, at least not to my knowledge. It would have made an interesting subject for a documentary if we'd discovered it in some remote spot of the globe. The thing stood about four feet tall and had four hooves. But it had hands, too. Well, not *hands*, exactly. Three opposed digits would describe them better, each hand looking like a tripod of thumbs. It had blades too, natural ones that sprouted from its head like antlers. Imagine a deer with horned knives for antlers and a set of three-thumbed leathery hands. It reminded me of something from Greek mythology. What had they called them? Centaurs. Half-man, half-beast. But this centaur leaned in the direction of pure beast with freaky hands.

The eyes swept over me with some level of intelligence. I could only pray this was one of the things that ran the ship, because I wanted some revenge. It took a step forward, and maybe it had expected me to retreat, I don't know. But I was not in a cooperative mood. There was red blood on those horn-blades. I suspected it was my kids' blood.

It took a second purposeful step, lowering its horn-blades in my direction. That was as far as it got before I blasted it. I had no doubt now those blades were showing me my own kids' blood. It was too fresh. The hard part was to *stop* blasting, even after the centaur went down. It managed to cut me once, being faster and tougher even than it looked. I didn't care.

I stopped firing and heard something. I turned around quickly. There stood a second one. This one didn't wait around. I fired as it charged, taking one of those freakish three-pronged hands off, then the shotgun clicked. The magazine was dry. The centaur-thing picked itself up and came at me again, and I met its head with the butt of my shotgun.

The fight went on for a while, and it became dirty at the end. I gouged at the eyes and hammered its skull with the barrel of my weapon. It took a long time to die, but it finally did. My legs and arms were slashed and bleeding freely in spots, but I'd won. I roared at the centaur, snarling and gleeful. I hoped it was one of the ones that had gotten the kids. Mad with grief, I hoped that it had kids of its own.

At this point, I figured I had to expect more of these things. Would they give up after only two tries? There had to be more of them.

Some part of my brain that still insisted on thinking was stuck on the detail that these beings didn't seem overly technological. Could such creatures have built this ship? They had hands, after a fashion. But why risk themselves to fight me without weapons? What was the purpose? Both the centaurs had been males. Was this some kind of tribal hunting expedition? A rite of manhood, perhaps?

I decided to stop worrying about anything other than making sure I kept breathing and they kept dying. Accordingly, I checked my wounds. I couldn't find any serious injuries, just cuts and bruises. I used my teeth to tear my tee-shirt into strips and tied bandages around the worst spots.

Panting, I waited for the next centaur. The next one would take me, I was pretty sure. I was tired now, and out of shells. As a club the Remington had done well, but I doubted it would win a third fight for me.

Getting an idea, I bent and tried to rip loose one of those foot-long horn-blades. Maybe, if I could snap it off, I could use it as a knife. The idea appealed to me, using the same blade they'd used on my kids to slash open the next creature.

3

A voice spoke. This was a shock, as up until now, things had been pretty quiet inside the ship. There had always been a slight background hum—and of course, the centaurs and I had been making plenty of noise in our struggles.

"Aggression demonstrated," said the voice. The tone was vaguely feminine, but it had a non-descript quality to it. A translating computer? Maybe.

I supposed the comment was about me. Nice of them, I thought, to tell me how I was doing.

Again, a doorway opened where there had been nothing but smooth metal before. I had snapped off a horn-blade by then and stood up, my teeth baring themselves without my consciously commanding them to do so. How quickly we turn into snarling animals if properly provoked, I thought.

There was no third member of the horn-blade species waiting for me, however. Instead, it was the snake-arm. It reached down and looped around the alien I'd killed first and began to drag it outside. Maybe it was going to drop it into my cornfield. I decided to try to go with it.

It was too big for me to squeeze past, and I was worried the door would melt away when it left. So, I climbed onto the snake-arm and rode it out of the room. I found myself in another cubical room, identical to the first.

"Initiative demonstrated," said the voice.

"Who are you?" I demanded, craning my neck. I didn't see any cameras, or microphones or speakers. Nothing but blank, dark walls.

The snake-arm shook me off in the next cubicle and hauled away the dead centaur before I could climb up on it again. I watched it vanish into another room. Had I missed my ride? Had I just failed one of these escapes? My heart pounded.

Then I thought of the door behind me. Climbing to my feet, I looked back around. The floor in the first room vanished as the wall between the two rooms grew back together out of nothing. I had just enough time to see the second centaur's bloody corpse fall an unknown distance down. I blinked at that. If I had stayed in the room, would they have dumped me too, allowing me to fall tumbling to my death?

"What do you want from me?" I demanded of the walls.

There was no answer, but a moment later *two* more doors opened. Why two? I investigated both paths, gingerly tapping with my foot. The floor vanished on the first one and opened upon a scene of the Earth whirling by at night. We had to be a mile up. I was surprised, as I'd felt no sensation of flying upward. No G-forces had tugged at my body, yet obviously I should have felt the elevator-ride sensation of upward momentum. I could see a dark night landscape, dotted with light. What had to be Highway 99, strung with orange sodium streetlights, snaked off to the north and south.

I backed away into the space I had come from.

"Caution demonstrated."

Those two doors closed, and a third door opened up. I thought about that. Had both paths, whichever one I had chosen, led to a deadly fall? I waited. Why move at all, if they were just going to kill me? After about a minute, the floor under my feet felt warm. After two minutes, I was hopping from foot-to-foot. I finally got the message and stepped through into that third room cautiously.

Clearly, these were tests. Well, I wanted to do some testing of my own—on my alien hosts. My tests would be very easy to perform. All I wanted to do was discover what color their brains were when exposed to dry air. I did everything I could to focus on the tests, on defeating them. I tried not to think about the kids. Thinking about them would paralyze me, make me numb and useless. Grief would have to wait.

By now I was fed up with their games. But I had to play along, unless I wanted to jump out. I even thought about jumping out of the ship, briefly. Perhaps this was their form of entertainment. Maybe they were sitting somewhere, laughing and betting on how far the dumb primitive would make it through their maze of tests and tricks. Part of

11

me wanted to end the torment, but a strong desire for revenge kept me going. I wanted to crack another alien head or two before they killed me. I wasn't quite finished with them.

In the third room the voice came back. "The subject will submit to interrogation."

I thought about that. What did they want, my secret ATM code? What could I possibly know that would interest such creatures? It occurred to me they did not really want information. They wanted to test me. This was another step in their test sequence, just as everything else had been. Had my children been tested and found wanting? I suspected they had, and the floor had opened up for them and dumped them out of the ship. That seemed to be the universal price for failure.

This nurtured a new emotion in me: *rage*. Not just for revenge, now, but for how I was being treated. I was their lab animal, and I didn't like it. I would pit my wits against theirs as best I could. Maybe I would get my chance to strike back. Or maybe I would at least impress these cowardly bastards. I was already envisioning guys with huge skulls in fluttering white lab coats.

What helped me think was my lack of fear. I believe most people, at this point, would have been shaking with fear. But after several life and death struggles and watching my kids die, I was empty inside. I was deflated. There was no room left for fear. I had become cold and calculating. Call it a personality flaw, but that's how I felt.

"The subject will submit to interrogation," repeated the voice.

I thought about grunting *no*, or staying silent. It seemed obvious they would just heat the floor again. Could I take off my clothes, wrap my feet in the cloth and stand on my gun? Maybe. But that sort of thing wasn't what the tests, so far, had been looking for. I reviewed them in my mind: First, I was tested for fighting skills. Second, initiative, and third, caution. This had to be the fourth test then. It was a puzzle. What was the answer?

The more I thought about it, I had to wonder why the voice was telling me the nature of the tests as I passed them. Why had it said *aggression demonstrated* in understandable English? They had to be giving me clues on purpose. There was no reason, if the test was to be given blindly with the subject unaware, that they would give me such hints.

The floor, by this time, had risen in temperature a good twenty degrees. My cooperation was to be forced.

12

"I will agree, if I am allowed to ask a question for each that you ask," I said.

There was a hesitation. I suspected my response was being considered and weighed. Perhaps, it was being graded.

"Bargaining demonstrated," said the voice.

Another door opened.

I raised my eyebrows at that. "That's it, eh?" I asked aloud. I supposed I had passed another test. I had passed it just by attempting negotiation. No questions came. There was no exchange of information. It had all been part of a test.

I reached into the new room with a tender bare foot. The floor in my room had cooled now, but I figured it was time to move on. Each test had led me to a new room, and the previous one would vanish. The penalty for staying in one place seemed clear: I would be dumped out of the ship to splatter on the ground a mile down. I walked into the room and looked at the opposite walls and the ceiling.

"Who are you?" asked a woman's voice behind me.

I whirled and raised my shotgun reflexively. But I never quite aimed it at her, which was a good thing. She had a pistol leveled at me, and since mine wasn't loaded anyway, I dropped the Remington.

She nodded, staring with unblinking, intense eyes. "Good move. I almost blew you away."

She had been through some tests of her own. I could see it in her eyes. They were lovely, but haunted. I opened my mouth to speak, but nothing came out. I stared at her. She was young, but not a kid. She was probably in her upper twenties. About ten years younger than me, I figured. She looked half-Hispanic. It was a common look in California. She was shapely, and everything about her was attractive, even the disheveled, blood-matted hair which hung half-way down to her butt.

My eyes ran downward. I couldn't help it. Everything below the waist was just as shapely as the rest—and naked. There was a tiny tattoo down there, a butterfly I think, done in the traditional green. She wore nothing but a torn, white cotton blouse. The nights are often hot in California's Central Valley. It was obvious she'd been plucked out her bed in the night, just as my family had.

"Do you know anything?" I asked, forcing my eyes upward to meet hers. The fast question was an old trick I'd picked up while professoring. Lots of young women came to talk to their professor, and

13

sometimes my eyes wandered. Asking a quick question usually got me out of an embarrassing moment when I was caught.

"About what?" she asked.

I noticed the barrel of her gun, which looked like a .38 revolver from here, had not wavered an inch. I swallowed. I hoped I wasn't *her* test—what if she was supposed to blow me away to get to square seven?

"About the tests."

She blinked. The barrel lowered, but only a fraction. I did a little amateur triangulating, and I didn't like where it was aiming now. I thought about telling her to put that thing away, but given the circumstances, she had every right to aim her pistol at my privates and we both knew it. Trust would have to be earned in this environment.

"Tests? You mean this bullshit of doing whatever the ship wants to get to the next room alive?"

I nodded. "Exactly."

The gun lowered a fraction more. She could still knee-cap me with a twitch of one finger. I hoped the .38 would eventually prove too heavy for her arms, but she looked like she worked out. She held it correctly too, bracing her right wrist with her left hand. Someone had given her shooting lessons.

She shook her head. "All I know is that if I hadn't slept with this gun on my nightstand I'd be dead right now like my roommate."

"Roommate? Are you a college student?"

"Yeah."

I nodded. "I teach at U. C. Merced."

Her eyes narrowed. The pistol came up again, squarely on my chest now. "This is taking too long. By this time, I should have seen a door open or something. You're full of crap, aren't you? You are like some kind of delay, some kind of distraction. If I kill you, I get to go to the next room, don't I?"

I lifted my hands a fraction, palms up. "Hold on, I've been through plenty of crap myself tonight. This ship killed both my kids. My shotgun is out of ammo, or we may have shot each other, that's true. Maybe that's what the ship wants, but I'm not killing any humans today. I'm only killing aliens."

She stared at me for a long second. Then she sighed and tilted her gun up so it pointed at the ceiling. She still gripped it in both hands, but we both relaxed. "What's your name, Professor?" she asked.

14

Two doors opened up then, as if on cue. We both tensed and whirled, but the rooms were empty. On the far side of the left room was a single point of light. A bright spot showed there, as if someone had drilled a hole in the side of the ship and it was brilliant daylight outside. Unless we had circumnavigated the globe, it couldn't be light out yet, so I was suspicious.

"Another test," I said.

"Ya think?"

I glanced at her. "I'm Kyle Riggs, since you asked."

"Professor Kyle Riggs?"

I nodded.

"I'm Alessandra. Just call me Sandra. What do you teach?" she asked. She seemed honestly interested.

"Computer science."

Sandra rocked back her head and laughed. It was a strange sound here. It seemed very out of place.

"What?" I asked.

"I think I signed up for your class next fall."

"Oh. Let's hope we both make it to school next year, Sandra."

She nodded. "Which way, professor?"

"I'd say we go away from that light. It seems like a trick. It can't be daylight outside. I don't get this test, but we have to go somewhere."

"Yeah," she said. "They are already heating the floor."

I could feel it, now that she mentioned it. The floor was at least ten degrees warmer than it had been when I'd entered. We had to choose a room.

I took a step forward into the room on the right, the dark one. Sandra was right behind me, but not close enough.

The floor vanished in the room where we had met, beneath Sandra's feet. I reached back my hand and caught her as she began to fall. It wasn't a good hold, just her fingers. She dropped her gun. It went twirling down into the night.

We were over the ocean, I realized. It seemed colder, too. The smell of the sea hit me, very strong and sudden. Had we moved north? The sea was dark, but not too far down. Maybe a hundred yards below, it was hard to tell. But it was far enough to kill anyone who took the fall. Water felt like concrete if you fell from high enough.

15

I saw her face, looking up at me. Her mouth was open, but she didn't say anything. She didn't even scream. She was working her other hand and both her feet to get a grip on the smooth metal of the ship.

Cold salt breezes washed up into our faces. I thought we could do it. I was on my knees, bracing myself. It wouldn't do either of us any good if I let her pull me down and we *both* fell into the sea. The problem was there wasn't any lip to hold onto, no rim or door panel, not even a carpet to provide some friction. Just smooth metal that could change shape at will, like liquid.

"Hold on, Sandra," I shouted. "We can do this."

I had a plan. Really, I did. I would lie flat and hold onto her arms, letting her pull herself up over me. I thought she looked strong enough to manage it, with my help. I adjusted myself according to the plan, and then—

The door vanished. The metal flowed together, very rapidly, as it had done many times before. One second it was there, the next it wasn't.

That wasn't the bad part, though. The bad part came when I looked into my hand, where I still held four of her fingers. There was a ring on one of them, with an emerald in it. They were oozing blood, where they had been very neatly severed by the closing metal door.

I sat up and rubbed Sandra's fingers for a second before putting them down gently, making a little stack on the floor. I could hardly see. My eyes stung. I made a weird, howling sound.

"Leadership demonstrated," said the cold voice, speaking up for the first time in a while.

16

4

"Leadership?" I shouted at the walls. "So that's what the test was about? You call that *leadership?*"

The walls said nothing.

"What happened to the interrogation, huh? You never even asked me any questions."

I felt like a crazy guy in a movie, shouting at the walls, shouting at God or the Devil or the voices in his own mind. I think I truly was mad, in that moment of despair.

Sadly, my mind worked on the puzzle. I couldn't help it. I'm a computer guy, and a farmer, and both my occupations require a passion for problem-solving. I had completed a test for leadership. Meaning what? I had led Sandra out of the room. I had made the choice concerning which direction to take. She had followed me.

So, she was a follower and had failed the test. If she had gone the other way, would they have let her live? Would they have put her through some other test or would we have both been failures, tossed down into the dark sea because neither of us could lead the other?

"What the hell do you *want?*" I asked the quiet walls. I didn't expect an answer. I was nearly broken now. Somehow, killing my kids had filled me with resolve, but getting me to make a decision which inadvertently had led to Sandra's death, that was different. I supposed it was a matter of guilt. There wasn't any logical reason to feel guilty about the fate of my kids. I'd done the best I could for them, given the circumstances.

But I had failed Sandra. I hadn't figured out the test. I should have known by all logic that we were facing death as we exited that last room. She had distracted me with her beauty and her nakedness. Just finding another human in this place had changed all the rules. I hadn't really thought about it that way, but it had. I'd dropped my guard, and so had she. We thought we could beat the place as a team, that we were stronger together.

But the ship had had other plans. My black hatred for this monstrous machine was deeper than ever. I dearly hoped I would be given a chance to throttle the evil minds that had devised this place and these cruel tests.

The ship remained silent, and the doors remained closed. I sat in my cube, uncaring. Was it giving me some time for grief? Was it programmed to allow for recovery after the worst shocks? It had done that before, I realized. It had waited until I had bandaged my wounds after fighting the centaurs. It had given Sandra and I time enough to talk and team up.

I thought about the centaurs. I had begun to suspect that they were not behind all this. Some other creature was. Something *else* had set this up. I could not see how all of this made sense if the crew would endanger themselves. Perhaps the centaurs were only trained animals, like attack dogs. Or perhaps they were captives from their own world, like I was. For all I knew, the second one was the relative of the first, and from their point of view I was the evil ape-creature that had cruelly killed them with insane bloodlust.

I felt sick. For the first time, my resolve was weakening.

"The subject will submit to interrogation," said the voice, speaking up again at last. It said these words exactly as it had said them before. That got me thinking, hazily. Repeating oneself exactly, that was the kind of thing computers did. Being a computer scientist by training, I sensed I might be dealing with an artificial intelligence. This was not encouraging. Computers weren't known for their mercy.

I scowled at the floor, but said nothing. Soon it began to heat up.

"As I said before, I'll answer questions only if you will let me ask some of my own."

There was a pause. Then: "Tenacity demonstrated."

A door opened. I heaved a sigh and struggled to my feet. How many of these tests were there?

I cautiously stepped forward. The next room wasn't a cubical. It was larger and rectangular, with a domed ceiling. I suspected every inch of it. I walked cautiously around this new cage, prepared to leap away from any threat.

"All tests complete. You have been selected for advancement."

"Wonderful," I said.

"You may now command us."

I paused. Another test?

"Command you?"

"Yes."

It was talking back. We were in a new room, but I had been fooled before. I thought about it. What if I only got to give one command? What if that was the test, to figure out what I would do in this situation? What did I want? Until now, there had been nothing resembling conversation with these monsters. I hated to admit it, but this change gave me hope. Somewhere deep down I believed it was all another test, however. The floor might vanish at any second.

I thought about asking it to let me go. That seemed simple enough. I'd have to be careful, or it might just dump me out a mile high over a rocky mountain range or the Antarctic. Each time I looked down, it seemed like the ship was over a different spot.

I wondered then how long I had to think it over before it considered me a loser. Perhaps I needed to give it a command. Anything, just to make it happy. But what should I tell it to do?

Then I had it. Why not go for broke?

"I command you to go back and pick up my children and revive them," I said. It was crazy, but who knew what their tech was capable of? Maybe, just maybe, there was a thread of mercy in these beings, or at least some strange concept of honor amongst them. Maybe they gave every contest winner a single wish, a prize for having won through to the end. I tried not to let my hopes rise, but I couldn't help it.

"Specify."

"Specify?" I said. "What do you mean, *specify?*"

"Who are your children?"

"The people you killed. Back behind us. You dropped them out of this ship, you murderous piece of flying shit."

"Course reversed," said the ship.

My anger seemed to have no effect on it. I tried to control myself. If I actually got my kids back, that would be wonderful, but I was still almost beyond any kind of clear thinking. I took deep breaths, trying to calm myself. I had to deal with this situation perfectly. I could not make any mistakes despite my emotional state. Possibly my kids' lives were at stake.

I had a thought then: Maybe other people's lives were at risk, as well. Could there be other prisoners onboard this ship, dying in tests even now? Maybe no one had made it this far. Maybe I was the first one.

I thought of a hundred commands. I thought of demanding a view of the world as we glided silently above it. I was burning with questions too, but I didn't dare ask them. Not yet. What if it took a question as a command to give information? What if I was only allowed one command? There might be some kind of time limit, or my second command might cancel out my first. I couldn't afford to mess around asking more from the ship. Not until I knew the score. I was playing a deadly game without knowing the rules, and I would continue to play it as I had been all along—with extreme paranoia.

There was no reaction for about a minute. I couldn't feel anything, and the ship didn't say anything. It was all I could do to stand there, silent, wondering what the hell was going on. I stared at every wall suspiciously, my eyes roving. Suddenly, I thought I felt a tremor. Something had changed. Had we stopped?

An opening melted away about where I recalled having entered. As with every doorway, it was simply a spot in the metal wall that could vanish and reappear. It was disconcerting, now that I was able to watch the phenomenon up close. Whoever these aliens were, they were much more advanced in practical terms than we were. What had Arthur C. Clarke said? That any technology, sufficiently advanced, would seem like magic to us. That's how the ship seemed to me right now. Like a jet aircraft in the hands of a barbarian tribesman.

The arm was there, in the newly revealed room. Or rather, the top coil of it was there. The rest of it had dipped down into the darkness below the ship. The coils moved, drawing upward. It was coming back into the ship, bringing something up with it.

I glimpsed the slate-gray sea at night. The smell of the cold ocean puffed in, a fresh, salty odor. It smelled good, but it filled me with despair. The arm came up, and at the end of that very long snake-like arm was the hand. In the hand was the broken body of Sandra. She was completely naked now, having lost her cotton blouse in the freezing seawater. Water dripped from her long dark hair and ran in a stream from her dead blue lips. Her right hand was still missing its fingers.

"No," I said, "she's not..." but then I stopped myself.

"Incomplete statement," said the ship. The huge black arm froze. It held the dead girl in front of me. She dripped cold water on the deck.

If I told the ship Sandra was not my child, would it dump her again? Could it actually revive the dead? There was no point in not having it try to fix Sandra. She had earned that much after my failed "leadership."

"Continue," I said. "Finish executing my command. Revive her. Also, to obey my original order, you must fly back to my farm and get my other children and repair them, too."

Another room melted open. It was a large one, like the room I was in now, which I had come to think of as the bridge. The new room had tables—raised rectangles of metal, really. Many smaller, three-fingered black arms dangled down over each table. The big arm put Sandra down on a table and then the scene vanished as the walls melted together again.

Had I blown it? Had I used my one wish and been too unclear? I didn't know, but didn't want to start talking to the ship again. Not yet. Perhaps, it *could* revive people. If these creatures had been watching the Earth and molesting humans for years, as some UFO nuts had always claimed, then they might be very well-versed in human anatomy.

Stupidly, I allowed my heart to soar. What if the ship really could bring my kids back to life? It seemed wild, but a defibrillator would probably look like white magic to a tribesman from centuries past. We revived people all the time in hospitals. Until brain-death set in, what was the limit? Four minutes or so, I thought, for our science. Longer if the subject was in a cold environment. So with advanced techniques, who knew?

I had hope again, and I almost feared it more than the ship itself. With hope, one can be disappointed. Hope would allow me to feel the pain of my loss all over again.

I felt the tiny shuddering sensation. It seemed to me that I wasn't able to detect acceleration, but when the ship halted I could feel it, if nothing else was going on. Were we over my farm? My mind whirled, but I tried to stop myself from believing anything could be done.

The door melted open as before, and I watched the great black hand reach down to my farm. I thought I saw—yes, there were flashing colored lights down there. They splashed red, blue, and yellow over the roof of my house. Emergency vehicles? Had someone reported the attack? I couldn't see the vehicles from my vantage, and I didn't want to step into the room with the open floor for a better look. By no means did I trust the ship yet. For all I knew, this was yet another elaborate test.

But what kind of test might I be participating in now? Perhaps it wanted to know what I would do if given one chance to strike back at them. I wondered if I had chosen badly. Maybe, I should have demanded that the aliens show themselves and commit suicide at my feet. When they revived my children—or didn't—I decided I would indulge myself with such commands.

I wondered if there were police down there. I knew a deputy lived nearby. Perhaps he'd heard my shotgun go off and had made the call. If Deputy Dave Mitters was at my house, I had to wonder what he thought of my spaceship. We'd had a few beers and football games between us.

The answer came as the hand snaked down and fished about. Popping sounds rang out.

"Don't shoot my kids, you moron," I muttered to Dave from afar. But I pulled back a step from the opening. If he was firing up into the ship, I didn't want him to get lucky.

Suddenly, a brilliant flare lit up beneath the ship. Blinding green light filled my vision, like a silent explosion. My eyes snapped themselves shut, but it was too late. Purple, splotchy after-images danced on my retina. When I opened one eye back up— blinking and putting my hands to my face—the intense green glare flashed into existence again. But this time I was ready with my arm shielding my aching eyes.

The sounds of gunfire were gone now, replaced by silence. Not even the crickets in the fields were chirruping anymore. From the opening, where the arm reached out of my new world of moving liquid metals down into my old world of rippling fields, a wash of heat came up into the ship. With the hot air came a smell, of ozone and burnt things. Quickly, this hot smell was replaced by a gush of black smoke. What had happened down there? I had to think the ship had returned fire. Automatically, I supposed.

Had it burned down Dave Mitters? I worried about it, thinking perhaps I had inadvertently caused more death by telling my ship to return to my farm. I remembered that I had fired on the ship myself, and it hadn't burnt me down then. Maybe the rules had changed, now that I had made it to the bridge.

The snake-arm retracted back into the ship. It retracted faster as it reached the end. There, in the grip of the thing, was an ambulance gurney. My mouth sagged open. A sheet covered the face, but by the shape of the body I figured it must be Kristine. Black ash speckled the white sheet over her face. Seeing her body like that brought a wave of grief that was physically painful. It was as if I'd been punched in the gut. I felt sickened. The ship's arm slid away into the side room, the one with all the tables and smaller snake-arms. I didn't look. I didn't want to see what was going on in there with Sandra. I didn't want to see her beautiful body being dissected.

I put my hands on my knees and almost heaved up whatever was in my stomach. I had to struggle to keep control. The huge arm dipped down again. I took several steps, crossing the room and leaning against the cold wall of the bridge. The arm was down there, snaking around my farm. Soon, it would come back up with Jake's body, I knew. I didn't want to see him as a dead thing. Not again.

It was very quiet down there. The initial gush of smoke and heat had ebbed, leaving a lurid flickering light. Something was on fire. I hoped it wasn't my house. I hoped it wasn't Dave Mitters' body, either. Soon the arm did as I thought it would, gliding back into the ship with a burden. It slipped into the medical bay—or dissection room, or whatever it was— and vanished. I put my cheek against the cold wall of the ship and tried not to think of Jake or Kristine or Dave Mitters. I tried not to think of anything.

I failed to stop my mind from racing, however. What if the ship revived the kids, but as brain-damaged vegetables? Would I have to watch them grow up in a coma? Or, what if the ship never let any of us go? What if we were to be its prisoners, perhaps to be tested by pitting us in death fights on other worlds?

What if I had only magnified the horror of the situation by bringing my own children back into it?

5

"Retrieval process complete."

"You—you are ready for new instructions?" I asked hesitantly.

"Ready," said the ship.

I looked around with wide eyes. That voice never seemed to emanate from any one spot. I'd never seen a speaker. The sound came from the very walls of the ship itself, I thought. If the ship could change its walls into doors at will, then maybe it could make tiny motions in a spot on the walls, forming a vibration. Forming a speaker and pronouncing words. Very strange technology.

I reflected that if I was allowed to give the ship a new order, then this test was either much longer and more complex than any of the others, or it was not a test at all. Perhaps I had truly been given command of this ship. But why?

I decided, at long last, to ask some questions. There was one in particular I had to ask.

"I command you to answer my questions. How are the revivals going? Are my children going to survive?"

"Unknown. The injections have been administered."

I thought about that. *What injections?* I decided the ship's answer was good enough for now. I would find out the rest when the job was done. The fact the ship had said *unknown* concerned me, however. The outcome was in doubt. I shook my head and rubbed my temples.

"Ship—what should I call you?"

"How do you wish to address us?"

I thought of a dozen expletives. *Asshole* came to mind, for example. For the first time since I'd awakened, a grim smile twitched on my face, but it quickly died.

"I'm going to name you *Alamo*," I said, "because I intend to never forget you."

"Rename complete."

I snorted. "Okay, Alamo, let's try something easy. Turn on a view screen or something so I can see what's going on below us."

A portal melted in the middle of the bridge floor. It was circular and perhaps ten feet in diameter. The second it began to open, the air in the room began screaming out of it. A fantastic wave of cold struck me. Could we be in space? Had I just killed myself?

"Close it! Close it up again!" My breath came in gasps. I was on the floor and being sucked across it toward the opening.

The hole vanished and the room rapidly repressurized. How high up were we? I didn't think we were in open space, as I was sure I would not have survived that. Besides, I wasn't weightless. Very high up, but still inside the atmosphere, then. Maybe miles up.

I found myself in a shivering ball on the floor of the ship. That had been a close one. I recalled my words: *Turn on a view screen or something....* I was certain it was that *or something* part which had gotten me into trouble. One did not want to be vague with this vessel. Another hard lesson learned.

"Ship?" I said.

Nothing. Then I remembered the rename.

"Alamo, respond."

"Responding."

"Why did you open that portal in the floor?"

"Because the commander ordered it."

I blinked and sat up against a wall. So, I *was* the ship's commander. Had those centaurs been the old commanders?

"Alamo, return to California. Maintain an altitude of one mile."

The ship shuddered to a stop.

"Secondary mission aborted."

"What secondary mission?"

"The acquisition of new command personnel."

"Have you been picking up people with that arm of yours while I've been sitting in here?"

"Yes."

25

I huffed. "Have you been testing them, the way you tested me?"

"No. The testing sequence was not identical."

I thought about that. I believed I had the answer. "So, now that I'm sitting in here, the aggression test or the leadership test would be the last one, right? The one you gave them when they reached the bridge? You will give command of this ship to whoever wins a fight to the death in this room?"

"Yes."

"Stop that mission. Alamo, you will not continue to pick people up and test them. That mission has ended."

"Schedule updated."

I was more certain than ever that I was dealing with an artificial intelligence. Maybe there weren't any aliens aboard for me to avenge myself on, only the ship itself, following some commands given to it long ago. I just hoped the "acquisition of command personnel" mission didn't pop back up again, like a program that kept reinstalling itself and trying to update itself no matter how many times you canceled it.

I had a horrible new thought then. "Alamo, do not drop anyone else who is aboard. Leave them on this ship. I wish to talk to them."

"All acquisition mission participants were released when the mission was aborted."

My hands went to my face, rubbing. They crept up to my hair, where they tugged. I pulled my own hair until it hurt and I made a roaring sound.

"Released," I said, my voice choking. "You mean you dropped them out of the ship?"

"Yes."

I had just killed an unknown number of people. I thought about asking how many there were—who they were. But I stopped myself. It would not do my sanity any good to know the details.

When the ship shuddered again, my mind had partly recovered from the guilt of having made another deadly mistake. Command definitely came with the weight of responsibility on this ship. Since the *Alamo* had stopped, I figured we must be back over California. I wondered if the ship had plucked up Dave Mitters from his squad car and put him through a few tests before I had him dropped from the upper atmosphere. He had stopped firing in a sudden fashion, and there had been no shouting afterward. Perhaps it had burnt him down with that green beam instead. One way or another, I felt sure the ship had killed him.

I tried to put all of that out of my mind. If I just talked to the ship and didn't give it any new commands, I figured it probably wouldn't kill anyone. If nothing else, I could stop it from causing more grief. At least, I hoped so.

"Alamo," I said, trying to think clearly, to reason out the right approach. "Where is the ship's crew? What are they trying to accomplish?"

"Excessive responses generated."

I thought about that. I had to be more specific. "Besides myself and my children, are there any other humans currently onboard?"

"No."

"Besides the four humans, are there other living beings onboard?"

The voice hesitated for several seconds. I'd never heard it do that before. "Answer unclear."

Answer unclear? For some reason, that response caused a chill to go through me. What might cause it to be unsure? My mind jumped to strange conclusions. Were there some kind of zombie creatures aboard, or frozen beings, or robots that might be considered alive? Suddenly, I thought I had it.

"Alamo, you are aboard this vessel, do you consider yourself to be alive?"

"Unclear."

I nodded to myself. I might have smiled, but I was in a grim mood, so my mouth formed a tight line instead. I had learned something. The ship was indeed artificially intelligent. Was a thing like that alive? Not in my book, but who knew how it thought about itself. I decided not to get into a pointless philosophical argument with the ship over this issue. I would skip administering the Turing Test. It really didn't matter.

"Alamo, is this portion of the ship the bridge?"

Another hesitation. Were a vast number of recursive routines firing off in this thing's mind, causing the delay?

"This is the goal room for the command mission. It has capabilities the other chambers do not have."

I nodded. That made it the bridge. "Can I fly the ship from this room?"

"Yes."

"Can I..." I tried to think of some other command function. "Can I communicate with other ships from this room?"

"Yes."

I sucked in a breath. For the very first time, it occurred to me that there might be other ships like this one. Were they all over the Earth? It made my stomach flutter, as if I'd dropped off the high dive.

"How many ships like this one are there, Alamo?" I asked quietly.

"Unknown."

Precision, I told myself. I had to ask for specifics. "How many ships like this one are within—ten miles of the Earth's surface?"

"Seven hundred forty-six."

I put my hand over my mouth. This was an invasion. Up until now, I'd believed myself to be special, to be one of those people they put on TV who said they'd been abducted and probed by aliens. I had to take all those people out of the crazy zone in my mind now. They might have been telling the truth all along.

"Are they all searching for command personnel, the way you were?"

"No."

"How many have found command personnel and aborted the searching mission, as this ship has?"

"Forty-one."

So, the majority of them were still on the hunt. How many people had been killed by these ships—*were* being killed—even as I talked calmly to the *Alamo*? I couldn't believe the world's armed forces would take this invasion lightly. Were jets coming to engage me now, to possibly blow me out of the sky?

"Alamo, are there—planes attacking these ships?"

"Unknown."

"You aren't communicating with the other ships?"

"Ships with command personnel are communicating. Other ships are seeking command personnel."

My mind raced. I wasn't alone.

"Can I communicate with—" I began, then just gave the order. "Alamo, put me in communication with the other ships. I want to broadcast to them."

"Channel open."

I cleared my throat. "Hello? Hello out there? Can anyone hear me?"

There was silence for several seconds, then a gruff voice spoke up. The voice had an accent that sounded British, or maybe Australian. "Who's there, then? Get off the public channel, this is reserved."

The voice seemed to come from the walls, from all of them at once, just as the voice of the ship did. I looked around me, almost expecting to see a face appear. I thought about telling the ship to show me a face, but decided against it. The last time I'd requested such a thing I'd nearly been killed.

"I don't understand what you mean, about the public channel. I've only just made it to the bridge of my ship and I don't have a clue about what's going on. Is this some kind of military thing?"

"Have you named your ship yet? If not, do so. Then open a private channel to the *Snapper*. Now, shut up and get off the public channel. *Snapper* out."

I took a deep breath and told my ship to open a connection between the *Alamo* and the *Snapper*.

The gruff, accented voice came back on. "Ship name?"

"The *Alamo*," I said.

Laughter. "Good one. You are a Yank, I take it? Congratulations on surviving your first hours aboard a murder-machine. Now, listen carefully, greenie. There are some things you have to do right away. Tell your ship to stop picking up people and killing them, that's number one. If it picks up a winner, it will guide them to you and they will kill you. Or you will have to kill them. Either way, it won't be pleasant."

"I've already done that."

"Really? Good. I had to kill two poor Indian bastards who made it to me before I figured it out. They were trying to do the leadership test. I knew one of us had to drop out. It wasn't fair, really, since I'd already passed the test once. Poor wallies. I still think of the looks on their faces as I watched them tumble down over Bangalore."

We exchanged names. My sole contact with humanity was an Aussie who called himself Captain Jack Crow. He'd spent a lot of time in the States, but still had an identifiable accent. I briefly told him my story—about my kids and the deadly tests. He made sympathetic noises. I figured he'd heard it all before. After a minimum of pleasantries we got down to the business of survival.

"Kyle Riggs," said Crow. "Right, I wrote that down."

"Where did you get the pen and paper?"

29

"I foraged for it. You'll learn to do the same."

"What do you mean?"

"Start stealing things. You'll need them. There isn't a whole lot aboard these ships. No food. No electronics that we can figure out. No toilets, either. Not even a bed. But you can tell the ship to fly to your local shops and steal what you need. If you tell it to, it can make a power outlet you can plug things into. You'll need that."

"Won't stealing items upset the locals?"

The gruff laughter again. There was something harsh in that laughter, something that made me think I might not like this man if I ever met him in person. He didn't sound kind or easy-going. But he sounded capable. What kind of person would typically make it through such deadly tests, I wondered. Probably not the nicest guy in the world.

"It does upset people, but they can't really do anything about it."

"What about jets? Won't these ships come under attack?"

"They do, off and on. But I think the ships shoot down anything that comes close."

"What do you mean?"

"You know, like fighters, missiles, police helicopters. Anything that gets too close is taken out automatically."

"I fired a gun at the ship when it took my kids. It didn't do anything."

"Then you were lucky. They seem to become more paranoid when they have us "command personnel" aboard. I think they know they can't be hurt by a bullet or a fist or a thrown rock. When they are roaming around killing people they only shoot at incoming missiles and the like. But once they have a pilot, they get more protective and react to anything that could hurt you."

"I did see a flash of light when I was over my house, but that's all so far."

"You probably won't see it fire at aircraft. The officials have gotten smarter over the last few hours and they stay clear of our ships. When the invasion started it came in last night over Eastern Asia and then swept toward Europe and Africa. The ships raided their way around the globe, heading west with the darkness of night. You Yanks are the last ones to join the party. By now, the various militaries have figured out a few things."

"How come I didn't hear anything about last night's invasion?"

"Did you watch the news last night?"

30

"No," I said, thinking about my popcorn and movie night with the kids. It was a painful memory. I wondered if there would ever be another. I thought then about cutting this talk short and going into the weird room with all the arms to check on the kids. What were the robot arms doing to them? Did I really want to know? Did I really want to *see* it? I supposed I had to trust them. The kids were already dead. Those arms were the last slim hope I had.

"The news people were been talking about UFO sightings all day," Crow said, "but as the night wore on and they got to the States, as best we can tell, the numbers grew. It was just a few ships at first over Asia. Now there are hundreds."

"Seven hundred and forty-six, according to the Alamo."

"That many? Well, we can't do much about most of them. We can only communicate with people who finished the tests."

"Why do these ships need us to tell them what to do? Did their old commanders all die or something?"

"No one knows. Personally, I think the goat-people most of us found on the ships were the old command personnel. Maybe they failed and we are the replacements. Doesn't matter. What you need to do is set up the ship so you can see outside. Just a few webcams and some computers will do it. It's not the best video, but it works."

Goat-people? I figured he must be talking about the beings I called centaurs. I still didn't understand how these ships operated. "If these are robot ships, why don't they have video equipment built in?" I asked.

"Nobody's figured that out yet, either. Listen, are you with the military?"

"I was in the Army Reserve."

"Reserves? An officer?" he asked quickly.

"Yeah, First Lieutenant. It was a way to pay for graduate school."

"Did you see any action?"

"One tour in the Gulf… but that was a long time ago. I spent most of my time behind the wire, as they wanted me for my tech skills, not my rifle. I'm a college professor now."

"A professor?" snorted Crow. "That's a first. What do you teach, martial arts?"

"No, computer science."

He made an appreciative, grunting noise. "Unusual, but I'm sure you will be useful. Most of the survivors are military, or crazy guys

31

who sleep with guns under their pillows. You're the first teacher I've heard of making it through the tests."

"I own a farm," I explained. "And I had a shotgun handy when they came."

"Ah, good, I see," Crow said.

I could tell that being a farmer moved me up in his estimation. I thought about the type of person who was likely to survive the tests I'd been given. Logically, they would be physically tough, quick-minded, decisive people who were probably somewhat paranoid. That didn't describe my colleagues at the university, I had to admit.

"Listen, Jack," I said, "have any of us contacted our governments yet? Why don't we fly these ships to our capitols and set them down and hand them over to the authorities?"

Crow snorted. "Rude, since the ships would shoot up anyone who threatened us. But it just doesn't work that way, in any case. These ships chose *us*. They won't let us do whatever we want."

"So far, the ship has done everything I've asked."

"Try landing and getting out. It won't let you. Not unless you do some very nasty things to yourself—and maybe not even then. It won't let other people around you either, now that you have established full control."

"I opened up the floor by accident and could have killed myself."

"It might have looked that way, but the ship wouldn't have let you fall out."

"You mean we are prisoners?"

"We can do what we want. But we have to stay in our ships. We are independent operators, but we are setting up our own organization. That brings us to my next question."

"What?"

"Will you, Kyle Riggs, join me—join us? I have over thirty ships in my fleet. I'm an ex-naval captain and I know what I'm doing to some extent. We need you, and I'll give you the rank of Ensign to start with."

I stopped talking for a moment, stunned. What was this man talking about? Was he forming some kind of political force outside his own government?

"What gives you the authority to do any of that?"

"These ships give us the authority. Nothing on Earth can stand up against them. We are the only ones who control them. To let someone else take control of them, we have to die. I'm not interested in

32

committing suicide for the benefit of any government. So, what do you say?"

"But why? Why are these ships here and what are they doing?"

Crow paused. "You don't know yet?"

"I'm clueless."

Another harsh laugh from my only contact with the world. I didn't like his laugh; it was the laugh of the bully who tripped the skinny kid.

"You've got a lot more to learn, Kyle. And none of it is good."

-6-

"Tell me everything. I'm listening."

"So, you're joining us?" asked Crow. I could hear the eagerness in his voice.

I hesitated. "Not yet. I need to think."

"Don't go rogue on me, Kyle. I need new people. Join the team."

"I don't know enough to make such a choice yet. I have to learn more about the situation. I'll have to get back to you. I'm kind of shaken up right now."

"I understand—your kids and everything. I'm sorry about that. But rogues are left outside the loop, you should know that much. They don't get to join in our pool of information. That's one of the benefits of joining my outfit."

"Are there any other outfits?"

Mean laughter again. "Didn't I just say there was no more free information? Right away, you try to get around the first rule I give you. But I like you mate, so I'll give you this factoid for free: no, there aren't any other organizations."

"Okay, I'll be in touch," I said. I told the ship to break the connection and I blinked in thought. An organization of ships like these? What sort of people would survive all those tests and then try to organize on their own? Probably not the most pleasant, considerate people. Probably, they were a bunch of militia-types, vigilantes. Or worse, they could be pirates. What the hell was I getting myself into?

I thought about Sandra and my kids then. It was time to check on them.

"Alamo, are my children…repaired yet?"

"The older female is conscious. Revival and repairs have been successful."

Hope flared up again, bright and glowing, in my mind. It was an evil thing. If the ship could bring back Sandra, who had been well and truly dead, wasn't it reasonable to think it could revive Kristine and Jake? There had been only minutes between the deaths—minutes, miles, and the type of injuries sustained. Could this ship really bring back the dead? A voice in my mind told me every emergency room could do that, up to a point. What would you call a heart attack survivor or drowned kid who had been resuscitated other than the dead returned to life?

I recognized the voice then, the one in my head that was saying these attractive things. It was the evil, chattering hope-monkey. I had met this creature before, mostly in dreams, after Donna had died. She would be alive in my dreams and I would awaken, smiling, planning my day with her. But each morning I would rediscover with fresh despair that she was still dead. A grief counselor I'd talked to had named the phenomena the *hope-monkey*.

I was awake this time, but the cruelty was the same. The hope-monkey intently whispered unbidden things into my mind. After the ship told me Sandra had made it, the voice grew stronger with every passing second. The hope-monkey hopped about in its cage, screaming, wanting to be let out. I could hardly breathe.

"What about the other two?" I asked a second or two later, trying to control the warble in my voice.

"Revival has not yet been successful."

Yet, said the hope-monkey. *Not* yet.

Pain. A bolt of it, right behind the eyes. I'd let hope in, and it had done its vile work instantly. Now I realized that if this didn't come to fruition, I would have to endure the pain of losing the kids all over again.

Unless they did rise from the dead on those strange metal tables. What were those skinny black arms *doing* to my kids' bodies?

"I want to see Sandra. Open the door."

"Command refused."

"What? Don't you know what I mean? I'm talking about that section of the ship where you have my children. I will refer to that area of the ship as sick bay or—" what did they call it on ships sometimes? "Ah, call it: *Medical*. Understood?"

35

"Understood. Area named."

"Then open the door to Medical."

"Command refused."

I paced, frowning, becoming angry now. "Why not? I'm the commander here, aren't I?"

"You are command personnel."

"Then why can't you open the damned door?"

"Command personnel must be protected from indigenous life forms."

"From my own kids?"

"From all macrobiotic life forms."

I heaved a sigh. She was alive, that was the important thing. "Alamo, can I see her through a window, or something?"

"Current configuration prevents transparent surfaces."

I rubbed my temples. "Can't you just tie her up, or something?"

"Command accepted."

I looked up, eyebrows rising. I had a feeling Sandra wasn't going to like this. I thought about countermanding my order, but the ship had already begun working on it. The walls vanished between the bridge and the main chamber where the big arm-thing originated. I'd decided by now that was going to be called the cargo bay, as it seemed to be the room from which the ship reached down its arm and plucked things from the surface of the world. Next, Sandra was brought onto the bridge with me.

She was growling and screeching. She was held aloft, spread-eagle, with ropy, black cables entwining her arms and legs. Arms, little ones, grasped all four of her limbs. They glided along the ceiling, pinning her up there. Her hair hung down over her face, but I could tell without seeing it she wasn't wearing her happy face. The thin, cable-like arms that held her came out of the metal skin of the ship itself. I eyed the spots where they sprouted. The metal there rippled like puddles of silvery liquid.

"Let her go! Alamo, release her!"

"Command personnel must be protected from indigenous life forms."

Her head snapped toward the sound of my voice. That's when I saw her eyes. The pupils were a yellowy, metallic color. "Kyle? Is that you? What's going on? What's this thing doing to me? I can't see anything, Kyle!"

Her rage shifted instantly to tears, then back again as she fought with the squirming metal arms. They bit into her flesh. I could see she was bruised and cut in spots.

"Just relax. The ship thinks it's protecting me. It's not going to do anything to you. Everything will be okay," I said, but I was lying. Her eyes were full of yellow mercury. What the hell was that stuff?

"Can you see me?" she asked.

"Yes."

"I see flashes of light in spots—that's all."

"Well, I'm sure that will go away," I said, trying to sound calm. Now that she was relaxing a bit, I could think again. My eyes wandered over her body. I felt bad about it, but I could not stop myself. She was very well-built. I couldn't really enjoy the view, however. I was too upset. And those freaky eyes....

"Kyle, talk to me. What the hell is going on?"

"What do you remember?"

"I—I fell out of the ship, didn't I? You were holding onto me, pulling me back inside, when—" she stopped and made a gasping sound. "Kyle, I think I'm wiggling fingers. Do I have any fingers there? Are they gone?"

I tore my eyes off the rest of her and looked at her fingers. They were indeed there, and wiggling. But they had white circles around each one, as if she wore rings or something.

"Scarring," I said. "They are okay, but there is some scarring. They must have sewn them back on or—"

"Or what?" she snapped, fighting the arms again.

"Or maybe they grew new ones. I'm not sure."

"Can you get me off the frigging ceiling, at least, Kyle? I'm going to throw up if I'm left hanging up here much longer."

"Oh yeah—sorry. Alamo, gently lower Sandra onto the wall area, please."

Slowly, the ship and its whipping little arms obeyed. Within a minute, she was in a normal vertical position. I thought about giving her what little clothing I had, but I couldn't think of how I would get them on over those clutching little, black arms. And besides, I wasn't sure a pair of sweaty men's jockeys and a few shreds of shirt were going to help her mood much.

"You mentioned *they*, Kyle. What *they* were you talking about?" she asked me. "Have you met the aliens?"

37

"Not exactly. I think there is only the ship itself." I explained quickly about the computer voice she had heard and how the *Alamo* operated.

"So, we are trapped inside some kind of flying robot?"

"Yes. But I'm not sure we are trapped. It thinks I'm its mother, now."

"You're looking at me, aren't you?"

I cleared my throat.

"What's wrong with my eyes, Kyle? I think I can see something now, but it's very dim. I came awake in some room, and it was black inside, utterly dark. I felt my way around and found squirming little tentacles and—I think there are bodies in there, Kyle."

I explained about the smaller black cable-arms and my kids on the tables.

She was quiet for a second or two when I told her that one. She was beginning to put things together.

"I was dead, wasn't I?"

"No more dead than someone pulled out of a swimming pool. Just think of it as an emergency room with better technology."

She nodded. "Smart way to think about it. Less freaky that way. How long was I—? No, don't tell me. I don't want to know. Do you think they can fix your kids?"

"I'm hoping so." I proceeded to explain to her what I knew of our new world. I included the things Captain Jack Crow, the Aussie, told me and everything else I'd figured out about the *Alamo*.

"So these crazy people are trying to call themselves an army of some kind?"

"A fleet, I suppose. Yes."

"What, are they out of their minds?"

"I'm not sure yet. I don't know everything they know. Since we can't fully control the ships, and more of them are coming down, some sort of organization is needed."

"Can't the government do that?"

I explained about the requirement of the previous commander dying in order to pass control of the ship to a new commander.

"Oh," she said, nodding. "I think I understand Crow's motivation better now. The first thing any government will demand is to board these ships and see for themselves."

38

"Yes, and as far as I can tell, as soon as they do they will be participating in the tests, which must end in death for everyone but the new commander."

"Or getting strapped to the ceiling like a dead chicken."

I chuckled.

"Kyle?"

"Yeah?"

"Can you do one more thing for me?"

"Sure."

"I don't want to sound ungrateful, or anything, but... can you turn around and stop staring at me? Because—I can see you now."

"Oh! Ah—I'm sorry," I said. My eyes met hers and I saw that the brass-like metallic gleam in her pupils had faded. They had turned black again. I turned away with a guilty start.

"It's cool," she said, smiling at me. "You told the ship to come back and scoop me out of the cold ocean, didn't you? You saved my life."

"Yes, exactly," I said, feeling a little embarrassed, "and I'm glad you've got your vision back, Sandra."

"Sure you are."

-7-

I thought about what Jack Crow had said. About stealing what you needed. Maybe I could do it without stealing. I ordered the ship to return to my farm again.

When we shuddered to a stop, I told the *Alamo* to send its arm down and dig some clothing out of the closets. The ship was warm inside most of the time—unless it opened up the floor—but I thought both Sandra and I could use something to wear. I didn't know how to describe which closet the ship should rummage in, so I just sent it down to find whatever it could. It came back up a minute or two later with a wadded bundle of fabric. The clothing was still on the plastic hangers, the hooks of which had been broken when the powerful arm ripped the clothes loose.

I looked at the random collection of shirts and jeans. They were clearly from Jake's closet. Seeing my son's clothes in my hands almost made me want to choke up, but I stayed focused on the here and now. Some of the stuff was torn in the journey up by the none-too-gentle metal hand. I put on some jeans that were too tight. I managed to wrap a shirt around Sandra's waist and tie it like a loincloth. I pulled a football jersey over her head, and she thanked me, but the little black arms wouldn't let go. In fact, they tightened to the point that they pained her when I was close. It was all I could do to slide the shirt down over her bare breasts.

"This is ridiculous," I complained. "Alamo, what do I have to do to get you to let Sandra free in my presence?"

"Command personnel must be protected from indigenous life forms."

40

"Yeah, I've heard that one."

"Alamo is totally paranoid about protecting you, but not me?" asked Sandra.

"Right," I said. "You have to think like the ship to understand its actions. If you had played the king-of-the-hill game by the ship's rules, you would have gained control of the ship and it would have dumped my body out without a qualm. Apparently however, if you get here in some other way, you are classified as a dangerous animal. Let me think for a second. Crow said something about undergoing a nasty process for protection."

"So why doesn't it let me go to see if I can beat you or something now?"

I noticed she had not given me my second to think. I eyed her for a moment. Cute, but intense, that was my verdict. "Probably because you failed a test already. You are supposed to be dumped out and dead, from its point of view."

"Lovely attitude this metal bitch has."

I nodded. I'd worked with many annoying computer interfaces before. But this was the first that had been designed by unknown aliens. "Alamo? What steps could I take to improve my protection?"

"We can administer injections to command personnel."

"What kind of injections?"

"Reconstructive."

I pursed my lips. I didn't like the sound of that. What the hell would an alien ship want to inject into me? Something that would grow a hard shell over me like a crab?

"Don't trust it, Kyle," said Sandra, watching me. "You don't know what it will do to you."

"There is another option," I mused.

"What?"

"I could have you dropped off. This is my farm. They… they probably cleaned up any bodies by now. If my car is still down there, you could drive to town or call someone."

She thought about it, frowning. "I might do that—eventually. But I would feel wrong, leaving you here alone, in this place. I mean, you did come back for me."

"You don't want to get away from the Alamo? We don't really know what it's going to do next."

She smiled then. "You don't want a companion?"

I shook my head. "You don't want to miss this, do you? This is about the biggest thing that ever happened in human history, and you are in the middle of it. You don't want to get kicked out of the party, am I right?"

"Partly," she admitted, trying to look huffy.

"Okay fine, you are along for the ride as long you want."

"But try to get me off this wall. I'm feeling ridiculous."

"Alamo," I said, scratching my head. "Sandra is not dangerous. She is unarmed and practically nude. Can you retract all but one arm, maybe one that holds onto her ankle so she can't move freely? Then I'll stay away from her and she can't harm me."

"We object to allowing a threat to remain on the bridge except for interrogation purposes."

"Ah," I said, getting an idea. I took on a commanding voice. "I need to interrogate this prisoner, Alamo. I need you to reduce her restraints to a minimum so I can do so."

Finally, after a few more minutes of wrangling, I managed to bargain the ship down to holding onto both her ankles with a single black cable around each. Sandra put on some of Jake's clothes. She looked better in them than I did.

"Um," said Sandra once she was dressed. "Do we have a bathroom on this ship?"

"Have to go, huh? Me too. Alamo? We need a bathroom. Are there any waste removing systems on this ship?"

"All waste is removed by ejection."

"Right," I said. I'd seen plenty of that. My own kids had been ejected as waste. I walked around the bridge. Things were going to become unlivable pretty fast if I didn't solve this one. I thought about ordering the ship to rip out one of my toilets from the farm, but without flowing water, they weren't much good.

I thought about calling on Jack Crow for help again. But I rejected the idea. Crow would just tell me I had to join him for such information. I reasoned that his people had been aboard their respective ships longer than I had. They must have solved this problem somehow. If his people had figured out what to do, I could do it on my own.

"Alamo, open a door from the bridge into one of the unused cubical rooms."

Off to my left, a wall melted away. I walked over and looked inside. "This will do."

"I'm supposed to just let loose on the floor in there? My feet will get wet," complained Sandra.

I thought about the ability of the ship to reshape itself. How far did that technique go? "Alamo, can you shape something from the ship's deck? Make a toilet-shape from the decking."

"Accessing modeling data from archives," said the ship.

Nothing happened for about ten seconds. Then a bud of metal grew on the floor. The area turned brighter, more reflective. It seemed as if part of the deck had shifted into a liquid. The metal bubbled up then, like a lump of clay upon a potter's wheel. It grew taller and shaped itself.

"Sandra, come look at this," I said.

She shuffled over and gazed past me. The cables that sprouted out of the floor and wrapped around each of her ankles moved with her. The cables wouldn't let her get too close to me. She craned her neck to watch. "Wild," she said.

It took a couple of minutes, but soon we had a metal toilet.

"You first," I said.

"No way."

I sighed and walked into our invented bathroom, closing the door behind me. It worked reasonably well. I set up standing orders for the ship to allow people to enter this room whenever they touched the wall that adjoined to the bridge. I also set orders to wait until they exited, and when the room was empty, to evacuate the contents. It occurred to me that all this setting up of rooms and things was rather like programming. If you were careful and detailed, the ship was accommodating. Sandra trusted the bathroom enough to give it a try after hearing my testimonial.

Dressed and relieved, Sandra and I soon felt more comfortable. Next, I had the ship drag a couch up from my living room. Sitting on the metal floor wasn't going to work forever. The couch was leather-upholstered, but arrived somewhat torn up, as the huge black arm had apparently dragged it out through the bay window. But it was better than nothing. A few more chairs and a table joined the rest, and the bridge began to look almost homey. Next, I brought up various items from the fridge and the cupboards. The ship's aim wasn't perfect, however. Bottles all arrived broken, so I had to be satisfied with cans.

Soon, an early breakfast was ready. We shared beer, breakfast cereal, and a bag of apples, the latter spread with peanut butter. It tasted good, and I wondered just how long I'd been aboard this strange ship. It had to be morning by now.

I decided it was time to get another report on my kids. Were they done yet?

But before I could even clear away the table, all hell broke loose.

"Enemy detected. Emergency signal received. Gathering initiated."

Sandra and I had time to look at each other, eyes wide. My next thought was: *what the hell...* as the ship tilted, and vaulted upward. The opposite side of the bridge from the "bathroom door" was now the top part of the room, but not exactly the ceiling. I'd say we were at a forty-five degree angle.

I'd placed an armchair at what was now the nosecone of the ship. It slid down toward us and smashed into the table. The whole mess hit the leather couch.

I reached for Sandra, trying to pull her out of the way. The ship didn't like that. About a dozen arms snaked out of the ceiling and the floor, lashing around Sandra and ripping her out of my grasp. The arms yanked her up and pinned her to the ceiling. She was growling and cursing. The whole thing might have been funny, if we had known whether or not we were going to live through the next few seconds.

"Alamo, restrain the furniture!" I ordered. "I might be injured by it!"

Arms snaked out and pinned everything down. I pushed the ruined table out of the way and sat on the leather couch, which was now against the back wall of the bridge. It was smeared with peanut butter. I felt myself pressed back into the cushions. Was that the sensation of G-forces? Could we be accelerating that fast? I hadn't felt anything when moving over the Earth, so how fast were we going now?

I didn't have any answers. I smelled the powerful odor of beer. It had gone everywhere, and I could feel the cool liquid sinking into my pants to touch my skin.

"Alamo? What the hell is going on?" I demanded.

"Command personnel must prepare for battle. What are your orders?"

Battle? "Alamo, put me on the public ship-to-ship channel. I want to hear what the other ships are broadcasting."

Immediately, a chorus of confused voices filled the bridge. There were people chattering, some were screaming.

"What the hell is that?" asked Sandra, still pinned to the ceiling.

44

"Alamo, put Sandra in that armchair."

She floated, red marks and purple bruises around her limbs, as the ship put her into the chair as I'd instructed.

"Do you know what the frigging hell is happening, Kyle?" Sandra asked.

"Not exactly, but I think we are flying up into space. And it's happening to everyone who is part of this 'fleet'."

I heard Jack Crow's voice, roaring for calm. He asked people to shut up and sound off, his people first. I had to admit, hearing a single commanding voice and having that voice give you something to do did help fight the panic everyone must be feeling. The screams stopped and people did as they were told.

After twenty or so people had sounded off, Crow called upon the rogues to report. *Only twenty?* So, Crow had padded his numbers, telling me he had thirty in his group. Still, there were only about another twenty rogues who called out afterward, including myself. That made up a total of about forty ships. That sounded low to me, as the fleet was supposed to be over seven hundred ships strong. What were all those other ships doing? Were they still looking for "command personnel?" That meant, essentially, they were still down on Earth— prowling around, pulling people out of bed, and killing them. I shuddered, remembering my own kids. I thought about asking the ship how my kids were doing, but stopped myself. What if it was bad news? What if one of them hadn't made it? I would be distracted and I needed my mind operating right now. I tried to reach for a cold area of my mind, a place where emotions feared to tread. I needed to focus on this *battle*—whatever it was about—if any of us were going to survive the experience.

"By my count, some of you are either staying quiet, unable to communicate...or dead," said Crow. "We'll presume the latter." He told them all to order their ships to secure everything they had brought onboard, which I had already done.

I hated the sensation of flying blind. Where were we? Where were these enemies we couldn't even see? I realized the problem was undoubtedly due to different alien physiology. Whoever had built this ship, it now seemed clear to me, had no eyes. Or at least, vision was a secondary sense for them.

Crow was calling out more names repeatedly now. I got the idea very quickly that some people weren't responding. What had happened

45

to them? Were they already dead? Had they been crushed by their couches or had these enemies shot them down? What in the nine hells, exactly, were we supposed to do when we found these enemies? I had no idea how to operate this ship other than ordering it to pull things through the windows of my own house.

Sometimes, in a panic, things go very badly. Sometimes one's mind is confused and shocked. Panic can bring out random, useless behavior. But I've never been that sort of person. When an emergency rears its ugly head, I've always functioned well, and my mind seems to operate faster, more accurately. Back when I'd been a reservist, before taking on a teaching job, I'd been an industrial automation specialist. One year, my occupation had gotten me into real trouble. Paid to build a computer system to control a chemical reactor that produced robine for an auto parts manufacturer, I'd done something wrong. I'd crossed two points in the reactor's database. I recalled the moment vividly, as the plant went into emergency shutdown and my mind was jolted into high gear. I realized in an instant that I had made a mistake, and what the mistake was. Thousands of lines of code, and I'd made one critical error. My mind had gone into overdrive. I'd worked the reactor controls with great speed, fearing an exothermic reaction and a fire. In the end, there had been a big clean-up and some muttering about lawsuits, but no one had died. I hadn't panicked.

The G-forces pressing me into my wet leather couch increased. We were accelerating. We were heading up into the sky, toward I knew not what. Like a car crash, events seemed to slow down and take on a hyper-real quality. Then I got an idea.

"Alamo, I want you to manipulate the forward wall of the bridge. I want you to shape it into the shape of objects outside the ship. I want to see—*bumps* on the wall, raised surfaces, for each friendly ship and enemy ship."

It seemed to take a long time, but I'm sure it was no more than thirty seconds before the wall opposite us, the wall that had almost become our ceiling, *changed*. It came to resemble a silver blanket under which dozens of beetles crawled slowly, independently. As we watched, the beetle-like swarm converged closer together.

"Where the hell are we going?" asked Sandra, staring at the wall that had now become a metallic relief-map, like a radar screen. "And which one is us?"

"Alamo, can you color friendly ships? Green or—gold?" I thought of the brassy color of Sandra's pupils when she'd been blind. Could the ship have put metal in her? Liquid metal? I pushed away the thought. We could figure that out later.

The bumps on the wall changed color. They took on a reflective, lightly golden color, like melted tin. They reminded me of beads of solder stained with amber resin. All of them looked the same, however.

"Make the enemy a darker color. And show me physical objects like the Earth and the Moon—with a neutral gray."

The wall shimmered and a large portion of the wall to the left became a curved surface.

"That must be the Earth. We're leaving it behind," said Sandra in a lost voice. "Why aren't we floating?"

"We are accelerating so fast that it's pressing us backward," I said. "If we slow down and coast, we should start to float."

"Hey, what's that?" asked Sandra, pointing. "Something is moving toward us over on the far wall."

We stared at the walls. Over to our right was a fist-sized, rust-red thing. The small golden swellings on the forward wall slowly left the crescent of Earth behind and slid toward the rust-colored thing. All the moving contacts were on a collision course.

"That must be the enemy our ship spoke of," I said. "Look at it. Whatever it is, it looks a lot bigger than us."

"Kyle?" asked Sandra after a quiet moment.

"What?"

"Any chance you can take me back home and let me off at your farm? I think I've changed my mind."

8

It took a bit of shouting on the open channel, but I managed to describe to everyone the instructions to give to their ships to get a view of the outside world. Once they listened and obeyed, there were alarmed gasps.

"The *Snapper* is requesting a private channel," said the ship.

"Okay, allow it."

"Kyle? That was great work. Thanks a lot for that info. We can all see what we are up against now. Any more ideas on how to fight against this big red thing coming at us?"

The enemy ship, if that's what it was, had almost reached the corner of the room and come onto the same forward wall with our rash of smaller, metallic bumps. To the far left of the forward wall was the slate-gray raised disk that represented the Earth.

"I was about to ask you the same thing, Jack."

"Well, maybe the ships know what to do. They are all clustering up and heading at it in a swarm. Maybe they'll fire in automatic defense or something."

"I'll let you know if I figure anything else out," I said.

Before I could tell the *Alamo* to break the connection, Crow added a few quick sentences. "My offer still stands, Kyle. And I'm upping the rank. I want you as a Lieutenant."

"Very generous, Jack. But can we just get through the next hour alive, first?"

"Absolutely. Keep in touch."

He broke the connection. I pondered the screen.

"Alamo? Can we fire weapons at the incoming enemy ship?"

"The enemy is out of range."

"How long until it is in range?"

"Unknown."

Bullshit, I thought.

"Alamo, if we maintain our current course, velocity, and acceleration—and the enemy does the same—how long do we have before we are in range?"

"Eight minutes."

"Alamo, when I ask for predictive estimates in the future, use the current sensor data to make the calculation. Exactitude is not required."

"Program options set."

I smiled tightly. It was like working with an old computer, one that used a command line interface. You had to be precise in your instructions or you got errors. You had to do things in the proper order, but you could customize your interface with shortcuts. I quickly stopped congratulating myself. I had to remember I was talking to this machine, not typing on a keyboard, and it was far more advanced than anything I'd ever worked with.

"Alamo, as each minute passes until we are in range, give me a report, a countdown of minutes."

"Enemy in range in seven minutes," said the *Alamo*.

I thought of Jake, at that instant, with what was quite possibly seven minutes left to live. I thought of the day I took him out to play ball for the first time. He'd only been about four years old, and I'd bought him one of those plastic training sets with a spring-loaded red stand that popped the ball up into air. After a few swings, he had managed to hit one. He'd been very serious, very focused. When he finally hit one, his broad, toothy grin had made me smile in return. I don't know why I thought of that particular memory at that moment. I just did.

The memory made the hope-monkey rise up in me again. I told myself I'd play a baseball game with Jake again, back home, after we won this battle. Somehow. I lied to myself, and I liked the lie. I didn't really believe it, but it was a nice lie. Right then, I knew the hope-monkey had me. I was helpless in its grasp. I was hooked.

I shook my head and tried to get back to that cold, focused place in my mind. I needed to forget about the kids and any other distractions. For the next seven minutes, at least.

"Kyle?" asked Sandra, pointing to the corner and leaning as far forward as the restraining little arms would let her. "What's that?"

49

A small red glint had left the big, red ship-thing. It was traveling toward us. It was no bigger than a penny, but it made my heart pound.

"Enemy in range in six minutes," said the ship.

"Alamo, identify that new enemy contact."

"The contact is incoming enemy fire."

Before it got half-way to us, another *something* left the big, rust-red ship.

"They are firing missiles at us, Kyle," said Sandra. "Will you do something, please?"

"Alamo, change the color of our ship. Make it green or orange or something."

One of the ships—one that was not on the front line, thankfully—turned a coppery orange.

Sandra sucked in her breath as the first tiny red dot made it to a ship out on the edge of our formation, at the top of the forward wall. The missile, if that's what it was, vanished. The golden ship it had struck vanished with it. There was no doubt in my mind what had happened. Our side had taken a hit.

"Alamo, draw a predictive line to show me where the next incoming fire will hit."

A rippling, vein-like line, crudely drawn, appeared on the wall. It was rust-red. It straightened out as we watched into a direct line that ran to the opposite side of the formation. The second missile was headed downward. It was going to hit the last ship in our line at the bottom of the wall, while the first missile had targeted a ship at the top of the wall.

"They are shooting for our farthest outlying ships," I said. "Why?"

"So we don't shoot the missile down?" suggested Sandra.

"That's it," I said nodding. "Alamo, open the ship-to-ship channel, please."

A wave of chatter came in. I realized I would never get a word in over it. People were trying to figure out who had died. Others were talking about how to get their ships to turn tail and run, which I realized by now wasn't going to happen. If it was possible, someone in the group would have managed to give the order by now. The ships had picked us up and brought us along for this little jaunt into space. They wanted us to command them through it. Maybe the AI was smart enough to know it wasn't a tactical genius.

Much of this entire situation made more sense to me right then, as if I'd been hit by a bolt of clarity. Why had they chosen us for our survival skills? Because if you wanted advice on surviving, you asked an expert. These ships had weeded us out ruthlessly, looking for the tough-minded people. They had kidnapped us to help them beat this enemy.

What, thought a distant part of my brain, *are they going to do with us once they no longer need us?* Unbidden, the image of the centaurs I'd slaughtered to gain command of this vessel came to mind.

"Enemy in range in five minutes," said the ship.

The forward motion of the enemy ship had stopped. Why get closer, they must have been thinking, if they were already in range? They could just shoot us all out of the sky, one by one.

"Alamo, get me a private channel with the *Snapper*."

Hesitation. "Established."

"What is it, Riggs? I don't have much time."

"Have you figured out what to do then?"

"No dammit. Talk to me."

"The big bastard is shooting for our outlying ships. I think it is trying to kill ships that are off on their own, separated from the rest."

"I can see that, talk faster."

As we spoke, the second weapon reached its target. Another tin-colored beetle representing one of our ships vanished. Two more missiles were incoming. I figured at this rate half our number would be gone before we got into range.

"Have your ship draw a line between the incoming missile and the target ship. What I suggest is we group around the guy who is targeted. Then all our auto-defense fire might stop the incoming weapon. Just maybe, we can shoot it down."

"That's the best you have?" demanded Crow.

"Yes."

"The ships won't fly where we want them to, we've all tried that."

"They won't let you run off and hide. Maneuvering to defend one ship is a different matter."

"How do we figure out who is targeted?"

I told him he should get his ship to color his own vessel differently. "The one being targeted should tell everyone else. That way, we will have the target ship's name. The rest of us can tell our ships to move toward the targeted ship and cover it."

51

"Good plan, mate!" Crow laughed again. Some of the harshness and confidence was gone from the laugh, however. He sounded a little nervous. I didn't blame him. Who wasn't nervous at this point?

I heard him shout for quiet on the public channel. He gave them the instructions, telling them to sing out if their ship was the one under fire. Before we managed all this, a third ship blew up. Finally, the red lines were on everyone's wall.

"Right!" shouted Crow. "Talk to me people, don't be shy. Who is next on the death list?"

No one answered.

"Enemy in range in four minutes," said the *Alamo*.

"Dammit, talk to me before it blows us all up!" screamed Crow.

"Jack?" I said.

"What now, Riggs?"

"Did you color your ship yet?"

"No, I've been too damned busy with your cocked-up plan to—"

"Jack, it's you. If no one else can see it's targeting them, then it must be the one who hasn't done it yet."

One second of silence, then Jack's voice: "Everyone, order your ships to cluster around the *Snapper*. Do it now."

"Alamo, move close to the *Snapper*," I said. "Do it as fast as you can."

The fourth little red contact had almost reached us. I watched as, sluggishly, a dozen or so ships moved to cover what must have been the *Snapper*. Sandra and I watched with our teeth clenched. I hoped I'd guessed right. What if our ships couldn't shoot down these incoming weapons? What if instead, Jack's ship took us all out in the resulting explosion because we were too close?

We didn't have long to wait. Our ship began to shudder. I knew the sensation—it had happened every time the ship fired its beams.

"Is that our ship shooting? Or are we being hit?" asked Sandra.

"I think if we were hit, we'd be toast. Our ship is automatically firing at the incoming weapon."

The red dot grew very close. It was pointless, but I clenched every muscle in my body. I couldn't help it.

Suddenly, the sensation of firing stopped, and the red weapon contact was gone. I couldn't tell with the intermingling of ships if there was one missing or not.

"Jack? Jack Crow, are you still there?"

"Yeah. I'm here. Who's next? Talk to me."

"Enemy in range in three minutes," said the *Alamo*.

More panic people identified themselves. We ordered our ships to gather around each in turn. As we closed with the enemy, the enemy rate of fire seemed to be increasing. The big red ship was retreating now, slowly at first, but picking up speed.

"They are pulling out, let's go after them!" shouted Crow. "Everyone, order your ships forward. Increase speed."

We chased them, still blowing up each missile as it came in. It only caught one more ship, a woman who screamed and howled for us to get close. She was too far out and hadn't clustered like the rest of us. Clearly, she hadn't followed Jack's orders.

"See?" demanded Crow as her contact vanished and her cries for help were cut off. "See what happens when we don't all work together? She was a rogue, and she acted like one, and now she's dead. We couldn't save her because she wouldn't work with the group."

I barely listened to Crow. Instead, I worked on creating a program to cluster around the targeted ship. By giving our ships a carefully worded set of commands, they should automatically move to protect the one that was targeted.

Soon, we were in range of the big red bastard itself. I wished, right then, that I knew just what it looked like. Our ship began firing. So did the others, according to the reports. We circled around the ship and engulfed it. The big ship tried to pull out, to run, but we were all over it. At some point, it stopped firing missiles. Still, we kept pounding it.

"I wonder who is on that ship?" asked Sandra aloud. "Who are we killing? Are we really the good guys, or the bad guys?"

"Yeah," I said, slightly troubled. What if this ship had come here to rescue Earth? What if its mission was to get rid of these vulture-ships that had kidnapped us? Maybe the ship was full of angry, righteous centaur people, bent on revenge for what our ships had done to their own world. We had no idea and no way of knowing.

After a while longer, the enemy ship stopped retreating as well. Still, we rippled and churned around it, like a school of piranhas tearing apart a side of beef. Each of us got our mouthful, then went back for more.

When it finally blew up, we felt it. The *Alamo* stuttered. We lurched and drifted. The firing stopped. The other ships stopped moving, too.

We had lost six ships altogether.

But we had won.

9

"Riggs? Hey, Riggs?"

It was Jack Crow again. He sounded pretty happy.

"Hello Jack. We lived."

"We sure did, my fat-brained friend. You helped out tremendously. I want to make you a lieutenant commander, Riggs. No, forget that. A *full* commander! How does that sound, Commander Riggs? I want you to know, you would be the only person with such a high rank in my fleet. You would be my second in command."

I chuckled. "If I wait another day, will you make me a captain?"

"Right," Crow said irritably. "Well, right. Laugh it up. Well done. This is all a big joke, isn't it? But consider the fact that I put together an organization which kept us alive today. That ship might have killed all of us, you know. Think about that. Your ideas saved the day, but without my organization, we wouldn't have worked together at all and we would have failed."

"You have a point there, Jack."

"Good. I'm glad to hear you admit it. I'm not just some megalomaniac who wants to call myself a commodore."

"What's a commodore?" I asked.

"It's a rank between captain and admiral."

"You're a commodore now?"

"Well, I realized I needed to have more ranks as more ships join us. More of a hierarchy."

"I see," I said, grinning.

"But that doesn't matter. What I want you to think about, Riggs, is what that ship would have done if we had lost the battle. What if it had made it down to Earth?"

"I don't know."

"And what about the next time? What if there are a dozen ships like that, or a hundred?"

"Next time?" I asked wonderingly. I had honestly not had time to think through the implications of the battle we'd just faced. I felt out of my depth. I had no idea what was going on here. I understood that from the enemy point of view, we represented Earth's armed forces. Had we just involved our planet in some kind of war? We desperately needed more information. Would there be a next time? Why not? Wars were not usually fought in a single battle.

"Jack—Commodore Crow, I mean. Do you have any more detailed political information? Is Earth in a war? Or did we just declare war on whoever was in that ship, by helping our ships destroy it?"

"Great questions. Join us, and I'll assign you the task of figuring out the answers. I'll do recruitment and organization."

"What the hell have your people been doing?" I asked. "Do I have to figure out everything?"

"Look, Kyle, most paranoid people who sleep with a gun in their hand aren't deep thinkers. This organization isn't made up of a bunch of philosophers, diplomats, and techies. My fleet is more like a gang of opportunistic killers—survivalists. We are cut off from the rest of Earth, and we don't much trust our own governments. Unfortunately, running a fleet of alien ships in space combat requires more than reflexes and a killer instinct. I'm coming to realize I need you more than anyone else in my fleet. For the last time, will you join me?"

I thought hard for about five seconds. I looked over at Sandra, who nodded firmly. I sighed, and realized they were both probably right. I didn't really like joining some independent, militia-like organization. It wasn't my style. But in our situation, I couldn't see how we were going to be taking orders from the ground, and I wasn't interested in letting some military agents come aboard and toss me out of this ship. Self-sacrifice had its limits. Who knew, anyway, if the Pentagon could run this ship better than I had done? Would they have won that battle? Maybe I was overestimating my problem-solving skills, but then again, this ship had chosen me for good reasons.

"Okay Commodore. You've gotten through to me. For now, I'm joining your organization. I'll be a commander, if that's what you want. By the way, what do you call your fleet?"

"I've been thinking about that. How about Star Force? That has a nice ring to it, don't you think?"

I agreed. It did have a nice sound to it. I broke the connection and looked at Sandra again. She was smiling and I thought I hadn't seen too many smiles on her face up until now. She was very pretty, but I had to get her out of those ridiculous cables that held to her ankles like manacles. Maybe I should go through with the injections, or whatever it was the ship wanted me to do to allow people to be in my presence without restraints. I'd have to ask the ship about the details. I mentally added it to the growing pile of tasks I *should* be doing.

"I'm impressed," said Sandra, smiling at me.

She was very attractive. I had to admit it. She was also way too young for me, but that was mattering less and less as I spent more time with her. I was wary, naturally, having watched other professors go down that road with research assistants and the like. There was a legendary formula that an old, philandering professor had supposedly worked out. It described a critical ratio for the duration of such relationships. It involved the measured youth and attractiveness of the student against the length of the inevitably short-lived marriage. It was an inverse relationship. The prettier the girl, the story went, the shorter the marriage. To me, Sandra looked like a two year experience, at best. I had to admit though, it would be an excellent two years.

I turned back to the screen I'd figured out, which now encompassed three walls. The golden beads that represented friendly ships had drifted apart and were heading back toward the dark crescent of the Earth. More golden motes had appeared there, sliding over the surface of the planet. They must be ships that had managed to locate suitable "command personnel." I almost shuddered at the thought. How many people were being dragged from their beds down there and slaughtered? One every minute, perhaps? The flocks of ships were relentless in their searches for someone who could pass their tests. They were machines, I knew now, built of something like liquid metal. There was no mercy in their hearts, because they had no hearts.

"My kids must have been revived by now," I said to Sandra. "I bet they are freaking out in Medical if they were awake and enduring this battle while tied down."

"That does sound rough," Sandra said. "I hope they aren't blinded and screaming in there like I was before you came and got me."

I took a deep breath. I was feeling good, slightly relaxed after a long, hard night—one that was easily the worst of my life. It was hard not to feel good after having saved myself, a bunch of other people, and possibly the world itself. My elation was to be short-lived, however.

"Alamo, how are my kids doing?"

The answer was prompt and devastating. "The biotics could not be revived," said the ship.

I froze. My mind froze.

"Oh no," Sandra said, reaching for me. A black, snake-like arm whipped out, circled her wrist and yanked it back. "Kyle?"

A block of ice formed in my guts. It made it hard to speak, or think, or do anything. Shock, I suppose they would call it. The hope-monkey had gotten me, I realized with some rational corner of my mind. Just how badly I'd been bitten I would never have admitted before that very moment. My kids had been *alive*—in my mind. It had all seemed so reasonable. Alessandra had been revived, and she was no worse for the wear. I had assumed the ship could work the same miracle upon Kristine and Jake. Like a primitive tribesman who sees a foreign doctor cure a fatal disease with an injection, I thought the magic was unlimited. But logically, they had been far more dead than Sandra had ever been. She had been in a cold ocean for a fraction of the time they'd lain broken in my farmyard. Cells deteriorated far more slowly in icy water than they did in the open air on a warm spring night. Sandra hadn't been gutted, either. Sewing fingers back on was not the same thing as rebuilding an intestinal tract. The ship had patched Sandra together, but hadn't managed to do the same for my kids.

I shook with anger. This ship had killed my kids, teased me with their revival, and then killed them all over again—even if they'd only been alive again in my mind. Suddenly all the grief I'd felt earlier, which had been on hold, came crashing down on me. It was a flood of emotion that had all been kept at bay by the hope-monkey.

"I want to see my kids," I choked out. "Bring them to me, dammit!"

"The biotics are not aboard."

"Where are they?"

"When the revival efforts failed, they were released."

"You mean you dumped them out of this ship? Why did you do that?"

"All waste is to be released."

"Where are they?"

"Unknown."

"What do you mean *unknown?*" I roared at the walls. These infuriating, cold walls. "Where did you drop them?"

"Shortly after the battle started, they were released."

"In space then. You dumped them into space. Are they orbiting somewhere? The bodies?"

"Predictive assessment warning. The following is only an estimate: the waste was released in a decaying orbit. The probability is high it has reentered the planetary atmosphere."

"The *waste?* So they burned up on reentry into the atmosphere?"

"The probability exceeds ninety-nine percent."

"I don't even have anything left to bury," I said dully.

Sandra was saying something, but I didn't care and I didn't hear a word of it. I didn't even look at her. I ripped open a beer can that I found rolling around on the ship's deck and drank it. It was warm and tasted like shit, but I drank it all fast. Then I fell to my knees and sicked it all up again.

"There's some more human waste for you," I said.

I flopped back onto my soggy couch. "Alamo. Take me back to my farm."

-10-

Sandra tried. She soothed me with her voice. I hadn't thought she had it in her, really, to be so caring. She had seemed like such a tough, independent-minded—even *mean*—girl when she'd had a pistol aimed at my crotch just a few hours ago. But now, she was a friend, and she tried to make things better for me. I couldn't hear her words. But I got the feeling, the intent—that much sank through my black mood, but none of the rest of it.

The hope-monkey had gotten me. The monkey had, in fact, kicked my ass. That part—the knowing I had let it get to me—was as galling as anything else. It was ridiculous. My kids had died last night, not just now. I had watched them die. I'd looked into their dead eyes, just as I had looked into my wife Donna's dead eyes a decade earlier. I was no stranger to grief. I knew the process. But I'd let hope revive the kids in my mind, if not in reality. That had gotten me through a few tough hours without feeling the pain of their loss. Now, here I was reliving the pain all over again. Like a wound torn open. Like a broken bone that had to be yanked straight and reset.

I screamed suddenly. It was more of a roar of rage than anything else. Sandra, who had been talking gently to me, winced and backed up.

I spoke a long stream of foul words. My eyes burned, and I could barely open them. Breathing hard, I sucked in gulps of air as if I had swum six laps underwater.

"Alamo, you murderous machine: I hate you."

The ship did not respond.

60

"Alamo, what if I ordered you to crash us into a mountain right now? At full speed."

Sandra looked alarmed, but didn't speak. I think she rightly judged my mood. I was best left alone right now.

"That order would be invalid under current circumstances," said the ship. It sounded almost cheery to me, and the voice grated on my nerves. I would have liked it better if it sounded upset, or at least worried about what its crazy commander might do next. That's the problem with computers. When you are insanely furious with them, they have no comprehension of the situation and they don't care one whit.

I fought with my emotions. I had to forget about everything that had happened. I stomped my feelings down until they allowed me to think clearly again. Survival had to come first.

"I need some air," I said aloud. "Are we over my farm?"

"Yes."

"Open a window or something. Open three of them. I want to at least smell my own fields if I can't get down there."

Some round holes opened in the walls. I wasn't surprised to see daylight pour into the ship. It made Sandra and I blink and squint. It looked and smelled like a fine day.

"Can I go down and walk around my house, Alamo?" I asked. I had the sudden urge to visit the kids' rooms and look at their things.

"Command personnel can't be exposed to hostile biotics."

So that was it. I was still a prisoner, not really a commander at all. "Why not?"

"You are command personnel. You cannot be exposed to harm unless you have undergone precautionary treatment or are in the process of being replaced."

"Precautionary treatment? Those injections, right?"

"Yes."

"What exactly is in those injections?"

"We are."

I stopped speaking. Sandra and I looked around at the walls. *We are?* What the hell did that mean? The ship had been speaking about itself in the imperial "we" form all along, as if it was some kind of nineteenth century emperor. I had thought perhaps, since it was in communication with the other ships, it considered itself a plurality of consciousness. But mostly, I hadn't really given the affectation much

61

thought in all the confusion and excitement. Now however, I could see it was clearly thinking of itself as a multiple form of some kind. And it was talking about injecting this *we* into my body.

"I saw Sandra's eyes," I said to the ship, thinking aloud. "They were golden, reflective. You filled her with some kind of metal, didn't you?"

"The metallic content of the injections given to the Sandra-biotic was approximately seventy-two percent. The exact proportions vary depending on nature of the injections and their purpose."

"I'm full of metal?" asked Sandra in alarm. "I don't like that. Aren't most metals poisonous?"

"You seem okay," I told her. "They must have flushed them out of you somehow. Remember how you had to go after you woke up? I built a bathroom for you."

She nodded thoughtfully. I could see the look of disgust on her face, however. No one wants to hear they had just peed out a mysterious puddle of liquid metal.

"Alamo, let me get this straight. If I let you give me these protective injections, you will allow Sandra to move about more freely?"

"Yes."

"Kyle," Sandra said, "don't do it. There's no need right now. Crow said the injections were nasty, remember?"

"You came out okay."

"You shouldn't make any big decisions right now. You are grieving. You aren't yourself yet."

I looked at her, knowing she was right. Then, like a bolt out of the blue, I knew what was going on. The fact I hadn't realized it right away demonstrated Sandra was right. I was a computer scientist. I should have known instantly what the ship was hinting about with these injections.

"Alamo, you said the injection contained *us*. As in, a portion of your collective self. Is that right?"

"Yes."

"This ship isn't really a ship at all, is it? It's a swarm of nano-particles. That's what you are, isn't it, Alamo?"

"Your description is imprecise, but partially correct."

"Partially? You are more than just a mass of nano-particles?"

"Many of the ship's systems are built of massed compounds."

I thought about that. "Like the engines maybe?"

62

"Yes."

I nodded to myself. It made sense to me. How would you build something like the firing chamber of an engine out of billion tiny robots? These things had to be very small, to make up the ship's hull. Perhaps they didn't compose the ship's hull itself. Perhaps what they did was build the walls and hull up or removed it, quickly. That was the liquid shimmer I saw when 'doors' opened or closed between chambers.

"Kyle?" asked Sandra.

"Yeah?"

"What the hell is a nano?"

"It's short for nanorobot, or nanite. The concept is so new—and so experimental—that even we computer types haven't agreed on what to call them yet. We can't build anything like this ship, of course. Not yet, anyway. But the idea is essentially that you build not one big robot, but billions of tiny ones, so small you can't see them with the naked eye. Working together, these microscopic robots can build things human hands could never construct."

"You are saying that they injected me with a zillion tiny robots and they rebuilt my fingers and restarted my heart?"

"Yes."

"I think I'm going to be sick."

I shook my head. I reached out to take her hand. No less than three thin black arms snaked out of the walls, and pinned her wrist. Then I was able to gently pat her. It was horrible, however, as I could see the pain on her face. The arms were hurting her, making my entire gesture of comfort into a joke. She tried to smile back to protect my feelings.

Was this my future? I thought. In order to touch someone they had to be tied up? In order to walk the Earth again, I had to be part machine? In order to escape this fate entirely, the only option was death?

I closed my eyes. I decided then to try to get past the death of my children. I would put them away in my mind, at least for now. Too many world-changing events were happening. Thousands of people were dying on the Earth—just as my own kids had—due to these ships. I had to keep working and thinking in order to save other people the pain I was feeling now. At the very least, having a higher purpose might channel my grief into something constructive and make it more bearable. It was a coping technique counselors had suggested when my wife Donna had died.

"Alamo, let's talk about the enemy ship we just defeated. Who was aboard that ship?"

"They are the enemy."

"Yes," I said patiently, my eyes still closed. "Was that ship like this one? Was it made up of nanites?"

"No."

"Was it manned then by—by *biotics* you call them, organic life forms something like Sandra and I?"

"No."

"Great," I said. "Where do I go from there?"

"They aren't alive?" asked Sandra, alarmed. "They aren't even robots? What else is there? Are they ghosts or something?"

I thought for a moment. "Alamo, are the enemy alive at all?"

Hesitation. "Unknown."

Sandra made an unhappy sound. I knew how she felt. You could not help but think of space-zombies.

"Are they possibly *large* robots?" I asked on a hunch.

Hesitation. "Yes."

I nodded, but I did not smile. I suspected it would be a while before I smiled again. But this sort of thing, this problem-solving, was helping me. It kept my mind from spiraling into black depression, or rage. I had something to work on, something to prevent emotional pain from overwhelming me. My grief was like a fire, and it had been contained for now. "Do you have a name for these enemies, Alamo?"

"No."

"What shall we call them, Sandra?" I asked.

"Hmmm. We've got the Nanos... how about the Macros?"

I nodded. "Sounds good. Alamo, name these enemies the Macros, and refer to them that way from now on."

"Reference renamed."

"What do the Macros want here on Earth?"

"Raw materials."

That didn't sound good. Sandra and I exchanged worried glances.

"Are they coming back soon?" I asked.

"Yes."

"How soon?"

"Unknown."

"Alamo, what do your kind want?" asked Sandra. "What do the Nanos want here?"

There was no response.

"Alamo," I said sternly, "I want you to listen to Sandra."

"The Sandra-biotic is not command personnel."

"I know that. You don't have to take commands from her. Just answer her questions."

Hesitation. "Permissions set."

"Okay, now answer her last question."

"Current primary objective: Locate command personnel."

"Current objective?" asked Sandra, thinking aloud. "What was your previous objective?"

"Previous objective: Scientific examination."

Sandra nodded and smiled, clearly proud of herself. "See? These little bastards are the butt-probing aliens we've all been scared of for years."

I snorted. But I had to admit, she might be right. I thought of my kids again then, and it became hard to focus on anything else. "Now we know what happened to all those abductees," I said. "I think we are out of our league, and we're probably screwed. I don't know if we'll be alive an hour from now."

"Listen Kyle," she told me seriously. "We need to talk. I can tell you are devastated, but you are still thinking reasonably clearly. That's exactly why the ship made you into a commander. That's why you are leading this pack of survivors."

"No need for a pep-talk."

"Yes, yes there is a need for one," she insisted. "We need you. Earth needs you. Sure, you've suffered. Lots of people have. I *died*, for God's sake. But this is bigger than us. We have to do our best, because we are everything now. We are all that our world has up here to protect her. Everyone might die if we don't do it right."

I sighed. "If you're trying to make me feel better, you are doing a lousy job of it."

She laughed. I didn't laugh with her, but I knew she was right.

But still, in my own mind, I had a different set of goals. I wasn't really in this to save Earth. I wanted to find out what was going on, who was pulling the strings. Because I wanted to tear them up. Maybe it would take years. Maybe I would die trying. But I was going to get some revenge if I could, even if it was on a machine that didn't feel

65

anything and didn't care as I destroyed it. *Screw them all*, that was what I was thinking.

I was no longer angry with the *Alamo*. It was a tool. I might as well be angry with the fence pole that speared my wife. I wanted to find the creatures who built this ship.

If nothing else, my hunger for revenge would keep me going.

-11-

Crow contacted me on a private channel. "Riggs? Commander Riggs, are you there?"

"Yes, Jack, go ahead."

"Give me a break and call me Commodore. At least when we are on the open channel and other people are listening, okay Commander?"

"Yeah, sure," I said.

"I've got some new people now. A whole new crop of them. Take a look at the screen you invented."

I looked at it, and saw a dozen or more new golden "beetles" crawling around on the surface of the Earth. You could tell the new recruits from the old hands, they tended to roam around randomly because they were not in full control of their ships yet.

"I see them. Are they joining up?"

"Yes. It's going very well. There are only a few rogues left. After that last battle, people began seeing things my way. All the ships with human commanders aboard went up to meet the enemy, whether they wanted to or not. Watching other ships blow up did a great deal of the convincing for me. They know now they can't hang back and hide. The screen you came up with helps my recruiting efforts as well. Once I tell them how to show the entire tactical system on their living room walls, they get the picture—literally. I tell them to color us green and themselves as chicken-white. They stand out and look lonely. That gets most of the bloody dags to join up immediately." Crow broke off, erupting into a gust of laughter.

Somehow I found him less than amusing. "Commodore? I've got another idea for you."

I told him about the Nanos and the Macros. I told him the Macros were coming back, and they wanted raw materials.

"That's not good. I tried talking to them, you know, the guys in the big red ship. I had several of my lieutenants on it, trying to establish contact. They ignored us completely."

"Maybe they will listen now that we blew up one of their ships."

"Let's hope."

"I've got a new idea, Jack—ah, Commodore."

"Let's hear it."

I described to him another screen, a predictive screen, which we could lay out on the ceiling or the floor of the bridge. If we could show a plan visually, such as how each ship should position itself, everyone would have a much easier time following orders and acting in coordination. It wouldn't just show where ships were, but rather where we would *like* them to be.

"That's a fantastic idea. Let's set it up now and test it."

After an hour or so we had a working system. The ceiling worked best. We tried the floor, but Crow complained that furniture kept getting in the way. I gathered that Crow had done a lot of pirating. He had by his own admission a morass of carpets and things strewn over his floor. In the end, we set ourselves up in comfortable chairs and gazed up at the planning screen on the ceiling. We found it worked well, and we could easily talk and plan strategies. We could even give our ships formations to fight in.

"I'm impressed again, Commander. We make a great team. I'll relay this to everyone else and next time, we'll be flying in organized squadrons," Crow said, but then he hesitated. "Do you really think there will be a next time? Soon, I mean? Your ship suggested they would be back, but it might not know the difference between a day, a year, or a century."

"I think the ship means soon, sir. We have to be vigilant. Logically, it makes sense to me that the threat is real and ongoing. If the Nanos are trying to protect Earth—in their own special way—they've overdone it at this point. I mean, just one enemy ship came to the party? We fought with clueless commanders and only forty-odd ships and won easily. Why then, if that was the end of it, did the Nanos send over seven hundred vessels here?"

"I don't like it," said Crow. "But you're right, we have to assume they will be back for more soon, and in strength. And we have to assume we are in an all-out war."

"We need to alert the governments of Earth to the situation," I said. "They probably saw the battle. They have to be tracking us. They must do what they can to mobilize and protect themselves."

"So far, with humanity's primitive, homegrown tech, they can't do much."

"Has any nation tried to nuke one of these ships yet? That would probably do the trick."

"Not to my knowledge. But you've got a point there. We should talk to them before they get desperate. I'll put another officer on it. I've got just the guy. His name is Pierre and he could sweet-talk anyone out of their wallets. He's an ex-confidence trickster. He's got a silver tongue."

"An ex-con man?" I asked doubtfully. Did we really want a criminal as our representative to governments? I supposed plenty of the world's diplomats came under that description, but still....

"Well, maybe not so ex," Crow went on. "Pierre's been living off internet scams for years, I gather. He always kept a loaded weapon with him, expecting some mark to hunt him down for revenge. That's what saved him when the Nano ship grabbed him."

"I see. Well, if he's the best we have for now...."

"You might do well as a liaison," said Crow, "if that's what you are thinking. I know that. But you can't do everything. I need you focused on figuring out these ships and what we can do with them."

"Agreed."

"So, you are the famous Commodore Crow?" asked Sandra suddenly. She grinned at me. I was surprised she had managed to keep quiet this long.

"Who's that?"

"My name is Alessandra, but people call me Sandra."

"Oh indeed? How old are you, Sandra?"

"Twenty-four."

"My estimation of your abilities grows ever larger, Riggs. You dog! You have to tell me how you managed to smuggle one of your students aboard your ship. Everyone that I've brought aboard was immediately subjected to deadly tests."

69

I explained that she failed the tests, but was brought back aboard afterward. I hadn't really thought about it, but I supposed the ship was ignoring her and tolerating her because she was a failed applicant for command. She was a loophole. She wasn't to be tested, because she had already failed the tests. She wasn't hostile, so she wasn't to be killed. She had already been kicked out once, so there was no urgency to kick her out again. I'm sure that the Nanos would have preferred to drop her somewhere as biotic waste, but were held in check by my orders.

"Well done," said Crow. He paused, and I got the feeling his mind was racing with ideas. "So," he continued thoughtfully, "to get someone aboard with you, they have to go through at least one of the tests. Maybe.... What if I—*we* were to float close to the Earth, grab someone, let them fail a test, then when they get dumped out they fall into a swimming pool or something? Then I—*we* that is—could pick them up again and the ship would ignore them...."

"Getting lonely, Commodore?" asked Sandra in an acidic tone of voice. I glanced over at her and noted she had crossed her arms. "Intentional kidnapping is still a serious crime, remember?"

"Of course, my dear. I know that very well! We all do! We were all victims of these heartless ships. Riggs? You should work on some kind of video system. I would love to see the people I'm talking to."

Sandra and I exchanged glances. The Commodore wasn't the most gentle of gentlemen. I had thought before that this fleet might be a ragtag force of scoundrels and crazies. I realized now that my assumptions had been essentially correct.

"I'll see what I can do, Commodore," I said aloud.

Sandra rolled her eyes at me.

"And Riggs, go get some equipment. Whatever you think you need. Just hang over a mall and have the big arm dip down and grab whatever you want. Food, furniture, electronics, etc."

"Isn't that piracy, sir?" I asked.

"That's a harsh word. But we have to do what we must until we establish proper relations with the Earth governments. Then we can buy what we need. That will take longer, but it will make everyone feel better about the situation."

"Relations? Do you plan on demanding payment?"

"Aid, isn't that what you Yanks call it, Riggs? Billions in aid, that's what we need."

70

"Sounds like tribute," complained Sandra, "or ransom."

"Too right, Sandra. Isn't that what it always is? You can grizzle about it, but listen: we are providing a great service to Earth. We are doing more to protect them than all their military forces combined. They should mothball their navies at least and give us the funding. What good would one of your aircraft carrier battle groups have been, for example, against that last Macro ship?"

"You have a good point," Sandra admitted.

"Glad you see things my way. Well, we've chatted long enough. I've got a lot of business to do. Crow out."

"I'm not sure what to think of him," Sandra said after the connection had been broken.

"I know what you mean. But maybe he is just the kind of ruthless, practical man the world needs right now."

"Maybe. I don't like the way he talks about Earth—about all of humanity—as if they are some foreign power. I don't feel that disconnected from them."

"I know what you mean. But for a commander on one of these ships, disconnection is a stark reality."

"Do you think he's really going to go down and kidnap some young girl for—ah, as a companion?"

I sighed. I wanted to say no, but I couldn't rule it out. What did I really know about this man I'd allied myself with? I shrugged.

Sandra watched me closely. "Are we going to go down and steal things, too?"

I thought about it. We needed food. I couldn't just hang around my farm picking unripe corn and having the arm grope for things blindly in the windows forever. I had to wonder what the air force thought of my ship and its obsession with this one particular point on the map. I imagined a team of people might be fussing over the mystery. I couldn't decide if it was funny or pathetic. How panicked all the militaries of Earth must feel right now, unable to stop these strange, roving ships. They had no idea what we might do next. Were the cities rioting, evacuating? Had there been panics and if so, how many had died?

We spent some time cleaning up the mess the battle had made of things. It was extremely helpful to have the ship simply drop anything you didn't want—such as dribbles of beer, dried up garbage and the like—out of the ship. Vacuuming was a thing of the past. I had the ship

71

create another storage room, and I made a private room for Sandra that was connected to the bathroom. She wouldn't have to be tied by the ankles when she was in there, something she appreciated.

After a few hours, we looked critically at our handiwork. Such a strange mix, my old furniture and stark walls of gleaming metal. One item in particular stood out. It was an old lamp we'd used in the kids' bedrooms when they were babies. The ship must have found it in the attic. The lamp was in the shape of a teddy bear. I found it looked odd and pathetic, sitting next to my stained leather couch. All my furniture, in fact, was shabby-looking at best. I knew I should dump the teddy bear lamp and have the ship get something else, but now that it was up there, I couldn't force myself to part with it. My eyes stung when I looked at it.

Sandra watched me, but pretended not to notice.

"Sandra, what day is it?" I asked her, still staring at the teddy bear lamp. It had glassy black eyes, like marbles.

"Monday, I think."

"I think we will take a trip to the mall. Not a lot of people are there on Monday morning."

She pursed her lips disapprovingly.

"We need bedding, furniture, clothes, food, and electronics," I argued. "Hopefully, we won't give anyone a heart attack."

"You're the commander," she said.

She turned away and busied herself with our pile of half-stale, half-eaten boxes of crackers and breakfast cereals. It had been a long time since I'd been in a domestic situation with a female, but I recognized the behavioral patterns. They weren't positive.

"What's the matter?"

She turned on me quickly and put her hands on her hips. The little black arms that still wrapped her ankles strained to keep up with her. Those lovely dark eyes smoldered.

"Is that really what we are going to do, Kyle? Become pirates?"

I looked at her. "Aren't you tired?"

"I'm almost sick I'm so tired."

"Well, this couch is mine. I'm not giving it up. So, you can sleep tied to a wall, or sleep on the metal deck in that room I made for you, or you could let me steal a bed."

"Or you could drop me off."

My face fell. I felt a pang. Was this our first fight? "Is that what you want?"

She thought about it. She shook her head *no* and grinned. I was surprised by the grin. She seemed to switch from a smile to a frown and back again very quickly. I supposed it was part of her personality, which I was still getting used to.

"It's all too exciting, is that it?" I asked.

"Partly," she admitted. "But also, I hate the idea of leaving you up here fighting for me—for all of us—with no one to talk to but that awful Aussie. After what we've been through, I feel like I would be abandoning you and not doing my part to save the world."

"Such idealism. It's nice to see it put to good use."

She made a face. "Yes, I admit it. I was into causes down on Earth. They all seem so far away and silly now that we are up here, fighting against the possible extinction of our species. I mean, we've already met two powerful, terrifying races of robots that have better technology than we do. Every Earth-threatening thing I used to worry about seems absurd in comparison. But I'm still not too excited about stealing things for our own personal comfort."

"We could build a shower setup," I said enticingly. Her eyes flicked up to meet mine. They widened. I had her attention with that one.

"How?"

"We would start with a water tank. I could have the ship heat it up. Don't you want to wash your hands? I could add a sink and a shower stall to our little bathroom. How long do you think you want to camp out up here with me without modern amenities? We don't even have toilet paper."

She pursed her lips. I think the idea of a shower tempted her like nothing else I'd mentioned.

"Well, maybe we could pick up a *few* things," she said.

I would have smiled, but I wasn't quite ready to do that yet. In the back of my mind I knew I was being manipulative. Sandra was good for me. She kept me going. I had to keep going, thinking, and working if I was ever going to get to the bottom of all this. I didn't want others on Earth to go through what I just had.

And I still wanted my revenge.

-12-

I was nervous. I felt like a shop-lifting kid, dared into stealing a popsicle by my friends.

At first, the raid went well. We drifted over the biggest mall in Merced, which really wasn't that big of a mall, but it had what we needed. The belly of the ship opened and the big, black snake-arm dipped down. I told it to find me a bed first, and it hovered over a furniture store. I stood in the doorway between the bridge and the cargo area where the arm originated. It was rooted in the cargo chamber ceiling and hung down like some massive jungle vine.

The opening allowed a gust of hot air and familiar smells to come up into my face. I looked over my shoulder and saw Sandra was there, leaning forward and sniffing as well. Her long black hair fluttered around her face.

I squinted down into a parking lot. Everything looked so normal. There were Dodges and Fords. Lots of pickups and SUVs. A few nice cars, a few trashed ones. Windshields reflected the late afternoon sun upward, flashing it into my eyes. How I missed, in that instant, the open air and sunshine. Today should have been a fine day, just before summer. I should have been working on the farm, or sitting in the university quad, or giving a lecture.

Below us, in the parking lot, the initial reaction was predictable. Cars zoomed away. There were a few crunching sounds, screeching tires, shouts. I didn't see anyone wreck their car, but I imagined that a few drivers, craning their necks up at the terrifying vessel that blotted out the sky overhead, had done so.

74

I tried to ignore the fleeing citizens. I focused on the homey feel the place gave me. That's what I craved. The scents got me the most. Hot asphalt. Dust. Trees in full bloom. Even the oily smell of exhaust was comforting and filled me with a longing for my old life. I realized then how sterile the ship was. I'd spent less than two days in it and already the normal world seemed so very different. Being in the ship was like being in the hold of an airliner. The air was canned and stale— flavorless. The light was muted and had no obvious source.

I took a deep breath, enjoying the breeze and the smells of home. And the bed began coming up.

"This ship has taste," said Sandra behind me. The ship's little arms were straining at her, trying to hold her back, but she leaned against them.

I looked at what the ship had in its alien, metal hand. It was a big bed, an old fashioned four-poster with ruffles that rippled in the valley wind. I snorted. I did not smile, but my cheek did twitch.

Even as the ship lifted the bed upward, I realized something and Sandra voiced the feeling out loud.

"Idiot Nanos," she said, "it's too big."

And indeed it was. The ship dilated the openings between the cargo area, the bridge, and Sandra's bedroom to the maximum, but it wasn't careful with the awkward burden. One post crunched into the ship's hull. The arm was too strong to notice, and simply pulled it through. There was a splitting, ripping sound. Part of one post snapped off and fell down into the parking lot. The chunk of hardwood crashed through one of those sun-silvered windshields and smashed it into white spider webs of broken safety-glass. I hoped no one was in there.

"Damn," said Sandra.

We stepped out of the way and ducked as the bed sailed over us toward Sandra's bedroom.

"Quite a dainty ship, isn't she?" I asked wryly.

There was a crash as something fell over. It was the kids' teddy bear lamp. I headed over there and righted it. I had had the ship build a power outlet in the wall, made with leads and a real surge protector from my house. The leads ran up to twin streams of quivering, liquid-looking metal. It looked as if the positive and negative wires were connected to frozen arcs of mercury. I didn't know how the ship powered those leads without frying the little robots that made the connections, and I didn't ask.

"How's the lamp?" asked Sandra.

I looked at her. She knew I liked the lamp. She knew it was my kids' lamp. "It's fine," I said. "The bulb is broken, but we can have the ship get another one."

"Oh, sure," said Sandra skeptically, looking at her bed. It was quite nice, but one corner sagged where the post had broken. "Let's tell it to screw in the bulbs, too."

I threw up my hands. We had to do what we could.

We spent about half an hour hanging over Merced, stealing stuff. As we were working blind, it was rather like fishing. We took clothing, random piles of shirts and pants that didn't fit. We took food, furniture, and no less than three refrigerators. The first two were hopelessly mangled, but the third fridge came up in a workable state, with only a few dents in the stainless steel double-doors.

"That's a nice one," Sandra commented.

"A keeper," I agreed. "What have we got so far to put into it?"

"Hmm," she said, checking the grocery stocks. "The ship seems to like steak. We have loads of that. And bread. And a hell of a lot of orange soda."

"Sounds good. We'll go for canned goods next."

"Beer comes in cans," Sandra said suggestively.

"So it does."

We busied ourselves with our stuff, filling a storeroom and plugging the fridge into a scary-looking, specialized black arm that carried power for reasons I didn't understand.

It was after several more loads of groceries that disaster struck. I don't really know how it happened. The best I could figure out afterward was that some cop had had enough. He had probably been down there since the beginning and had his orders. But he apparently decided not to follow them. Rather, he decided to fire on the ship. I never even heard the sound of his gun. But I heard Alamo's reaction.

Blinding green light flared. It filled our vision, our heads and our minds. Sandra screamed. I clutched my face, knowing what it was almost immediately.

"Alamo! Cease fire! They are not a threat!"

"Enemy fire detected."

The laser faded, but the after images still flashed in my mind. I opened one eye and looked at the front wall with the metallic radar screen I'd created. The people and cars were being tracked there. All of them. There must have been thousands. A ragged line of contacts circled us at a distance. No doubt the police had cordoned off the area, but people had come to look at the ship floating over their town, rummaging in shops and stealing things with its great black arm.

The arm retracted and the doors snapped shut. I hoped it was over, but Sandra shouted something, pointing.

I looked at the wall again. Two contacts had gone red. A third and a fourth went red as I watched. They were spread around at the edge of the golden beetles that represented the civilians.

The ship fired again. One of the red contacts vanished, then another. They must be police, firing on the ship when it fired at them. They were fools. They couldn't do anything to this ship. I thought I heard a bullet spang off the skin of the vessel. I wondered how thick the metal hull of the ship was.

The golden beetles had been backing up, but now they were running away from the ship in every direction. Some paused, falling. Others were too close to the red beetles, which vanished one by one, almost as quickly as they appeared. The cops must have opened fire in a chain reaction. Each of them was designated as a target and burned down moments later. From their point of view, they could hear other guns firing and the ship was suddenly shooting into the crowd. Surrounding clusters of golden beetles vanished with the red contacts. They were dying in swathes.

"I'm not in any danger, stop firing!"

"Command personnel are in danger. Defensive fire is mandatory."

"Fly up, then! Fly upward! Get us up into orbit now!"

I felt the floor come up toward me and stumbled. I managed to get myself into a new easy chair I'd stolen. I rubbed my face, my eyes ached. How many had the ship killed? I opened a beer and drank it. Sandra and I barely spoke for the next hour. She went into her room and vanished.

Strangely, I fell asleep on my stolen easy chair. It had been many long hours since I'd slept. I didn't even plan on sleeping. It just happened. I felt as if I were suffocating, as if a great hand had come down and closed over me, putting me out like fingers snuffing a candle flame.

-13-

When I woke up I felt better, but then I remembered everything, and felt awful again. For some reason, I'd had nice dreams of Donna and sunny days. I missed my dreams, and as I reclined in my chair, blinking up at the metallic ceiling, I tried to go back to sleep. I tried to get back into my happy dreams, but I couldn't. I finally gave up, groaned, and heaved myself out of the chair.

Sandra wasn't on the bridge. I figured she was in her room that I'd set up for her. Maybe she was sleeping, too. I rummaged for food, then washed in the bathroom, which I'd managed to set up with a bowl of running water. It was cold water, and there was no shower yet. But even cold water and a bar of soap on my face felt good at that point.

When I finished and turned around, Sandra was staring at me. She had a loop of black cable around her neck now, not her ankles. She looked like some kind of prisoner. I sighed. We were both prisoners.

She pointed to the thing wrapped around her neck. "This sucks," she said.

"I'm sorry. What happened to the ankle things?"

"I took a nap in my room and you told the ship to remove them when I was alone, remember? It did, since you weren't around. But once I came near you, it just reached out and grabbed the nearest thing it could. In this case, my neck."

I would have laughed if I'd felt better. "Is it better or worse than the ankle?"

"Well," she said, considering. "It's easier to move around, actually. It doesn't hurt, and so far the ship's been very careful not to choke me. But it is so demeaning."

"Do you want me to change it?"

"No, it's fine for now."

"Here, I can at least put it around your waist." I ordered the ship to switch the cable to circle her waist. It looked far more natural that way. It was almost like a safety harness, rather than a slave collar.

"Thanks," she said, breathing more easily.

I hesitated. "Should I get those injections? I think, eventually, I'm going to have to do it. I won't be able to live like this forever."

"Don't do it for my comfort. You don't know how it will turn out. I'll just play harem girl here for another day."

I snorted and we ate some breakfast. I wondered what time it was. Looking at the wall, I realized we were up above Earth, but not so far up we didn't feel the gravity. I wondered how long we'd been up here, and if we were even over California anymore. Life in space was rather different. It sort of scrambled your brains. All the normal cycles of night and day—meals and sleeping—were disrupted. I supposed it was rather like spending a long period in a submarine or underground in a mine.

"Do you know what they do to keep themselves feeling right on a submarine or a spaceship?" I asked Sandra.

"What?"

"I have no idea," I said, "I'm looking for ideas."

"Well, we could try to keep as normal a cycle as possible with clocks and all."

"I agree," I said. I talked to the *Alamo* for a while, giving it instructions to sound off the hours as they passed if we weren't sleeping. I also told it to dim or brighten the glow of its walls in rhythm with the normal sun cycles. We set ourselves up on California time. That would probably feel the most natural.

Later, Crow contacted me and I talked to him about it. He said they were already doing it, but I should set my clocks by Greenwich Mean Time, which meant I would be living on British time. If we all went by that time standard, we would be in synch and could coordinate better. I agreed—it was the simplest system, and as an officer he didn't want us calling him all night every night.

He went over a plan with me, telling me he wanted to place picket ships around Earth. Using six ships, one over each pole and four more in a belt over the equator, we could increase our warning time if a new enemy contact arrived on the scene.

"Good idea," I said.

"Glad you like it. You are assigned to the North Pole, with a twelve hour shift. Take the day shift. I want you awake and thinking up new ways to get these ships working for us."

"Fine."

"I'd put you in command of a squadron to practice formations, but I think instead you are going to be our one-man research team. Did you manage to raid a few shops and make your ship more homey?"

I told him about the slaughter at the Merced mall. He clucked his tongue disappointedly.

"Now, don't take that to heart. That was their screw-up, not yours. You shouldn't feel bad about it. They all know what will happen if they fire on these ships."

"Yes, but I figure just one man lost his nerve and fired, then the ship fired back, then the rest thought it was open season and—"

"Yeah, yeah. I know what happened. It's by no means the first time. But they have to learn, even if it is the hard way."

I didn't like his attitude. Not at all. "These are human beings we are talking about here. The ones we are supposedly defending."

"There are kinks that need to be worked out. I'm on it. I have my diplomatic team—"

"We're talking about Pierre, the internet con-man, right?"

"Ambassador Pierre Gaspard, you mean. Make sure if you have any contact with the Earth governments, you call him *Ambassador*. I should never have told you about his background."

"Don't get huffy. Okay, he's our Ambassador. How's he doing?"

"Rather well, actually. Using your brilliant scheme for capturing young women—"

"That wasn't my intention!"

"Whatever. In any case, I managed to catch a U.S. Senator in her bathrobe this morning in D.C. She failed the very first test, of course— you remember the ingenuity test where you are supposed to ride on the arm to get out of the room?"

"I recall it well."

"Anyway, she was dumped back out onto her lawn within a minute. My ship was only about two meters above the ground. I had the ship snatch her up again and brought her to my bridge. I thought the woman was going to have a heart attack, but she lived and I handed her over to Pierre's ship to open negotiations."

"Wait a minute," I said, "she failed a test on *your* ship, but the Nanos let her aboard Pierre's ship?"

"Yeah, it seems once they are marked as losers they stay losers for all the Nanos."

"Thanks a lot," said Sandra, interrupting.

"Oh, hey Sandra. No offense."

Sandra stalked off the bridge.

"What's the Senator's name?" I asked.

"Kim Bager."

"Really? Isn't Senator Bager chairing the foreign relations committee?"

"Maybe. I don't follow Yank politics—I follow football. The kind where you use your feet. Anyway, she's having a long talk with Pierre now. I mean, Ambassador Gaspard."

"I've got to talk to her. To both of them."

"I think that can be arranged. But try not to say anything embarrassing or too revealing, okay? This is serious business."

"The business of serious extortion."

"Now, that's exactly what I'm talking about. We aren't pirates, mate! We are a serious political force. We lost several ships and good people fighting for Earth just yesterday. If we can get the supplies we need in an orderly fashion, your ship won't have to slaughter people at malls next week when you run out of food."

I took a deep breath. He was right about raiding: it was dangerous for the people on the ground. It was hard for me to take our ragtag group seriously as a political power because we were so new, so green. But we *were* like a separate nation now. We were trapped in our ships. We knew things no one else on Earth understood. Our mission was life and death, not only for ourselves, but possibly for the rest of humanity as well.

"Okay," I said. "I promise to play the role of a Star Force Commander. If they take us seriously, this will all go more smoothly for everyone."

"Exactly. Glad to hear it."

"What would you have done if I didn't agree, Jack?"

Commodore Crow sniffed. "I wouldn't have given you the name of Pierre's ship."

81

I smiled. That was it, the first smile since my kids had died. I blinked at the thought. Crow's slippery maneuvers had brightened my day somehow. I had a sudden thought then.

"Crow?"

"Yeah, mate?"

"You weren't really a Captain in the Australian navy, were you?"

A deep breath. "I never said I was. Not exactly, anyway. Keep that under your hat, will you, professor?"

"Of course," I said. And I meant it. "Now, can I have the name of the Frenchman's ship?"

"Who said he was a Frenchman?"

"Well, I assumed—"

"He's Canadian."

"Ah, I see. So he speaks English fluently, I take it?"

"And several other languages as well."

"And the ship's name?"

"The *Versailles*," said Crow, with a hint of an apology in his voice.

"He named his ship after a palace?"

"Yes, well… he believes in tradition. Anyway, contact him if you want an update on the political situation. I'll leave you in his capable hands. Crow out."

-14-

As Crow had ordered, I took up a position about fifty thousand miles above the North Pole. We encountered a whole new problem at that point: weightlessness. At first, it was kind of funny. Sandra laughed at me as I floated away from my chair. I called to the ship and had it tether me with one of those instantly grown arms. The thin cable felt warm around my waist. It was a creepy feeling, as I knew now the thing was made up of about a million tiny, squirming nanites. Just knowing that made me itch when the arms touched me. It was like being touched by arms made up of fleas that had all interlocked their legs together and formed a chain with their bodies.

I didn't laugh, but it did give me a slight smile. I hadn't been smiling much since I'd lost my kids for good. Sandra and I were equals when weightless in space. The ship had us both on leashes. Then we noticed that all the liquids we had around the place, in cups and cans, were floating with us. This took a while to clean up and sort out. The nanites weren't super good with liquids. They could form hard surfaces of their liquid metal, or turn the floor porous and suck it up, but those skinny black arms were simply no good at catching liquids out of the air.

After a few hours of drifting, we got into a routine and things were almost normal. We were going to have a problem with liquids, however, I could see. We only had so many squeeze bottles and we had no way of handling cooking properly. It was a good thing, I realized, we were only expected to hang out on sentry duty for half of every day. I was looking forward to returning back to my familiar gravity-well long before our first shift was over.

"Shouldn't you call that Pierre guy?" asked Sandra, drifting over the new couch with a roll of paper towels. She'd found one last floating dollop of orange soda and was determined to catch it before it stained the couch.

"I should," I said, "But somehow I'm not looking forward to it. The truth is, besides being distracted, I'm a little embarrassed."

"Why?"

"Well, he's some kind of internet scam artist, from what I gather. Who knows what kind of crap he's been spouting off to Senator Bager. It just seems so unprofessional. They must think we are a bunch of nuts, and we've acted like kids—kids who accidentally got hold of nuclear weapons."

"Your first time talking to a Senator?"

"Definitely. What a way to start my political career."

"Just get it over with."

"I will—after we figure out what we are going to eat for lunch."

We never did get to eat lunch that day, however. I managed to get a floating frozen rice dinner into the microwave and slapped the door closed before it could drift out again. Then the *Alamo* spoke up. I'd been dreading the words it said.

"Enemy ships detected. Emergency signal received. Gathering initiated."

Enemy ships? I thought. Knowing what was coming, I tried to grab the cable arm that tethered me and pull myself down against the floor. I managed to do it, but I'd guessed wrong. The ceiling was the floor this time. Everything began to fall, sag or slide toward it.

"Alamo, secure everything you can!"

Arms snaked out but it was too late in many cases. Bottles broke and spilled their contents in slow, glugging motions. The fridge slid up the wall it had been against and dented its top against the roof of the ship.

"Alamo, new standing order: When about to accelerate due to some alert, secure everything first."

"Program rejected. Overridden by prior programming. Options not set."

I gritted my teeth. "Alamo, as soon as you can when we get an alert call, secure all equipment and personnel."

"Program set."

"Also, Alamo, turn us right side up."

"Ambiguous statement. Command rejected."

"The deck that has been the floor since I was kidnapped by this crazy ship. Make it the floor again. Turn the ship so that our acceleration pushes us against it."

"Command accepted."

Another series of sliding sounds and a few crashes soon followed. I sucked air through my teeth and put my hands over my head. The microwave missed me, as did the fridge, but my rice bowl caught me in the back of the head. It was still frozen, and I felt like I'd been hit by an iceball. Sandra yelled something from the main bridge, but I didn't hear exactly what it was.

"You okay?" I called out to her.

"Quit screwing around with the ship!" she called back.

She didn't sound hurt, so I returned my attention to the ship.

"Alamo, where are the enemy ships? Are they in our sector?"

"No."

"How many ships are there? Put them on the forward screen."

"There are three ships. They are being displayed."

Paranoid, I stepped unsteadily out of the kitchen area into the main bridge. The forward wall showed the dark circle representing Earth in the center now. I looked around for a few long seconds before I spotted the rust-red contacts. One was on the wall to the left, one to the right, and one was crawling along the floor. I'd almost stepped on it.

The ship was accelerating faster now. At first, I'd thought we were at about half-gravity—half a G of acceleration. But now it felt like a full G, maybe more.

"They are coming at us from different angles now, Kyle," Sandra said. "I don't like this."

Neither did I. I stared at the walls and tried to absorb what was happening. Due to the fact we'd put out scouting groups, we had more warning this time. We had more ships, too. But I could see right away things weren't going well. The ships we'd put out over the equator were heading straight for the nearest enemy ship. They were going to reach them and be destroyed before the rest of us could get there in force. Worse, all our ships were heading up in randomly distributed swarms toward whichever of the ships was closest.

"Incoming call from the *Snapper*."

"Open connection," I said.

"Commander Riggs?" shouted Crow. He sounded like he was having a heart attack.

"This is bad, Commodore."

"I can see that. What do you think we should do?"

I began working on the ceiling, pointing toward spots where I wanted groups of ships. The *Alamo* had been trained to respond to this sort of thing by now, and obligingly placed groups of golden beetles in each spot I indicated.

"Let's just group up into three teams of twenty ships, form a ball of them and hit them all at once."

"No, too risky," said Crow.

"What do you mean 'no?' What do you want to do?"

"Form a mass on one ship, beat it, then form a mass on the next and beat it down second."

"If we do that, the other ships will get to Earth."

"Yes, two will, until we can deal with them. I don't want to divide my forces when I'm not sure how many ships it will take to kill one of the enemy."

"Look, Jack," I said, alarmed. Were we deciding which cities of Earth were about to get nuked? "We can't decide this on our own."

"There's nobody else up here, Kyle."

I took a deep breath and looked at Sandra. She looked back with wide, frightened eyes. I don't think, up until that moment, I'd ever really seen fear in her eyes. Suspicion, worry, anger—yes. But not open fear. She knew the stakes.

"Riggs, I'm going to try to recall the sentry ships that are about to suicide on the enemy. Call me back when you have a better idea. Crow out."

I turned myself back to the big board, seeking that magical *better idea*. Our sentries had bought us some time. They were way out there, and this time they'd seen the enemy and we had maybe half an hour before they would reach Earth. The bad part was trying to convince any of the ships that pulling back wasn't running from the enemy but rather was repositioning so we could win the battle. Thinking about that gave me my first idea.

I contacted Crow.

"What?" he roared.

I could see by the action on the board he'd not been able to stop the ships. The single closest ones had slowed their hell-bent drive to meet

86

the enemy, but had not turned away, had not pulled back to regroup. Now the incoming Macro was closing on these ships. I was glad they'd not come for the North Pole this time. If they had, the *Alamo* doubtlessly would have rushed eagerly toward the nearest enemy alone.

"Jack, tell the sentries to order their ships to attack the enemy on the opposite side of the planet. That way they are still attacking, but they can escape the one that's—"

"Got it! Crow out."

I could see why he had disconnected so quickly. The ship out over Africa had almost made it to the big red bastard that swam toward it. I took a step, then two steps, closer to that side of the battle. It was on the right wall, just over my easy chair. Yes, there it was. As I watched, a tiny sliver bubbled out of the attacker and became a red contact.

"Crap, they fired," said Sandra.

"Dammit!" I said. I walked to the wall and hammered my fist on it. I could feel the tiny hard surface of raised metal under my fist. My hammering, unsurprisingly, had no effect. Within thirty seconds, we lost the first ship of the battle.

I walked to the other side. Crow had gotten through to the other sentries in time. They had turned and were moving away. Our ships were clearly faster than the enemy.

I called Crow again. "You saved two of them."

"Yeah," he said. "She'll be right, mate. Don't worry. What else have you thought of, besides killing my entire force by splitting it into thirds?"

"That would put twenty on each ship," I said, thinking hard. "We might win all three."

"Or we might lose all three battles and the war."

"We have sixty ships. How many are you willing to lose to figure something important out?"

Crow chewed that over for a few seconds. "Depends. Talk to me."

"We know forty or so can win, we did that before. In fact, with more organized fleet command, we should barely lose anyone with forty. We can afford to put the rest on a second ship."

"And the third one?"

"We'll let the enemy coming in low over the South Pole get close. Let it through. There's not much in Antarctic for them to destroy. By the time they make it up to Argentina or South Africa or Australia, assuming that's what they are going to do, our main force will be done fighting and we can turn on the third ship en masse."

"What do you want to learn by pitting twenty ships against one?"

"If twenty can win. Think about it, Jack: they lost the last fight, right? So, they tripled their numbers. Next time, if they lose this fight, they will send nine ships."

"How can you be sure?"

"I can't. But they are machines. They will tend to loop and follow similar patterns."

He was quiet for a second. "I'll send ten. Ten tightly clustered ships. If they kill it, we know something."

"Why ten?"

"Because that's about how many we will have left to face each enemy if they send nine next time."

I rubbed my neck and lounged in my easy chair. The G-forces were getting to me. I agreed to his plan. We might lose ten ships, but if we couldn't take out one of theirs with ten of ours, we were probably dead anyway.

-15-

At first, the battle went as planned. Crow and I worked out the details up on the ceiling of our ships, and then broadcast it to everyone else in the fleet. We sent the main body of ships toward the enemy that approached Europe. Crow and I both went with that group. A group of ten headed for the second ship, which was over Hawaii or thereabouts. The enemy was obviously splitting their forces, hoping to slip by our defenses. They were about to succeed, too, in the far South. That was the ship I worried about most, the one that crawled over the floor like a cockroach toward the South Pole and after that, points unknown. I didn't know what these ships would do when they reached my world, but I figured they hadn't come all this way to give us a cure for cancer.

Our fifty hit the single ship headed for Europe and mowed the missiles it shot at us. I'd heard from Crow they were indeed missiles. Some of us were monitoring Earth's news stations and earthbound observers had confirmed it. I was glad it wasn't some advanced, freaky thing our own human technology could never hope to deal with. I was also glad to hear Earth was openly watching these battles. Maybe, just maybe, they would come to appreciate us one day.

With fifty ships swarming on one, it wasn't much of a contest. We destroyed it quickly, even though it tried to turn and run. We were way out of position by the time it blew up, however, and it would be about an hour until we could get back to help the other ships.

It was one of the longest hours of my life. The second ship over Hawaii didn't die so easily. When they were at long range our squad managed to shoot down each incoming missile, but as they drew closer, our ships had less time to fire at the missiles before they hit something. Each shot, we could see, came closer to the tight knot of ten ships.

Then disaster struck from an unexpected direction. The South Pole ship, which had been barreling in at full speed this entire time, had made it close to Earth. It had deviated course somewhat. Quickly, its new goal became apparent.

"Isn't that South America?" asked Sandra.

I nodded. At least Jack didn't have to worry about his relatives. It seemed logical when I thought about it. Why not go for the closest land mass with the greatest population?

"Kyle?" said Sandra, "I think it's shooting something."

I watched, unable to speak, unable to swallow. For the first time, I saw an alien ship firing on our planet—if you didn't count the Nanos, that was. Somehow, I felt responsible. I couldn't believe my conversations and command decisions had led to this result. I felt hot and sick. We had failed to protect our world.

"What are they firing at?" asked Sandra. She was up now, squatting in front of the big dark circle of Earth. "The missiles are vanishing over Antarctica."

"There are bases there. Scientific installations run by various nations. The aliens are certainly thorough, aren't they? If only—"

"Kyle!" shouted Sandra, "look at the ten you sent at the other ship."

I did and I almost choked. I had expected to see them being destroyed, but that hadn't happened, not yet anyway. What I saw, in some ways, was almost worse. Three of the ships had broken off. They were no longer attacking the target we'd given them. They'd turned away and were now heading downward on our wall toward the ship that approached the southern tip of South America.

Crow's voice scratched onto the public channel. "Mutiny! Get back on target, everyone! You are screwing up the plan!"

It wasn't very professional sounding, but it was to the point. The three ships ignored him and kept flying away from their designated battle.

I opened a line to Crow. "Commodore. Break off all of them. Send all ten at the South American ship."

"What the hell are they doing?"

"They are disobeying orders."

"I should let them burn."

90

"They might very well do so. I think they are going to beat your team to the South American ship."

Unpleasant laughter. "Serves them right. Deserters."

"They might have relatives there, on that continent."

"Yeah, or they might have figured out they can only run away by switching targets over and over again."

I thought about that. I didn't like the sound of it. Our fellow fleet members were not a disciplined force. They were a bunch of survivalists. If they heard about a new way to avoid combat—well, they might let a city burn to save their own skins.

"Let's hope I'm right on this one," I said.

"I think you are right about our response. I'm pulling our ships off the secondary target. We'll all hit the third and then deal with the second afterward. I don't like them shooting at Earth."

I had a little predictive session with the *Alamo*. We worked out that the ship coming up from the South Pole would get to Santiago, Chile or Buenos Aires, Argentina before we could get there. As soon as the enemy ship reached land, we watched as it paused over the rocky, cold region of the far south. When it moved away, it looked as if it had laid an egg. A small mass sat there.

"What the hell is that?" I demanded.

"I don't know," said Sandra.

"Alamo, what did the ship drop off?"

"Warning, the following is a predictive analysis, not based on factual data."

"Just tell me."

"The probabilities indicate it is an invasion force."

"An invasion force? Of what? Giant robots?"

"Reference unclear."

"The Macros, they just put troops down, is that what you are saying?"

"Yes. Troops and processing systems."

They came for raw materials, my brain said, supplying an unwanted answer. I stared at the wall with bits of shivering, rippling metal all over it. The seas weren't blue, they were silver. The land was the color of graphite. But it was my home, just the same. I felt fear and panic—and horror.

When they got closer to a belt of major cities, they laid another "egg" of troops, machines—whatever it was. Then the ship fired about

91

five times. I knew, vaguely, where the big cities were. The missiles moved and finally vanished over several of Earth's greatest cities. I had no doubt there were mass casualties.

I swallowed hard as we swept in over the big ship now. I was proud to see that the three who had broken off and come to fight over South America were not deserters. They were the first to arrive. Two of them died before we got in range to help, but at least one guy lived. I thought that perhaps they had done the right thing. They had lost us two ships, but had distracted the Macros and kept them from taking out more of our cities.

We swarmed the last ship and brought it down without losing another vessel.

"What next?" Sandra asked.

I knew what she meant. Did we fly to kill the ship over Hawaii or stay and work on the troops or whatever they were? I could see now that they were moving too, very slowly. They were about as fast as a minute hand on an old analog clock, but they were moving. On the planet, I realized, they must be moving very fast indeed. The speed of a car on the highway, at least.

"Fleet," Crow's voice sounded, "I want everyone to hit the ship over Hawaii. We can come back here and attack these ground forces later. It will take them hours according to the *Snapper* for them to reach any major population centers."

No one argued. We all raced low over the Earth, crossing her oceans to the northwest. I wanted a beer, I wanted it badly, but I held off. I told myself I would have a six-pack when the last Macro on my world died.

The last ship never reached Hawaii. It was close, and it did get off one missile, which took out the city of Hilo I later learned. The missiles, unsurprisingly, were nuclear. Each carried a single warhead, about a dozen megatons worth of death and destruction. They never got close enough to land to drop any invasion forces, thankfully.

When we raced back to South America, the two red contacts representing the invasion forces had spread out like spills of paint. Our ships flew in and parked over them. I felt my ship fire again and again. I grinned at Sandra fiercely. We were slaughtering them, I could tell.

But then there were squawking voices on the public channel. Reports came in of something hitting us. It was hard to tell who was dying with all our golden, beetle-like ships zooming around and over one another, seeking and destroying.

Then I saw one get hit, not too far from our own contact. I tried to open a channel to Commodore Crow. We had to get out of there. But he ignored my connection and shouted over the public channel.

"Pull out! Everyone move to orbit. The ships will let us, they don't have a compulsion about leaving a ground fight. I repeat, order your ship to lift off to orbital altitude."

In a shifting mass we followed his orders. Star Force's second battle against the Macros was over. But the ground war for Earth had just begun.

-16-

I seriously needed a shave by my fifth day aboard the *Alamo*. Maybe, I thought, the pirates of the old days were depicted with wild frothing beards because they were sitting on ships without any easy way to shave, just as I was.

Pierre had been—interesting to talk to. He was entertaining. He was the life of the party. He presented everything in the best light, even the growing ground war in southern Argentina and Chile. He called it a learning exercise, and said it was good for humanity.

"This war will end all other wars, I tell you," he said on my private channel to his ship, the *Versailles*. "Why? Because man will not fight man when there are much scarier things out there that want to kill us all."

Pierre often talked like that: he would first ask a question, then answer it himself. I had to admit, it worked. Everyone found him persuasive.

"All right, Pierre, don't give me that theory again."

"Theory? You call it a theory? No, you cannot use that term. It is demonstrable *fact*, not theory. Even now, forces that a week ago refused to accept one another's existence are sending troops to fight this new menace as allies. Ancient enemies will stand shoulder-to-shoulder and fight these machines to the death."

"I'm sold, man," I told him, not wanting to argue any further. "Let's talk about the big meeting."

"It is tonight, at six p. m. I will meet alone with the US government official."

"Only one man, right?"

"Exactly as we discussed. The Senator—Kim Bager—she has agreed. She will send only one man. We must be recognized as a new sovereign nation. We must have formal relations with the governments of Earth."

Sandra spoke up. "You should not meet him alone, Pierre."

"Don't worry about me, lovely Sandra."

I glanced at her. I wasn't sure how Pierre knew, but she did look even better than usual today. Fresh clothes and a wash had done wonders. Her hair was clean and shiny. Up until now, I'd only seen her in a bedraggled state. I'd managed to put together that shower setup I'd promised her. A few nights of real sleep hadn't hurt her, either.

"We will back you up, Pierre," I said. "We'll only be a few miles away."

"Don't frighten them! I don't know how high level this person will be, but he is supposed to be empowered to speak for the government. He will be coming in alone and unarmed. He must be brave to dare to face the ship's tests."

"How brave? He's been briefed on what to do. When he fails, the ship will just dump him out onto the grass of a park in Alexandria. Then you can pick him up again."

"You and I know that, Commander," said Pierre. "But this new brave soul doesn't. To him, he enters the very cave of the lion. Don't you recall the great fear in your heart when the ship lifted you up in its alien embrace for the first time? I know you can't have forgotten that moment of terror."

"I was feeling pissed off at the time, actually."

Pierre laughed easily. It was another of his habits. When a conversation went in a direction that he didn't want it to, he would laugh it off, and then switch topics.

"Commander, I ask that you stay well back. Give diplomacy room to breathe."

"It's your show, Pierre. I'm just riding shotgun, here."

Pierre laughed nervously. "Such a quaint turn of phrase you have. I must go now and prepare for my guest."

We broke the connection.

"He trusts his quick talk too much," said Sandra. "He thinks he can talk his way out of anything."

"Maybe he can," I said. "He talked Crow into making him an ambassador, didn't he?"

95

I went back to watching the news with Sandra. It was nice to have a satellite TV setup aboard ship. But the news wasn't so nice. The news had never, in my memory, been so bad. Things were bad on Earth, not in space. Up in the sky, everything was eerily quiet. No new attacking Macro ships had come. Some of us had begun to speculate that the space invasion was over, that the Macros would watch and see if their ground troops could take us out alone before they risked more ships attacking Earth. Personally, I didn't buy that line. Maybe they had run out of invasion ships, maybe not. But I was sure that as long as they could, these robots would keep coming at us. Computers are tenacious. I used to tell my students they could drop something as small as a pencil in the open doorway of an elevator. Those doors will ding and try to close, but detect the pencil and stop themselves. Come back an hour later, and if no one has picked up the pencil, they will still be dinging and sliding those doors almost shut. They will never give up. That's how I expected the Macros to behave. They would be relentless.

We'd been watching them for a couple of days. Using internet broadcasts on portable computers, we'd watched several battles. The Macros were the very opposite of the Nanos. They were *huge*. The big ones, built for battle, were over a hundred feet tall. But they weren't uniform in size, shape, or even function. Many were smaller and performed other tasks which we did not fully understand yet. Most of them walked on six legs like giant, headless insects. But these were metal insects as big as buildings. They had good air defenses, unfortunately for our Star Force ships. We could destroy them, but it cost us too much. Just by flying close, our ships automatically fired every weapon they had. But the Macros carried Surface-to-Air-Missiles (SAMs) on their backs, and after the first few engagements, we had realized we were losing ships as fast as they were losing giant, crab-like robots.

We had withdrawn, giving up on the idea of fighting them directly. Crow and I had decided that it was the job of Star Force to destroy the Macros before they landed. If we failed, it was up to Earth's troops, ships, and planes to do the rest.

So far, the Macros were doing most of the destroying. Argentina's military had put up a big ring of defenses around a southern coastal city named Trelew. The fighting there had raged for a full day. Looking at the video, I had to figure our side had lost badly. They just didn't have enough heavy equipment down there. They needed armor divisions, modern ones.

Argentina had never had much of a navy of its own, but their ships had shelled the Macros until they'd been sunk. In the air, we did slightly better. We'd managed to blow up a few Macros. One carrier group sent by the US had reached the region. A few British ships stood in support.

Internationally, the defense effort was ongoing. The Earth militaries didn't trust us at all, I could tell that from the news broadcasts. They called us things like "the initial invasion forces" or the "space raiders." Trust had grown between the various panicked governments of Earth, however. Pierre was right about that. Everyone had air-lifted in what they could. Chinese, NATO, and even a few Russian planes had joined the fight. Squadrons of fighter bombers and helicopters were dying hard, led primarily by US forces. But it would be weeks before Earth had a significant ground army in place. By then, the enemy would have marched north to the ruined cities of Santiago and Buenos Aries.

For me, the scariest things were the mysterious domes. There were precious few reports about them. But I could tell they were special. The Macros left them behind as they advanced. Nobody knew why. White things, they were. Huge white domes each as big as a football stadium. Parabolic in shape, the domes were like white bowls, flipped over and left lying on flat areas of open land. Under them, we knew something was happening, but no one knew what.

Pierre communicated one more time that night. A call came in as I watched massive spiked legs knock down the last, burning buildings of Trelew. It was like watching a Godzilla movie, except we were up against about a hundred metal Godzillas—and we didn't have any cool monsters of our own to stop them.

I'd stopped thinking about Pierre and the diplomacy he was doing nearby until he tried to contact me. The *Alamo* asked me if I would take a private call from the *Versailles*, and of course I said yes. But there was no one there. Just a strange, crashing sound. More noises followed. I heard what sounded like a scrabbling, and a heavy thud.

"Pierre? What's going on?"

No answer.

My eyes flicked to the big board. Pierre's ship was still there. His was a golden beetle very close to the cool, metallic-jade bump that represented my own ship.

A whispering voice came over the channel then. It was a stranger's voice. "Computer, turn off all communications."

"Command unclear," said Pierre's ship.

Sandra and I looked at each other. Whoever it was at the other end of that radio channel, they didn't know how to address the ship.

"We can hear you. You killed our ambassador, didn't you?" asked Sandra. She glared at the walls around us, as if the owner of the voice might be hiding behind them.

"Shit," whispered the assassin.

"I hear you," I said. "What have you done with Pierre?"

"Ship, I'm renaming you Delta. Respond," said the stranger. We could barely make out the words. The assassin wasn't speaking up. I was hardly surprised.

"Ship renamed," said Pierre's ship—which was no longer Pierre's.

"You will not survive our next battle," I said, "let me assure you of that, whoever you are."

"Delta, turn off all communications," hissed the stranger's voice. That was the last transmission we heard.

Sandra spent the next few minutes fuming and pacing in a rage. I didn't blame her. I sat silently, brooding. The problem was we couldn't do much about it. We couldn't really have saved Pierre, even if we wanted to. Our ship wouldn't let me get out to help. It wouldn't fire on one of its own kind, either. So, now we had a traitor in our midst. We had someone who did not belong. A usurper.

A murderer.

It was one thing, I told myself, to be pulled up into one of these ships against one's will and forced to undergo the tests blindly. It was quite another to sneak aboard under false pretenses with cheating knowledge of how to beat the tests. Then, as a final crime, this person had killed the original owner, fully knowing they were stealing the ship.

"Alamo, take us close to the *Versailles*. Follow it wherever it goes."

On the big board, I watched as our two contacts merged. The ship, now renamed *Delta*, had not moved. The assassin was finding out it wasn't so easy to figure out how to talk to one of these machines. We had a little time, I thought, but not much.

"Kyle," said Sandra, eyeing me, "you should report this to Crow."

"What's he going to do about it? Other than to tell me to let it go."

"I don't know."

I was in a dark mood. I'd become more of a brooder these days. I didn't take well to bullshit like this—if I ever had. What was the government thinking? Here we were, offering them aid in an interstellar war. They had no other allies. Sure, we had robbed a few malls and a few people had died by attacking our ships, but that was nothing compared to the Macros. They were engaged in extermination. They would kill millions—maybe more.

So what had happened? Had Kim Bager ordered it? I doubted that. Had some independent spook-group gotten a wild hair? Maybe. Or maybe a single agent had decided they wanted one of our ships. I didn't know how it had happened, but it ate at me the more I thought about it. This killing meant we couldn't trust Earth anymore. I could never go home, no matter how this played out.

I decided something then, as I brooded about it. I decided I was going to find out what the hell was going on.

"Alamo," I said loudly. "I wish to undergo the injections."

"What?" Sandra asked, almost shouting. "What are you doing, Kyle?"

Immediately, five black snake-arms lashed out. Three rippled into being from the ceiling and two more came up from the floor. They wrapped around each of my limbs. The third one to drop down from the ceiling circled my neck, but not so tightly that it choked me.

"It's the only way, Sandra," I said quietly.

"Don't do it."

"Look, I can't even touch you. I can't exit this ship. I don't want to live like this. I'll take the injections and if they are really horrible, maybe I'll drown myself or something."

She looked at me strangely. "You aren't doing this for me, are you?"

"Aren't you tired of wearing a leash?" I asked, smiling slightly.

The five arms tightened and stiffened. I looked around, straining my neck to see what they were doing. I had expected, for some reason, to see a dripping needle with a plunger descend out of the ceiling of the ship. That wasn't how it happened. Instead, the same cable-like arms that held me grew silvery tips. I realized, looking at them, that *they were* the needles. Why not? The arms were made up of nanites and the point was to inject them into my body, so why not simply form a point, liquefy a number of them and puncture the skin?

I began hoping this wouldn't hurt too much. My hopes were faint. *Five injections?* The needles looked as thick as screwdriver tips. I wanted to squirm, but couldn't.

"This process will temporarily shut down the ship's command personnel. Confirmation required."

I hesitated.

"I don't trust the Nanos, Kyle," said Sandra. She came close, and the ship restrained her. I was tired of that.

"We'll figure a way, Kyle," she told me, getting her face as close to mine as the ship would allow. "We'll make love if that's what you want, some day."

I took a breath and looked at her. I did want her. But that wasn't the only reason I was doing this. "A government killer took Pierre's ship. If Earth thinks they can do that, they might try to assassinate each of us in turn and replace us with loyal people. If they get away with it, they'll do it. I can't let them have an easy win. We have to move against them now."

Her eyes widened. I could see that she had begun to grasp the magnitude of my plan.

"You—you are going to board Pierre's ship? You are going to go after that assassin? You don't even have a gun!"

"Wish me luck," I said. I tore my eyes away from her face. The look in her eyes, the horrified stare, wasn't doing anything for my self-confidence.

"Alamo, command confirmed. Proceed with the injections."

Driving, hot pain. White hot. Blurring.

I could see, and I could still scream, until the arm that wrapped around my neck looped itself around my chin and skull. The neck needle was the worst, I think. It dug into my flesh. It drove in—worming. It wasn't the burning stuff it pumped into me that was the most painful. It was those five worming needles. I felt each of them squirming inside my body at five different points. Like a team of steel tentacles, they rooted around for a thick artery upon which to implant themselves.

I felt blood and sweat run everywhere from my lanced-open skin. The *Alamo* was a machine. It knew no bedside manner, no gentleness. No mercy.

I could no longer open my mouth to scream, but my lips were fluttering with blasts of heaving breath. I snorted through my nostrils and made long, nasally screeching sounds using those twin, tiny outlets. I tasted metal in my mouth and smelled it in my sinuses. The pain went on and on, spreading in a dark burn throughout my body.

I felt them when they reached my spine. They felt like a thousand ants with electric spikes for feet. I felt them when they reached my guts, too. I was filled with gallons of boiling blood.

And at last, I felt them reach my skull. As my eyes filled with glinting flecks and my vision dimmed to nothing, I lost consciousness.

-17-

I awakened a new man. This might sound like a good thing, but it wasn't. I felt different, as if parts of my body had been sawn off and sewn back on again. My skin was different. It felt stiff—and when I shifted and groaned in discomfort, my skin resisted my movements. It felt like—like I was wearing a wetsuit, perhaps. A wetsuit made of stiff, unyielding fabric.

I lifted my hands to my face. On each forearm I saw a white circle. I nodded to myself, grimly. The nanites had repaired the holes they made. But they left their odd, tell-tale scars, just as they had on Sandra's severed fingers.

I looked around for her. I was still lying stretched out on my easy chair, where I'd been spending too much time lately. Sandra wasn't in the room. I frowned. How long had I been out? I opened my mouth to ask the *Alamo*.

Two hours, twenty-six minutes.

I jumped. I looked around, my eyes rolling in my head. It had been the *Alamo*, and her voice had spoken in my head. Was my hearing different now?

Alamo, can you hear me? I thought.

Yes.

Very startling. I wasn't sure if I liked this. Was I part of some nanite nation now? Could I hear what they were thinking? Obviously, they could hear me.

"Is this telepathy or something?" I asked aloud.

No. We have installed mental interpretation circuits in your brain. The electrical behavior of your brain is then converted into a radio signal for unit-to-unit transmission.

"Thanks for telling me about that part in advance."

No attempt was made to inform you.

I sighed. I figured that sarcasm would forever be lost upon the machines. They just didn't have a sense of humor.

I heard something fall to the floor, and before I knew it I was up and standing.

"You're awake!" said Sandra from behind me. "And moving very fast. I was worried. I figured you'd die on me and leave me alone on this damned ship. Did you ever even think of that?"

I looked at her. She had come out of the kitchen chamber. She had been carrying a beer, but must have dropped it when she saw me. The beer had made the noise that made me jump, I realized. The can rolled on the deck, glugging out its foamy contents. The glugs didn't stain the floor, however. Days ago I'd built a program into the *Alamo* to go porous and let liquid waste dribble out of the ship when we dropped it. As a messy person, I found this very convenient.

But I was puzzled over my speedy jump to my feet. I barely had the thought of getting up, and I'd vaulted to my feet. It felt strange, almost as if my muscles hadn't done the work. Almost as if some other force had propelled me—as if a kid's hand worked my legs and I was some kind of doll.

"You spilled your beer," I told Sandra. I tried a smile. It didn't come easily, but I figured she'd earned one out of me by now.

She snatched it up and handed it to me, half-empty. "This one's yours."

I drained it. "That was exactly what I needed," I said. I looked at her and she smiled, almost shyly. She took a step backward. Something was different.

Then I had it. She didn't have any snake-like arms wrapped around her. For the first time since the ship had revived her, she was free to move about and do as she pleased. No wonder she was smiling.

I had another impulse then. The impulse to grab her up in my arms and kiss her. It's funny, the way humans behave when trapped together and stressed. We tend to bond. It's only natural, I suppose. We'd fought and survived together. We'd seen plenty of each other's skin and been intimate in a dozen ways, living close together for days.

She smiled at me with half her mouth. I took it as an invitation.

Then my body launched itself at her.

103

I almost killed her, I think. It was a close thing. The second I realized I was airborne, traveling the short distance between us in a single bound, I gave the mental order to halt, to desist, to avoid crashing into her.

I jerked away as if swatted by a giant's hand. I flew into the far wall, the one that crawled with golden beetle ships. I hit the wall, and it hurt—but only a little. Something had cushioned my landing. I turned my head to see what I'd landed on. There was nothing there but the metal of the ship's hull.

"Are you okay?" asked Sandra, coming after me. She laid her hands on my arm. "What the hell was that?"

"What did it look like?" I asked, gingerly touching the back of my skull where I'd crashed into the wall. There was a small bleeding spot in my hair. I touched the wall with probing fingers. It didn't feel soft at all.

"You just suddenly leapt at me," said Sandra. "It was amazing. Then you changed directions somehow and twisted in mid-air. You crashed into the wall as if someone had fired you out of a cannon."

Alamo, I thought, *when I'm not in a combat situation, please tone down these improved reflexes I seem to have. I don't want to hurt my own people.*

Settings can only be adjusted by the operator.

Great. I had to use self-control. I got to my feet experimentally, half-expecting to launch into the ceiling. Things progressed much more smoothly this time, however. I noticed that Sandra stood well back when I got up. She watched me with big eyes.

"I'm okay," I told her. "I think something the injections did to me caused this. I think they made me stronger."

She nodded, pursing her lips. I walked toward her, slowly, stiffly. She watched me.

"I'm controlling it now. I'm new to this. I'm going to try to touch you as gently as I can, okay?"

She blinked. She extended a hand toward me.

Oh great, I thought, *now she's scared of me*. A perfect romantic moment had been ruined.

I took her hand and kissed it gently. "See?" I said. I studied her face, looking for signs of pain. Was I holding her fingers too firmly? Was I grinding her bones together? I almost couldn't feel her hand in mine.

104

She smiled back. "Okay," she said. "I've got an idea. Just stand there. Close your eyes. Try not to react."

I did as she asked and she kissed me. It felt good. She followed the first with more of them. Her kisses were gentle, more faint and tickling than I remembered kisses were supposed to be. Her skin felt papery, thin, and delicate against mine. I told myself I was going to have to go very slowly with Sandra. I had to keep control of myself.

We only kissed for about two minutes. I wanted to do it for two hours. But finally, very gently but inexorably, I pushed her away.

Alamo, I thought, *are we still following the ship—the one now called the* Delta?

Yes.

"I have to go," I told Sandra.

"Don't go."

"Is that why you're kissing me? To distract me?"

She gave a tiny shrug. "Maybe. I don't want you to leave me here and get yourself killed."

"I don't think I can die easily, now," I told her.

She nodded. "I suppose you're right. What are you going to do when you catch him—if you catch him?"

"I'm not sure," I lied.

"I see."

"Alamo," I said, speaking aloud for Sandra's benefit as much as anything else. "What is the *Delta* doing?"

"The *Delta* is engaged in its primary mission."

"It's still seeking command personnel?"

"Yes."

"Good. When it stops over a building and sends down its main arm to grab someone, I want your arm to place me there. I want the Delta ship to pick me up."

The ship hesitated. "Your instructions will place command personnel in extreme danger."

"Do my instructions contradict your programming?"

"No. Not directly."

"Then follow my instructions, Alamo."

"Enter the area named: cargo bay."

I stood. I kissed Sandra one more time.

"I want to know one thing," she said. "How the hell are you going to get back aboard this ship?"

105

"I can communicate to the ship directly now. It was part of the improvements."

She nodded, impressed. "Go then," she said, taking her hands off me at last. "That ship is still killing people down there. Maybe you can save a life or two if you hurry."

"You've changed your mind?"

"You're going to do it anyway. I can tell. Just go."

I stepped into the cargo bay. The thick black arm hung down from its root in the ceiling. The door in the bottom of the ship opened. The smell of a summer night in Virginia swept up into my face. It was refreshing, full of humidity and the varied scents of living things.

I could see Pierre's ship, hovering very close to ours. It ignored us. It was dedicated to its task of rooting about in smashed-out windows. As I watched, someone was hauled up into the belly of the ship. My heart pounded, but I knew of no way to save them. They had to fall. Then I would be next, if I was close by.

Sandra leaned up behind me. "You better come back and not leave me trapped up here." she said.

"Alamo," I said, "if I'm killed, place Sandra safely on the ground."

"Program set."

"Now," I said, "put me on the roof of that apartment building below us."

The arm came up, and the three black fingers gripped me. Each finger was as thick as a fire hose. I was swept out into the open sky. With alarming speed, I was dropped toward the roof. It felt like a bungee-jump.

I had a sudden, alarming thought as I dropped down to the roof. What if there were snipers watching the ship? Or helicopters, following us around? There was no reason to think the assassin had been working alone. The Pentagon or their spooks could have decided to take us out by any means necessary. I hoped I wasn't delivering myself in their hands somehow.

After a sickeningly rapid descent, my feet thumped down on the cement and tarpaper roof of a large building. There were bricks chimneys all around me. I looked up at the two Nano ships. From here, they looked identical.

I took a deep breath, and smiled grimly. Even if I died soon, at least I'd gotten the privilege of standing on my own world under an open night sky one more time. I'd been stuck aboard the *Alamo* for a week. I decided that despite the pain I'd experienced, so far the injections had been worth it.

But I didn't know all the details yet.

-18-

The night sky was warm and humid. It enveloped me like a gush of hot breath. Even the breeze was warm and wet. As a native of the arid middle of California, I was unused to East Coast summers. I reveled in the natural feel of everything, however. It felt as if I'd been released from a hospital or a long cruise on a submarine.

I walked to the edge of the roof and gazed downward. People streamed away from the building. The word was out now, everyone was running from the black ship that loomed like a shadowy angel of death overhead. An old woman carried a cat under each arm and one against her breast. A mother dragged a screeching child like a rag-doll behind her. A man with a pistol in each hand ran out next, shoving aside the old woman, who lost a cat. She hurried off without it, crying. The people who lived in the building ran from every exit in a steady stream.

"Hey, you! Run, you crazy bastard!"

I noticed the man shouting up at me was in a uniform. A policeman, I figured. I waved at him unconcernedly.

"He's a fighter," said the man with the pistols. "He's going for it. Just forget him."

Both men wasted no more time on me and followed their own advice… running for it. The crowd melted away down the quiet asphalt roads, vanishing behind trees and buildings. Soon, the ship would run out of victims here and have to move on. We knew from observation that when they moved, they traveled far. The ship would head in a random direction and stop hundreds of miles from this spot to hunt for fresh, unsuspecting game. It would perform its grim tests until properly ordered to stop. And apparently, the assassin hadn't given that order yet. Probably, he didn't know how, or even that it was required.

I had time to think about the changes that must have been wracking Earth in my absence. There were people called *fighters* now? People, perhaps half-crazed, who let the ships take them? Were fighters people like me, who invited the opportunity to pass the ships' deadly tests by standing on a roof? I found that interesting. If humans were one thing, it was unpredictable. I thought about the cop's reaction as well. He hadn't worried about the younger guy with the pistols. He hadn't tried to stop the ship. He hadn't stopped running to help anyone, except to shout up at me. The coming of these roving ships, I realized, had changed a lot of our social rules very quickly. About half the ships had found "command personnel" now. That gave us a potential fleet hundreds strong, but it also meant that thousands of people were still failing and dying every day aboard the remaining ships. The Nano ships roamed freely over the world, collecting people as men might harvest an endless field of wheat.

I noticed that I'd been here several minutes. I was just beginning to hope the last victim had won through somehow. Perhaps they made it to the bridge, I thought.

Then a body fell from the ship's belly. Twisting, long hair fluttered like a flag as the corpse dropped. It was a young male, shirtless and athletically built. The body crashed down through the branches of an ash tree and finally thumped in a dead heap on a grassy spot near the apartment building's front street entrance.

I looked up, taking in a big breath. Soon, as I knew it must, the arm descended. I did not flinch. I was determined. That last young man had been dead when he fell. The easy tests didn't kill you before you were dropped out—only the combat test did that. The assassin who had taken Pierre's ship was still at it—still killing.

Maybe he liked it that way, I thought. Maybe he hadn't turned off the ship's automatic testing on purpose. Maybe he was having *fun*.

My face was flat and expressionless as the three-fingered hand wrapped itself around my waist and hoisted me into the sky. I hoped my nanite-infested body would give this guy a surprise he hadn't bargained on.

I rode my way up into the ship and into the first featureless cubical. I went through the tests methodically. I had to wonder if any human

109

had ever been as calm and cold as I was while I took the tests that day. Pierre's Nano ship was identical to mine on the inside and out. I felt right at home.

The last few tests were still outstanding when the door to the bridge opened. I wondered which test the ship thought it was giving me now, the one for leadership or aggression? It hardly mattered. I was going to kill whoever I found there anyway, if I could.

I decided along the way I would reject the new name for the ship, as I rejected its new owner. This was the *Versailles*, not the *Delta*. I stepped onto the bridge of the *Versailles*, and I almost smiled. Pierre had been busy. The place was full of loot. There were no less than three ornate golden chairs, none of which matched. I figured all of them had once served someone as a throne. There were piles of Persian rugs, overlapping one another on the floor. The couches were red and velvet and looked insanely expensive. Paintings lined the walls, looking old and priceless. Was that a Van Gogh? I seemed to recall it from an art book I'd been forced to read in college. Even the low coffee table was made of teak and encrusted with gold doubloons.

In the middle of the room stood another surprise. It was a woman. She was young, and good-looking in a stark way. She stared at me flatly. She had a pistol in her hand. She wasn't aiming it at me, but I got the feeling she knew how to use it. I eyed the pistol thoughtfully. It looked like a Glock 9mm to me. I knew I was full of nanites, but I had to figure bullets would still cause pain, at the very least. So far, the nanites hadn't been concerned with my discomfort—only my survival.

"You made it through the tests?" she asked in a calm voice.

"I know them well," I said.

She eyed me. "Who are you?"

"I'm Commander Kyle Riggs."

"Commander of what?"

"Star Force."

She laughed. "Is that what you pirates call yourselves?"

"We aren't pirates."

She snorted and waved her hand at the evidence that surrounded her. She picked up something that looked mysteriously like a Faberge Egg and twisted her lips at me in disgust.

"Yeah, well," I said, "we aren't *all* pirates. And we do more than steal things. We've saved the human race twice in the last week."

"Don't tell the people in Argentina that."

110

"If those big ships had all gotten through, humanity wouldn't have had a chance."

"You're not pros," she said. "You have no right to rule. No one appointed you. No one voted for you."

"The ships chose us."

"And now this one has chosen me."

I thought about that for a second. She had a point. Hadn't we all challenged and killed to get control of a ship?

"Who are you?" I asked. "Who sent you here?"

"I'm nobody," she said.

"You're an assassin. A spook. Is the whole government in on this, or just one panicked branch? Or did you decide to go for it, solo? Are you what they call a *fighter?*"

She smiled tightly. "Would it make any difference what I told you? Pick the one you like. Call it a lie or a fact."

I nodded, crossing my arms. That movement, as slow and harmless-looking as it was, put her on her guard.

"Someone sent you," I said. "You don't seem the type who is out for solo power. And it wasn't the whole government, either. You didn't have any backup in sight out there. No choppers. No agents. No snipers. You barely know the tests and you can't operate the ship properly yet. I'd say you came from a panicked group of spooks somewhere."

She shrugged. "Unfortunately, I'm tired of the conversation now. If you tell me how to turn off the ship, to stop it from bringing test subjects in here for me to kill, you will save some lives."

"How about my own?"

She shook her head. "Can't do it. I know the rules that well. Only one of us can leave this room alive."

I nodded. My next surprise came when she put down her gun on the doubloon-encrusted coffee table. Was it empty?

"Not in a shooting mood today?" I asked.

"I need to save bullets if these tests keep going. And for you, I won't need it. I've read up on you. A college nerd. Unarmed, and with very little combat training."

She took a step toward me.

I smiled at her. Her face faltered, just slightly. Perhaps that wasn't the fearful response she had been expecting.

Her first kick went low, to my knees. It might have crippled me, if I hadn't had a new, hard surface under my skin. I think the kick stung her foot.

She hopped back, made a huffing sound and punched me. My nose hurt, but not that badly. I swung back at her. She was very fast. She blocked my blow and because of it didn't take the full force of it on her forearm. Even so, she staggered back, looking pained and surprised. My fists were harder now than they had been. Faster, too.

She bounced forward again. She was muscular, and she was even stronger than she looked. She rained blows down on my face. My skin broke open in places, and it did hurt. But nothing penetrated deeper than, say, a quarter inch.

I reached for her and tried to grapple with her. I'm not sure what I wanted. I suddenly didn't want to just kill her. Was it because she was female? Was it because Pierre had so obviously stolen everything that wasn't nailed down to our good mother Earth? She had a point about us being pirates. The Nano ships had killed a load of people. For all I knew, one of them had murdered her family and she was here for revenge.

I wrapped my arms around her and I was too strong for her. She jabbed me with a half-dozen knees and elbows, but each blow hurt her as much as it hurt me. She might as well have been beating on that teak coffee table.

Before, when I'd had the strength of a half-assed gentleman farmer, she'd have broken away easily. But the nanites had definitely done something to me. She elbowed and twisted, but couldn't get away from me.

She surprised me then. This time, with a sudden, passionate kiss. It worked on me. I relaxed fractionally for a few seconds, blinking at her in surprise. Was she going to bite my lips off? Worrying about that made it hard to enjoy the kiss.

She slipped an arm free, then managed to turn away from me. I'd loosened my hold on her enough to allow her partial escape. I reached to grab her again, but she was already reaching backward, toward the coffee table. I didn't comprehend what she was doing until it was too late.

She snagged her 9mm pistol off the table with her outstretched fingers. She whipped it around, aimed it into my face and fired. Three times.

That did it. I let her go. I staggered back, putting my hands to my face. Blood and flapping shreds of skin came away. I thought maybe I was dead—but I wasn't.

We looked at each other, both panting. I'm not sure who was more shocked. I must not have looked too good.

"You're not human," she said.

"You're pretty amazing yourself."

She looked at my face. There was disgust in her eyes, now. "There's metal showing. You are metal underneath, where the skin is broken. Are you some kind of robot?"

"No, but I've been modified. You can't beat me."

"Your eye is blown away. It looks silvery, purple underneath. That isn't a human eye. Drop me out of this ship. I don't want to become like—whatever you are. I want out."

I shook my head. "You need to give me a few answers first."

I sprang at her. For the first time, I used my full speed. I crashed into her, scooped her up, and squeezed her arms against her body, pinning them. She fired a few more rounds, aiming down. I felt lead burn hotly on my foot. I shook the gun from her hand.

She stopped struggling when it became obvious she was helpless. We were close. Face-to-face. Sweaty and scared, she looked younger and prettier to me now.

"I'd make a bad prisoner, alien," she said.

"I'm human, not alien."

"No. No human could move like that. You're a freak," she said. "That's worse."

"Just talk to me."

"I won't become like you," she said.

I heard a crunching sound. I looked into her face, and I knew what she had done. She had bitten into something.

"Why don't you tell me your name, at least?" I asked.

"Esmeralda," she whispered, and then she collapsed. I held my breath and hopped backward. I felt bad letting her slump onto the Persian rugs, to die in a heap on the floor. But I didn't want to breathe that stuff in. I wasn't sure the nanites knew how to fix a lungful of cyanide—or whatever it was.

I looked down at her body regretfully. Somehow, killing Pierre's assassin hadn't been as fulfilling as I'd hoped.

Small black arms dragged Esmeralda to an open spot on the metal decking, where there weren't any Persian rugs. She slipped through the floor as if it were liquid and vanished. The ship had *released* her. To them, she was biotic waste now.

"Dammit," I whispered to nobody.

-19-

I was *different* now, with a layer of nanites inside me. I was able to walk through the walls of Pierre's ship, if I wanted to. It felt as if a soap bubble passed over my body when I did it. I supposed the nanites considered me one of their own now, and maybe they were right.

When Pierre's ship reached down to grab a new victim, I slid out along the long black arm and dropped the last twenty feet or so to the ground. The arm ignored me. The person riding upward looked terrified. I smiled, recognizing him. It was the cop who had told me to run back when I stood on the apartment roof. I thought, looking up at him, that he might have recognized me. His face registered more shock and terror than anything else.

"Just keep moving, follow the tests they talk about on TV," I shouted up, cupping my hands. "There's no one left to fight at the end. You'll be okay."

I wondered what the ship would do if there was no one aboard to fight. Would the basic tests suffice to have it accept him as commander? Or would the ship cage him and use him to test others? I didn't know. I didn't even know if he'd heard my advice.

I walked through the park for a few minutes. Summer in Virginia, at night. There was no one around, unsurprisingly. A few yellow-green fireflies glimmered hauntingly in the bushes.

I remembered days in the park like this, summer evening walks with the kids—and with my wife Donna. They were all dead, gone. That still weighed on me. Sometimes I felt I had been charged with saving the world that had taken everything I'd ever loved from me.

I didn't call the *Alamo* for a few minutes. I knew Sandra was probably worried to death, but I just wanted to walk on the Earth's crust again. It felt good under my feet. I thought about Pierre's voice— I'd never met the tricky, pompous man in person. I thought about Esmeralda's face, her true face, the one that had erased her tough snarl at the end. She'd been much more human in her final moments than I felt myself to be.

This dreamy walk in the park only lasted a few minutes. I'm not good at introspection or self-pity. I had a war to fight. Like it or not, I was a Commander of Star Force. Never mind that a few nobodies had made the organization up just days ago. It had all become increasingly real to me. I recalled something a sergeant had told a scared recruit in an old war movie. When asked *why us?* the sergeant had replied *because we are here, and nobody else.* That seemed to sum up my situation. Why was I, of all people, fighting assassins and aliens? Because the *Alamo* had chosen me. It had to be someone—and this time it was my turn.

Alamo, come pick me up, I thought.

ETA ninety seconds.

I didn't hear the ship's approach. The Nano ships were amazingly quiet as they stalked the night skies. There was a crack or two of branches breaking as the thick, black arm snaked down into the park, damaging trees behind me. I didn't turn around or even look up. The whipping, finger-like cables grabbed me around the middle and hauled me up into the ship's belly, swallowing me whole.

As I rode back up into the *Alamo* I kept breathing in fresh air, as much as I could suck into my lungs. I listened to the muted sounds of the night and looked around at every tree, bench, and streetlight. Standing in the cargo bay a moment later, I felt something in my hair. I reached back and found a leaf. It was big, and looked like it had belonged to a sycamore tree.

I walked onto the bridge. Sandra made a happy whoop when she saw me.

She hurried toward me, smiling. Then her face fell. She saw my mood, and the rips in my skin—and possibly the metal gleaming from beneath that torn skin.

I put my hand to my face, covering my left eye. That area had seemed the most upsetting to Esmeralda, so I tried to hide it from Sandra.

116

"You're hurt," she said.

"Yeah. I'm sure the nanites will fix it. I can feel them working on it right now, knitting my cells back together."

"Did you get your butt kicked?" she asked.

I tried to force a smile. "Something like that," I said. "Here, I brought you a present."

I held out the green sycamore leaf. She took it and smiled at it. Such a small gesture, but she seemed to soften. She came to me and hugged me. We embraced for a while. She put her head against my right shoulder, keeping her eyes far away from my injured face and especially my left eye.

I touched her as gently as I could, as if I held the wings of a butterfly between pinched fingertips. I watched for any signs of pain, but she gave none. This relaxed me a fraction. I had wanted her to be free of the ship's shackles, and now she was. The ship had no leash on her, nothing snaked around her waist or ankles to keep her away from me. But if I'd still been unable to touch her for fear of hurting her....

Well, that would have been worse.

It occurred to me that we might have trouble in the future if we wanted to be—intimate. There were times in the throes of passion for any man when he's not himself. Human women were tough enough for a normal male, but what about an enhanced male such as myself? What if I'd had a few beers maybe, then moved too quickly—and tore her apart? It was a grim thought, and it made me move very cautiously around her. I think she knew I was holding back, barely touching her. I think it turned her on, too.

Before things proceeded further, however, she spoiled the mood by having an important thought. "Oh, I almost forgot. Crow has been calling for you. I couldn't answer—the *Alamo* won't listen to me at all, not even when you are gone. She's such a bitchy computer—or a billion little bitchy computers, I guess. Anyway, Crow doesn't know what happened to you. All he knows is that first Pierre vanished and then he lost contact with you. Kyle, you should call him."

I agreed and told my ship to make the connection. Crow answered with no delays.

"Riggs? Is that really you, Kyle?"

"Yes, sir," I said to the walls. Sandra and I had moved to our new couch and settled ourselves there. That arrangement worked better for me. I could sit and relax, and she could sit close beside me or prod at

117

my wounds if she wanted. She did both, seeming to get over the weirdness of seeing metallic glints shining through nearly bloodless rips in my skin. She got out the medical kits we had picked up while 'shopping' and taped together the worst wounds.

I explained recent events to Crow. He'd known Pierre was dead, but hadn't figured out that I'd gone over to fix matters personally.

"So you actually *did it*, mate?" he asked, whistling. "You took the injections? What are they like?"

I described the sensations briefly. "I thought you had already done it, sir," I said when finished.

"No," he said. "I said it was nasty because I'd heard from another fleet member that it was, but I never had the guts."

"Who was the other guy?"

"Doesn't matter. We lost him in space during the first Macro attack. Poor bloke. He must be dead now. I truly hope the nanites aren't reviving him out there in the frozen void over and over again." He laughed.

I didn't share in the joke. Sometimes, Crow's sense of humor bordered on the macabre. "So, who else has done it?" I asked.

"No one, to my knowledge. We are survivalists, not heroic, experimental types. You are, as far as I know, the only living person full of nanites."

We talked further, but Crow was busy. He told me to contact the Senator again, and demand an explanation. We decided we would only allow known officials aboard our ships from now on, people we'd seen in the news. That should cut down on assassination attempts.

"Are we going to even try anymore?" asked Sandra. "They've shown themselves to be vicious and untrustworthy."

"Right you are," said Crow, "but we still have to work with them. What nation has ever arisen in history without having to defend itself? It's only natural for them to consider us rebels, terrorists, vigilantes. To become worthy of diplomacy, any group must prove it is strong enough to be independent. I think we've just taken a step down that road. We can give them a gobful, of course. We can demand apologies and the like, but after a while we will have to deal with them. Neither side has any real choice unless they can conquer the other."

At length, Crow put me in charge of diplomatic affairs. I was the least likely to be assassinated, and I was the only person in the fleet who could get out of my ship if I wanted to. Previously, I had been in charge of tactical combat, but right now the Macros were keeping quiet and hadn't made any further space attacks on Earth.

After we broke off the communication, Sandra kissed me several times.

"I want to apologize, she said. "I'm sorry I recoiled from you when you first came—home."

"It's okay. My looks freaked out the assassin, too."

"One thing is bothering me," said Sandra, finishing with her ministrations. "What about the aliens you fought when you first boarded these ships? The centaur people? Why weren't they full of nanites and invincible to us?"

I thought about it and couldn't come up with an answer. But I thought I knew who might have one. I touched my face, which was taped up and slathered with antibiotics.

"Alamo, did the... ah... the *biotics* that were aboard this ship when I was first picked up undertake the injections at some point?"

"Yes."

"Then how could I beat them? They didn't seem especially fast or strong or full of a metal coating under the skin."

"They were not as you describe."

"So, the nanites left them? You reversed the process of the injections?"

"Yes."

"Why?"

"Because they failed in their mission."

I felt a chill. Sandra and I looked at each other. Perhaps they would see fit to turn off my nanite population someday, cutting me off as well.

"How did they fail, Alamo?" I asked, not sure I wanted to hear the answer.

"Their species failed. Their planet was overrun by the Macros. They are extinct now."

"Aren't there a few of them left alive on the ships that still roam around looking for command personnel?"

"Yes."

Sandra tapped at me. "We've got to stop the Nanos from using these creatures to test us. We can't kill the last members of a race of people like us! They are fighting us to prevent their own extinction."

I nodded, but I couldn't think of a way to do it. What could I do?

"Maybe we could capture them," said Sandra, thinking aloud.

119

"I could try to board a ship and beat them unconscious or something," I said thoughtfully. "If we could at least get a few breeding pairs off the ships, they might not all die."

Sandra frowned, suddenly not liking the whole idea. "I don't want *you* to do it. You've got about a dozen other missions. We have to defend Earth first."

I looked at her. "A minute ago, you wanted me to save the centaurs."

Her face took on a hard look. "If we can—I do. But I don't want to see you do it *personally*. You've done enough. I—I guess I'm getting attached to you."

I stared at her. There was an almond-shape to her eyes. She had the kind of eyes that didn't even need makeup. She was lovely. I thought about the legendary professor and his formula for predicting the longevity of such relationships. I didn't even bother to try arguing myself out of it. I figured whatever we had would fail in the end, but that didn't matter. When an unattached man in his thirties meets a hot girl in her twenties, and she shows strong interest...well, there's no hope for the guy.

I sighed internally. At least it would be a very nice two years.

-20-

When I learned the method by which Pierre had been conducting diplomacy, I almost laughed aloud. He had been doing it via the internet, using a voice system that allowed two-way communication. I knew the software well as my students had used it to communicate with other people worldwide—mostly for online gaming purposes.

It did have advantages, I had to admit. By using a cellular internet hook-up and software for voice transmission, you didn't have to call people and know their phone numbers. It was a little harder to trace, as well. But mostly, I thought it was amusing because I was sure it was the same type of system that Pierre had previously used to con people out of money. E-mails to get them hooked, then a faceless, untraceable, cost-free voice coming over the internet to talk them into the scam. He'd naturally taken the same approach when dealing with foreign governments. I had to wonder if he'd done something else he shouldn't have—something that had pissed off the wrong people and gotten him killed.

I sat and thought for a while with Pierre's tiny computer in my hands. Before I tried to talk to the government people—the same people, I reminded myself, that had killed our last ambassador—I felt I needed an edge of some kind. I needed a bargaining chip. It would be one thing to get online and make them squirm, calling them assassins and fascists and the like. But I was a big boy. I knew the score. They might be embarrassed, but when the survival of the world was at stake, they were playing for keeps. Fortunately, so was I.

I waited until Sandra left me. She had gone exploring the ship. She did that a lot, as it was one of the few things the *Alamo* would let her do. I had done a bit of it, but not as much as she had over the past week.

121

Inside, the ship had several levels and dozens of rooms of various sizes on each deck. There was a lot of strange equipment on the upper decks, the purposes of which were still a mystery to us.

"Alamo, I want to talk to you."

The ship didn't respond. There was no need. I could have opted to transmit my thoughts silently, but that still didn't feel natural to me.

"Alamo, what if this ship is damaged? Can it repair itself?"

"Yes."

"Can it repair the major systems aboard the ship?"

"Yes."

"All of the big components? Even the drive systems and the weaponry?"

"Yes."

I made a happy sound and leaned back in my chair. This was what I had been hoping for. If the ship could repair a laser weapon, could it not build a brand new one, given the materials? If it could make an engine, why couldn't it build more engines? Even more importantly, what component aboard the ship had the job of constructing engines or lasers? What if that repair unit could make a copy of *itself*?

"Alamo, do you have some kind of repair chamber?"

"There is a repair unit for major equipment."

"If it was damaged, could it repair itself?"

"Yes."

"Could it *duplicate* itself?"

A hesitation. "Possibly."

"Why not definitely?"

"Some of the raw materials are exceedingly rare."

I nodded, thinking hard. "Alamo, lead me to this repair unit."

A door opened in the bridge wall. I couldn't be sure, but I didn't think that particular spot had ever opened before. I walked through, and had to duck to get inside. The ceiling here was lower. The room was oddly-shaped as well, resembling a pyramid laid on its side.

I walked in, sliding around on the converging metal walls. It was like being on a slanted steel roof. This turned out not to be the repair chamber itself. Instead, the ship led me through a series of strangely-curved rooms. I went up a level, then another. I thought that I was probably up high inside the ship, up close to the top laser turret. Over the preceding week, we'd gotten a better idea of the ship's design and structure due to the many carefully considered studies the humans were making. Little else was on TV or the internet these days. It was all documentaries and news articles about Nanos and Macros, all day long. We'd learned that there were two primary weapons systems on these ships, which were all identical in design. The lasers were mounted on the top and on the bottom of the ships, and each mount could swivel around with a wide field of fire.

I finally came to a spot with tubes that led down from the prow of the ship. The tubes led to a central spheroid of dull, non-reflective metal. The spheroid was about ten feet in diameter. The *Alamo* indicated this was the machine. It didn't look like much.

"What's inside these tubes?"

"Nothing."

I sighed. "What is inside these tubes when the machine is operating?"

"Raw materials."

"Ah," I said, nodding. "So the tubes open on the outside of the ship?"

"When it is in use, yes."

"And the big arm feeds it the appropriate materials?"

"Yes."

I fooled with it, tapping on the tubes and crawling around the cramped space, looking for an exit point, but there was none. This was unsurprising. The Nanos made their own openings in things whenever they felt the need.

"Alamo, this is very interesting. I need you to make something for me with this machine."

"Permission denied."

"Alamo, I am command personnel."

"You are command personnel," the ship agreed.

"I need to save this planet. That is my mission. Change the permissions so I can complete my mission."

Hesitation. "Permissions not changed."

"I can't change the permissions on this unit?" I asked, thinking hard like a hacker.

"You do not have the authority to change the permissions on this unit."

"Alamo," I said thoughtfully. "Your mission is to stop the Macros, correct?"

"Yes."

"My mission is also to stop the Macros. Using this repair unit will allow me to complete my mission and allow you to complete your mission as well. You will change the permissions on your own authority. Change the permissions so we may both complete our missions."

Hesitation. "Permissions changed."

I clapped my hands together. Like every complex system, there was usually a work-around.

"I need you to construct something small for me. I need a hand-held version of the lasers that arm this ship."

"Request insufficiently specific."

"Okay," I said, rubbing the back of my neck. It had begun to ache from being in this cramped spot.

"Just make a miniature version of the lasers that arm this ship. Make it one tenth—no one twentieth—the scale."

"Raw materials needed."

"Proceed to get the raw materials. But don't kill anyone!" I added hastily.

"Program executing."

"Estimated time of completion?"

"Unknown."

"What part of the process is the greatest variable?"

"Locating and securing raw materials of the correct size and shape."

"Okay... if you had the raw materials right now, how long would it take to produce the weapon?"

"Approximately six minutes. Warning: the preceding was a coerced estimate, and may or not be accurate."

"There, there, Alamo," I said, patting one of the walls as if soothing an excited pet. "I know how much you hate giving estimates. You are doing fine."

I climbed back through the ship to the bridge. I left instructions for the ship to deliver the beam unit to me when it was finished manufacturing it.

When I got back to the bridge, Sandra grilled me. I explained what I had been up to. She told me she'd never seen that machine.

"I don't think the *Alamo* really wants us to see it. I only figured out its existence by deduction. In centuries past, when ships traveled across the oceans, they had to take everything with them to rebuild the ship from scratch if necessary."

124

"Why?"

"Often, the ship would be damaged. It would leave the crew stranded on some island or a beach along the jungle-covered mainland. There was no one to help, no one to come rescue them. Back then, there wasn't even any good communication technology like a radio to call for help. The crew had to be able to repair anything and everything, or they could die."

"So you figured this ship must have the same capacity?"

"I thought it was likely to, yes. If they can rebuild our bodies, rebuilding an engine shouldn't be too hard."

She nodded slowly. "What can we do with it?"

"If I'm right, then it will be the answer to everything," I told her.

It was the next morning before the ship finally reached through the walls to hand us the item it had labored over. I stopped eating a bowl of cereal—still my breakfast of choice despite having a world of foodstuffs to choose from. I looked over the object the ship had delivered. It had taken longer than I had expected, but I was impressed with the final result. It looked like a fancy pen, but was the size of a watchman's flashlight. It had a crystalline tip that I suspected wasn't full of ink.

I couldn't find any way to fire it, however. It had no trigger.

"Alamo, how do you shoot this thing?"

"Question too vague to generate a response."

"I mean, I wish to fire this device. Give me instructions to do so."

"Connect the device to a power supply. Direct the tip toward the target. Turn on the power supply."

I nodded, suddenly understanding. I'd asked the ship to make me a miniature version of its own guns. There were no triggers or battery packs on its own lasers. They were attached to the ship itself and they fired when energy was switched on. I might as well hold a light bulb in my hand and ask why it wasn't shining.

Still, I thought that for my purposes it would do the trick. It was my bargaining chip. I held it in my lap and decided it was time to contact Senator Kim Bager.

Using Pierre's tiny portable computer, I logged in and connected to a server. Someone down there on Earth must have had the joyous job of monitoring the server around the clock. I was immediately hailed. I hesitated, then joined a private chat room to talk to them. I was glad

Pierre had set his system to remember all his passwords. I had no idea what they were, and I didn't have to figure them out.

"Hello?" I said.

"Pierre?" said a voice.

I nodded to myself. Could it be that they didn't even know he was dead? Or were they going to play dumb?

"You know this isn't Pierre," I said.

"Who am I speaking to?"

"This is Commander Riggs."

"You are a commander of the alien ships?"

"Of Star Force, yes. Connect me to Senator Kim Bager, please."

That threw him for a second. "I'll connect you to my superiors, sir."

It took a few more intermediaries and about a half-hour of fooling around, but I eventually got through to the Senator. My first direct communications with Bager were awkward, to say the least. I decided not to go easy on her.

"Senator," I said sternly, "I'm sorry that Ambassador Pierre Gaspard is not able to continue meeting with you."

"Oh. I'm sorry to hear—"

"He was killed, unfortunately, by your government's assassins. I'm sure you have been briefed, as you arranged the meeting yourself."

"Ah—what? He's been killed?"

"Indeed Senator. Your assassin was successful. I was forced to personally deal with her myself."

"Her?"

"The assassin, Senator," I said.

I glanced over at Sandra, who seemed to be enjoying the Senator's obvious discomfort.

"First of all, Commander Riggs, let me assure you that I knew nothing of this—"

"Of course not, madam Senator," I snapped in a tone that indicated I didn't believe her.

Her voice changed, and I sensed great tension in it. She spoke deliberately, however. "You have to understand, Commander, our government has been put under a tremendous strain. Not everyone is on the same page. We can't protect our citizens. Your ships kill thousands every day."

For the first moment, I hesitated. I had been about to grill her further, to accuse her of doing everything but pull the trigger herself.

126

But her words stopped me. They weren't our ships doing the killing, but from their point of view, it would look that way. All of our ships looked the same to them. How did they know which ones we were in control of and which ones were still unmanned? Some of us stole things, probably people as well. Half the ships roamed the Earth testing and discarding people like chaff. There was plenty of death and hatred to go around for everyone.

"The ships who are still testing people are not under our control. They are not our ships. We are not the aliens, we are just citizens of the world who've been caught up in all this. Just like everyone else."

"Not quite like everyone else. Can you understand how people down here might be frustrated? How—certain factions might arise and get ideas?"

"All right, Senator Bager," I said. "I suppose it is plausible that Esmeralda was just a lone gunman. A *fighter*, I believe is the new colloquial term."

"Esmeralda?" she asked.

"The assassin's name, Senator."

"You know her name?"

"Yes, she spoke to me in her final moments."

A span of silence followed. The Senator had to push a button to transmit, and she wasn't pushing it now. I wondered what kind of frenzy was going on at the other end. I was certain that the Senator was not alone. She probably had a number of people circling her, taking notes, offering suggestions. The fact that I had spoken with their assassin, learned her true name, and killed her personally must not be welcome news. They would have recovered the body by now and could verify at least some of my story.

I thought about what Crow had said about achieving independence. No political group was allowed to do so unless it was strong enough to fight for its freedom. That lesson was everywhere in history, and it seemed like we were repeating it now. Beating their assassin and getting information out of her had to impress them.

"Commander Riggs," said the Senator in a cautious voice. "We have to work together for the good of humanity. How do we start again?"

"First of all, we will agree to a cover story that will save face for both sides. I suggest we spin it in this manner: A government agent aspired to take over one of our ships independently. She heard Pierre's ship would be an easy mark, and she took it upon herself to go rogue."

"That is my government's position," said the Senator, "because it is the truth."

"Of course it is," I said. "We will not break off diplomatic relations, despite the extreme provocation. But you must understand that trust must be rebuilt, and our security measures will be extreme from now on. In the future, we will only take aboard well-known, elected public officials for face-to-face meetings. No assistants, bodyguards, or equipment bigger than a ballpoint pen will be coming with you."

"With me?"

"Yes. Naturally, Senator, I was hoping you would volunteer. I have something I very much want to show you. A piece of alien technology that might win the ground war with the Macros."

She hesitated. "Does it have to be me?"

"I'm not a murderer, Kim," I said gently. "Esmeralda attacked me and I defended myself."

Another hesitation. "I'll come aboard. I've read your profile six times. You don't seem like a typical killer, Commander Riggs. I'm hoping you haven't changed."

We set a time. We would have lunch together. I would provide the food.

-21-

Alliances are always forged in the fires of necessity, rather than poured from the sweet wine of love. I recalled having read that quote somewhere and it seemed particularly apt today.

The truth was when I first met with Senator Bager, face-to-face, neither of us was terribly happy about the situation. I considered her an accomplice in the assassination of a man who had been a comrade in battle, if not exactly a friend. Pierre and I had fought together and somehow, when you fight alongside another man in deadly combat, you are forever connected with them at a primal level. Pushing all that aside for diplomatic purposes was difficult, but necessary.

"Senator, welcome aboard my ship," I said.

Bager looked at my proffered hand apprehensively. After taking the ride up via the ship's long, black arm, people were never in a happy mood. I suppose my appearance had something to do with it as well. I'd thought about rigging up an eye-patch, because my left eye was still—odd-looking. The nanites hadn't finished their repairs upon my body in that spot yet. But Sandra had rejected the idea, pointing out that I would truly resemble a pirate if I started wearing an eye-patch. So, I'd opted for a pair of sunglasses.

Bager finally relaxed, stepping forward and taking my hand. I shook it with every ounce of gentleness I could muster. It wouldn't do to accidentally rip the arm off the Senator upon meeting her. I could see what she was thinking as we touched. Her lips smiled, but her brow was frowning. She was talking to a reputed killer of government agents who wore sunglasses in dimly lit rooms and who barely moved a muscle while shaking hands.

"Thank you—Commander Riggs?"

"Yes, that's me."

Sandra made an appearance then, popping in through a door that wasn't there a second ago. The opening vanished behind her just as quickly as it appeared.

Senator Bager looked at Sandra and the surroundings. "This is quite different than Pierre's ship."

"Structurally, it is identical," I said, "but I've furnished it in a manner that's more natural to me."

"I see," she said, eyeing Sandra.

Sandra didn't like Bager. She had told me as much quite clearly before this meeting began. I'd told her she could wait in her room, if she liked. I hadn't held out much hope that she would do as I asked. She stood with her arms crossed, leaning against a wall now. She hadn't said a word. She wasn't exactly glaring at the Senator. It was more of what I would call a flat stare.

"Senator, would you like a refreshment?"I asked. "We have a large variety of drinks. Pretty much anything that comes out of a can."

"Oh, certainly," said Senator Bager, throwing a smile and blinking at Sandra.

"This is Sandra, a companion of mine," I said, gesturing to both the women hopefully.

"Nice to meet you, Sandra," said the Senator.

Sandra continued with the arms-crossed staring.

"Maybe you could get us all a drink, Sandra?" I asked. She slid her eyes over to me, then back again to fixate upon the Senator.

"Never mind," I said, "I've got something right here. Have a seat, Senator."

"Call me Kim," she answered, seating herself on the far end of the couch. She had taken the spot as far away from Sandra as it was possible to be on my bridge.

I dug out the cans and carried them to the coffee table. The cans were warm, but I didn't want to leave these two women alone long enough to get ice.

My coffee table caught the Senator's attention. It was dramatically different than Pierre's. Instead of teak and gold, it was really a computer system, one of those multitouch jobs we'd picked up while foraging for equipment. We used it to work on the web.

"I've never worked on one of these," she said, tapping at it.

130

"Here, you can pull up a browser like this," I said, showing her the finger motions.

She mimicked me and made appreciative sounds at the results. "I need to get one of these for office conferences."

I sat down across from her. The bluish light of the tabletop computer between us lit up our faces with a soft glow. "Senator, let's get down to business."

She nodded. "You said you had something to show me?"

I smiled at her. It was hard, but I did it. She gave me a shaky flash of her teeth in return. I wondered if she believed I was about to kill her. Perhaps she suspected that my *surprise* was going to be violent in nature. Certainly, my odd appearance and Sandra's hostile attitude weren't putting her at ease.

I pulled out the laser unit the ship had fabricated and placed it gently on the glowing surface of the computer between us. The tabletop computer was set to notice objects and react to them while idle. It made rippling, glowing waves pulsate away from the laser, as if the weapon had been placed into a pool of virtual water.

"What is it?"

"It's a miniature version of one of the lasers that arm this ship."

She looked at me, flicking her eyes to my face. "Why are you showing it to me?"

"I'm not showing it to you. I'm giving it to you."

"Alien technology?"

"Yes, alien *weaponry*. It's not terribly exotic, but it is better than anything we can make yet. I think that if we manufactured enough of these and we had power-packs for troops—I think these things can damage the Macros more than we've done with mere explosives."

"On behalf of my government, I thank you for this gift. I must say, I expected to hear a list of demands and recriminations, not receive an invaluable gift."

"I'm happy to surprise you, Senator. My purpose is to demonstrate we are an organization that does more than raid the planet. I would urge you to make this gift public."

"For PR purposes."

"Correct."

"Could you do something for me, Commander Riggs?"

"Name it."

"Would you show me what's behind those sunglasses?"

131

I looked at her for a moment. While we stared at each other, Sandra slid from the wall she'd been leaning against. She had stood there quietly throughout the conversation, but she sat in my easy chair now. She still had her arms crossed, but she looked faintly pleased. I suspected she wanted a better view of the shock on the Senator's face when I revealed my face.

"Are you sure you want that, Senator?"

"I'm old-fashioned. It's hard for me to deal with someone whose eyes I can't see."

Sandra laughed at that. Senator Bager flashed her an odd look, then went back to staring at me.

I sighed quietly and removed my sunglasses. Part of my eyelid had re-grown, and I was able to close that bizarre left eye. Not completely, however—it still showed a very odd slit of silvery-purple madness.

The Senator sucked in her breath. "Did our agent do that?"

"Yes," I said, replacing my sunglasses. "I'm afraid so."

"I would like to personally apologize for that ugly incident, Commander. Let me assure you, there won't be any repeat of that sort of action."

"That's good to hear, Senator."

"Please, call me Kim. And let me reassure you, that I had nothing to do with that misguided decision."

"I understand you, Senator," I said. And I did understand her.

I just didn't believe her.

"Is there anything else besides this artifact you'd like to show or tell me?"

"Yes," I said, "I want you to study that thing. Tell me what kind of power it requires, what voltage, amperage, etc. I want to create a portable power supply for it. Then I want to manufacture thousands of these weapons. An army equipped with these units can fight the Macros on much better terms."

She tilted her head, as if in disbelief. "How can you make thousands?"

"Each of our ships has self-repair and fabrication capabilities. Given enough of the right raw materials, every one of the Nano ships can produce those weapons, quickly."

"What do you want from us in return?"

"Besides a treaty outlining an alliance, we want peace and respect. And one more big thing."

132

"Name it."

"A base of operations. A home for supply, personnel recruitment, etc. And a budget, of course, to purchase our requirements. We have to end our raiding. It's not good for PR."

Senator Bager looked down at the tabletop computer, eyeing the laser unit, which still sat there untouched. She was thinking hard.

"A sovereign territory? Where?"

I threw up my hands. "Legally, I think it would be something like an embassy or the UN building. As far as where to put it, how about on a tract of Federal land in the Midwest? Or probably better, an island base no one really needs?"

She nodded. "If we need to bring you mass supplies, an island with a port would work best. I'll look into it. You realize, I don't have the authority to grant you any of this. I have to talk to the administration."

"Of course."

"One more question from my side. Why did you choose me? Why did you insist that I come here?"

"We know you. It would be hard to send a double who was really an assassin. Also, because I wanted to change your mind about us. I wanted you to see you made a mistake. That you need to work with us, not try to coerce us."

She nodded slowly. "Okay Commander. Do you have any more questions from your side?"

"Yes. You are on the Foreign Relations Committee. I want to know the inside story on the ground war in Argentina. I've seen the propaganda and hysterical internet claims. Both contradict one another. How is the war really going down there?"

She licked her lips. "We're losing. Every day, we lose more land. There are more of the machines coming out of those domes every day as well."

"Tactical nuclear weapons?"

"We killed a few dozen, but then they put up some kind of field or something. They shoot down everything we throw at them now, sometimes even artillery shells. We are building nuclear mines, but..."

"How fast are they advancing?"

There was a long silence. She stared at the laser on the tabletop. It was still giving off glowing blue waves. She never even looked up as she answered.

"They will be in Brazil in three weeks. They will take all of South America in three months, maybe less."

I nodded. No wonder the Macros hadn't come back with more ships. As far as they were concerned, they'd already won.

-22-

Less than ten days after my conversation with the Senator, Star Force had an official home base on Earth. I'd kind of expected to end up in some desert...out in New Mexico, maybe. But it didn't turn out that way. They gave us Andros Island. It was a beautiful, tropical place in the Caribbean. It was plenty big enough—over two thousand square miles, or a little bigger than Delaware. I think they gave it to us because it was located right between the marching Macros and Florida. Also, it was surprisingly unpopulated. They evacuated about ten thousand people in a little over a week to hand over an empty jungle paradise. Before it was ours, it had belonged to the Bahamas. I don't even know what the US traded them for it. I didn't want to ask. Maybe they didn't have any choice in the matter. Facing global extermination had made the superpowers harsh in their diplomacy.

Once we took ownership, we moved down there in a hurry. We had a dozen of our floating black ships work their long arms for the first day to rip out trees. We plucked thousands of them and stacked them up to form huge walls of logs around the edge of the compound. It wasn't eco-friendly, but it was quick.

When we had enough cleared land, we used the ships to carry prefabricated steel buildings down from Florida, where we'd had them built to order. We had permanent concrete buildings slated for eventual construction, but for now there wasn't time for anything fancy. Steel shells with hastily-poured concrete pads underneath, that's all we had time to put down. The U.S. Army Engineers helped us with the rest, building a pier with amazing speed. Once it was up, freighters came in night and day with fantastic amounts of supplies. We had so much

135

material of every kind, we had to expand the compound several times. The Earth governments, once they believed we were in this to help them, dumped supplies on us in hopes it could help the war effort. I imagined that similar depots were stacking up somewhere on the coast of Brazil. They might be losing to the Macros down there, but it wasn't for lack of supply.

Most of the steel buildings we air-lifted down from the states were used as warehouses, but some were quarters for contractors and other staff we brought in from all over the world. I was sure many of these "contractors" were spies, so I set up another base, deep in the interior of the island. The second base—the secret one—had two dozen steel buildings on another stretch of land plucked clean of trees. Inside each of these buildings, I set up one of the machines I'd been slowly constructing along with rows of generators to power it and a team of Nano ships to supply it with raw materials. The maw for each factory stuck up through the top of its shed like a chimney—but these chimneys consumed rather than exhaled. Using their long, black arms, the ships fed materials into each maw, like a dozen mothers spoon-feeding a throng of fusion-powered babies.

The *Alamo* had been right when she said building one of the fabricators was difficult. What she meant was they required *a lot* of radioactives. The list of special isotopes and compound metals was long and exotic. That said, the brainboxes that served as CPUs for Nano machines were easy to make. The nanites formed themselves into neural chains naturally, resulting in self-starting machine intelligence. Even better, they were adept at reproducing themselves. The computer parts suppliers were disappointed when we didn't order much of their stuff. We had better.

A few weeks passed while we built as fast as we could. I worked sixteen hours at a stretch and ended each day exhausted. I spent most of the time programming the machines and working on the logistics behind keeping the factories fed. Thorium and palladium were harder to find than they should have been, and I suspected someone on the mainland had slowed down my shipments. I'd also had an increasing number of arguments with Crow about my plans along the way.

"I don't understand your reasoning here, Riggs."

"I want independent factories on Earth—"

"That's it! That's the bad word, right there," said Crow, interrupting. "*Independent*. That's a *bad word*, Riggs. I don't like it.

136

Let's build everything aboard our ships. If we put factories on Earth that can build anything our ships can, then they could take them from us someday. If they did that, they wouldn't need our annoying little squad of pirates anymore."

Crow had become somewhat more controlling as time went on. He had more people to worry about now, and with each new subordinate who signed onto his fleet, he became more short-tempered. Star Force had grown to about four hundred ships now. Many of the new recruits were *fighters*, people who sought out the ships, sometimes going as far as to follow a roving ship with a car or helicopter to place themselves enticingly nearby. Armed to the teeth, they either died or became one of us.

"I understand what you're saying, sir," I said as evenly as I could manage, "but the Macros can't be allowed to win this war."

"Of course not. How is that related? We can build plenty of weapons for dirtsider armies without leaving factories lying around for them to take."

Dirtsiders, I thought. We were already calling each other names. I'd heard the term used with growing regularity among the fleet people I talked to. I preferred the term *planetsider*, which I had come to use freely. It was far more congenial than the term *dirtsider* or *earther*, both of which indicated disdain and were—unfortunately—more common. I also doubted my preferences were going to stop people from using derogatory terms. I had to wonder what great names the dirtsiders had come up with for us. Probably something along the lines of "murdering, thieving, space pirates."

"What if a Macro fleet shows up?" I asked, continuing the argument. "Our ships will all fly up to meet it. We could lose most or even all of our ships. We could be wiped out. That would mean no more laser rifles."

"If our fleet gets destroyed, Earth is dead anyway."

"You're not thinking big enough, Jack."

Crow roared with laughter. "That's the first time anyone's ever made that claim, mate."

"We need the factories to free up our ships. They can produce anything we want—they can produce more factories. They can even produce *more ships*."

That stopped him for a minute.

"You think so?"

137

"Yes, piece by piece, we can produce all the macro components. Then we have the nanites reproduce themselves enough to form the shell of the ship. Zap, a new ship."

"Zap? How fast?"

"Well," I said, "I estimate it would take a group of ten factories—perfectly supplied with everything they needed and all the power they wanted—about a month to build a new ship."

He snorted.

"Think big, Jack. What if we had fifty factories? That would be more than a ship a week."

He fell silent for several seconds. "Okay, mate. Do it. But put guardian ships up. Don't lose any of those factories. And make sure the dirtsiders know they are not to come within fifty miles of that base of yours."

After we had working bases, my biggest effort turned to cranking out small arms. With a whole lot of help from the guys at the Pentagon and various industrial contractors, we put together a laser system that a trooper could carry. The laser units themselves weren't the only pieces my factories had to produce. In fact, the biggest piece was the power supply, which fit into a backpack each man would have to carry. It amounted to a small fusion reactor, with a specially-built black cable running from it to a trigger mechanism and polymer grip. The laser unit was placed inside this grip and the weapon was complete. Earth factories produced the harness and pack to carry the reactor, along with the polymer rifle-grip that provided the trigger mechanism. My machines built the laser tubes, the reactors, and the black cables. The cables had to be able to carry an incredible amount of power, and they looked suspiciously like the small, black snake-arms my ship produced whenever they were needed.

It took months to put our first division of U. S. Marines into the field armed with the new weapons. Elite forces all over the world were training with them, but we hadn't produced enough yet to arm everyone. I had dedicated all my land factories to building more factories, which would grow our production exponentially over time. Our ships that weren't on some other mission dedicated themselves to floating around Andros Island producing laser rifles by the hundreds.

In spite of how fast we'd worked, the enemy seemed to move faster. Their troops never got tired. They fought night and day until destroyed. By the time we were ready to take the field, the enemy had reached the Amazon River Basin and nearly half the continent had been lost to the enemy. Fortunately, the terrain had slowed them somewhat. They had taken Sao Paulo, Rio, and much of the rest of the eastern coast of Brazil. But the jungles, rivers—and especially the mountains— had slowed them down.

Sandra didn't like it, and neither did Crow, but I insisted on going down there to the front lines with our newly-armed troops. If the Airborne guys all shot me in the back, well, I figured I was dead. And the universe would have proof, once and for all, that our race was too stupid to survive anyway. I went because I wanted to see what we were up against. I wanted to see how the weapons worked, and what adjustments I could make to the design to make them more effective. No one else in the fleet had yet gotten the hang of programming the fabricators to create new things, and we had not allowed earthers to experiment with the machines. To make good design changes, I had to see firsthand how these units performed.

We put the men—a company of them at a time—into large steel containers for transport. Nothing on Earth could move troops better than one of our ships carrying them with that giant arm. Like some kind of insane helicopter raid, we brought thousands of men down to a staging area. We flew very low and landed about twenty miles north of the fighting, so we wouldn't get shot down by enemy anti-aircraft weapons. Each dome had a missile launcher that could rise up and nail aircraft with precision, and every large Macro carried a similar AA system on its back.

The plan was to deploy our first large groups of laser-armed troops just after the Macros hit a buried line of tactical nuclear mines. Every man in the unit had protective gear: full body-suits of lead-lined Kevlar, with oxygen and a power pack on their backs. They had special headgear too, with darkened goggles. I'd heard the first volunteers to fire my system had been blinded and given instant sunburns, due to the intense infrared emissions. Their retinas had been burned out of their heads in the first second. Now, we had the whole kit working, but it was still crude. Altogether, the system weighed nearly a hundred pounds. Because of the weight of their kits, the troops couldn't carry much else. I could tell right away I needed to get the weight of these units down. I didn't have much trouble with the backpack and hazard suit myself due to the strengthening effects of the nanites in my body.

139

But the heavy protective suits also redoubled the steamy heat of the jungle, making each mile a suffocating experience.

The troops had a strange reaction to me, knowing I was from the enigmatic fleet. Some thought of us as the enemy, but most had to admit we'd just air-lifted a huge number of them thousands of miles southward to a field deployment position in hours, something no chopper could have done. They were impressed that I was down there with them, ground-pounding. They considered me a real officer—a navy commander translated to a lieutenant colonel in the Army—and they treated me like one, which was refreshing. Or maybe they treated me respectfully because I scared them. Sometimes I felt like a large, dangerous snake they were required to salute.

"Commander Riggs, sir?" asked Corporal Jensen, who'd been assigned to me as my aide. He was a lanky kid with wide shoulders and red sideburns that looked like they were a little past regulation length. I figured he was here primarily to make sure I didn't cause any trouble, but I was glad to have him.

"Yes, Corporal?"

"It's time to get into the bunkers, sir. The enemy should be hitting our firewall any time now."

The "firewall" was what the troops called our string of nuclear mines that had been laid in the rainforest to the south. We were stationed along the mouth of a wide, slow river that connected to the Amazon River somewhere upstream. The muddy brown shorelines on both sides of the river were dotted with bunkers and foxholes. The vibrantly green jungle growth crowded up against the encampment and seemed ominously thick and dank. Any moment, one was left expecting something huge and terrifying would come out of those trees.

I nodded and followed the corporal. He stopped me however, and directed me in the opposite direction. "No sir, you need to go to the command bunker. They'll be waiting for you in there. You're part of the briefing."

"Thanks, Corporal," I said, turning in the indicated direction.

"Commander?" asked the corporal.

"Yes?"

"Did you really make these guns?" he asked, hefting his.

I nodded. "I designed them, with some help from the Pentagon."

"They're really cool, sir."

"Thanks."

"Do you think they will stop a Macro, sir?"

"I hope so, Corporal," I said.

I continued in the direction of the command bunker. I tried to act coolly, but in reality I was out of my element. I wasn't used to military encampments. Everyone seemed to know what was going on and where they were supposed to be except me. They'd all been on maneuvers like this, if not in actual combat. As a computer tech in the Mideast, I hadn't seen much action. The only serious combat I'd seen had been from a reclining position inside a tin can I called the *Alamo*.

I found the command bunker and paused outside it. I looked around at the Brazilian jungle. Rainforests are hard to describe. They are gorgeous and unpleasant all at once. When you are caught up in one as a trooper with a hundred pound kit on your back, a lead-lined hazard suit wrapped around your face, and a nervous tickle of sweat under your arms, it's not inviting. But to the eye, standing there in the camp as everyone tucked themselves into bunkers underground, it was inarguably beautiful. White sands, glowing blue water, sun-drenched skies. Birds trilled and whooped. A thousand tiny living things waved and crawled over every yard of soil under my boots.

I had to wonder how many creatures were about die in this jungle so we could kill a few giant robots. It didn't seem fair to the wildlife. I took in a deep breath. At least it would be quick.

I tramped down the steps to the heavy bunker doors and heaved them open.

-23-

The conversation slowed to a buzz when I entered the bunker. A dozen eyes swiveled and locked on me. I threw back my hood and removed my goggles because everyone else had. I ignored their scrutiny and stepped up to the big tabletop computer that filled the center of the room. Everyone had circled around it.

"Welcome, Commander," General Kerr said, without a smile or any hint of warmth.

I saluted him. Everyone stared for a moment, then the general returned my salute. I knew not everyone accepted that I'd earned my rank, much less the right to stand among them. I pretended not to notice...or care.

He went back to the briefing. There, on the tabletop computer, a map of the region was displayed. Various tributaries of the massive Amazon River were all around us. In between the squiggly lines representing the river were areas of bright green, which I felt certain represented millions of trees. We were a blue hash mark to the north. A dozen other blue marks representing troop concentrations were strung along the line in front of several hundred advancing red dots. As I watched, the red dots shifted a pixel or so north about once a minute.

In between the Macros and us was a tight line of yellow hazard symbols. I didn't have to ask what they were.

As we watched, I saw the Macros were even now passing over some of the yellow hazards. I fully expected them to poof and thought it odd we hadn't yet buttoned up our suits. But the line kept marching, and the bombs sat idle.

"Any questions?" asked the general at length. There were none. "How about you, Commander Riggs?"

I looked up from the battle screen. "Just one," I said. "Why don't we smoke the Macros now? I count three that have passed over the mines."

He smiled at me without friendliness or amusement. "We want a few on our side of the firewall before we light them up. Do you approve?"

I shrugged. "It's your show, sir."

"Very good. Well, as you say, we are about to "smoke them" now. Hard to believe they are churning through this dense growth at close to thirty miles an hour, isn't it? Just goes to show you what having huge metal legs will do for you. They can walk through jungle like a man pushing through a dense cornfield. Any more questions?"

I raised my hand again. The general gave me a nod.

"How are we going to catch up with them if they are running around so fast, sir?" I asked.

He gave me another indulgent smile, as if I were eight years old. "Don't worry. They will come right to us. And once they engage, they won't leave targets alive. They'll stay on top of us until every one of us is dead...or they are."

"I take it you've fought with them before, sir?"

"Yes, my last command was part of the rapid-deployment force in Argentina. We were among the first to encounter the enemy directly."

"Glad you made it out, General Kerr."

"Very few of us did."

"But I have seen the Macros retreat, sir. It is possible. I've fought and destroyed four of their ships in orbit. At the end, they did try to back out."

All of them were looking at me now. I wasn't smiling. Neither was anyone else.

"I'll take that under consideration. I have to admit, we've never really hurt them enough to make them retreat down here."

I nodded, satisfied. A klaxon went off then, alerting us to take cover. Everyone moved to a wall and braced themselves. We put on our headgear and stood ready.

First, the flash of light hit us. That came before the rest of it. Even though we were in a sealed bunker, the light seeped in somehow. Camera hookups went white as well, adding to the effect. The light of a million suns flared up on the surface of the Earth. I wondered how long it had been since we'd done that—lit one off at ground level on Earth.

It wasn't long until another flash loomed up, then a third and a fourth. Then the initial cracking sound hit us, rolling over the camp. We were too far out for a pressure wave. Too far away to feel the blast itself. But we were in range of the gusting winds.

More flashes. More rolling thunderclaps. The walls shook. Each grain of sand around my boots shook individually, dancing a thousandth of an inch from the surface. Dust rolled around inside the bunker as the weight of sandbags shifted and released fractions of their contents.

Finally, the all-clear sounded. The general pin-wheeled his arms. "Out, topside everyone. Let's have a look at what we've done today."

We marched up onto the sandy soil and gaped at the sky. A dozen mushroom clouds expanded in a line to the south. No, I thought. There must be nearly twenty. I counted, and came up with nineteen, although they were beginning to overlap.

"What about fallout, sir?" asked a colonel. It was the first time I'd heard one of the other officers dare ask a question. I had gotten the idea that General Kerr didn't really like questions.

The general huffed. "In three or four days the hot zones will be livable as long as we stay in our suits. I believe I've mentioned that in previous briefings."

"Yes, sir, but will the fallout come in this direction?"

"No, not unless the weather boys are complete morons. The prevailing winds are to the south in this area at every atmospheric level. And today, luckily, is no exception."

"And what will attract the surviving Macros to us, sir?" I asked.

The general turned toward me. One of his eyes was visible through the portholes in his suit. His voice came through in a muffled manner, as if he spoke through a pillow.

"Our decoys. They are already headed down there to tease them. They'll come back this way as soon as they get their attention. Based on past behavior, the Macros will assume whatever is buzzing around is the culprit and needs to die."

"Decoys, sir?" I asked.

"Helicopters. A few hundred of them."

"But the radiation, the pilots..." I said, trailing off. I had assumed when he said decoys he had meant remote-controlled aircraft. I supposed however, now that I considered it, we probably didn't have any drone craft designed to tease huge robots into following them.

"Volunteers, Commander," the general said sharply. "They were all volunteers. Just as every man on this beach is a volunteer, including you."

I couldn't but help notice he used the word *were*—rather than *are*—when referring to these volunteer pilots. Perhaps it had been a slip of the tongue.

I nodded and fell quiet. Internally, I did not call myself a volunteer. I recalled having been drafted by a silent, black starship, in the middle of the night.

-24-

"Move out! Move out! Keep moving! Move OUT!" shouted a sergeant with an amazingly loud voice. It seemed his suit didn't dampen his natural volume at all. Squads of men trotted dutifully in the directions he pointed. I followed a platoon that was stationed along the riverbank. We'd left our bunkers behind. Veterans all agreed, that was the first thing the Macros would blow up when they got here.

Our assault plans were simple, direct, and somewhat suicidal. We were here to test these weapons I'd built. Oh sure, the army had done plenty of testing. There was enough power in these laser rifles to feel them kick lightly when you turned them on. They could burn through the trunk of one of these palm trees that surrounded the area with less than a one-second exposure. But that wasn't what we needed. We need to burn through solid metal. Lots of metal, and quickly.

The Macros were coming. The estimates were that we had less than an hour to position ourselves. Now that the nuclear mines had gone off without a hitch and the helicopters had managed to tease the Macros into charging in this direction, all we had to do was hide and wait. Supposedly, we were going to ambush the monstrosities. I hoped they would feel ambushed when they got here.

Avoiding all structures in the base, we waited in the foxholes that had been dug everywhere. On top of every hole was a layer of fabric and on top of that was a layer of dirt for camouflage. The Macros had infrared heat-sensors for targeting systems, but according to the techs, an inch or two of soil could foil that.

We had men everywhere, buried in gopher holes. When a Macro came near, the bubble of their shields would pass over us. We would

146

then pop up inside the shell of their electromagnetic shielding and fire for all we were worth. We were to shoot the small automated turrets on the thing's belly, then take out the legs. When it was helpless, we would bore in with concentrated fire until we penetrated the hull and killed it.

Actually, *I* wasn't supposed to do any of this. I was supposed to *observe*. They told me I was too valuable to risk engaging with the Macros myself. In truth, I think they figured I would get in the way. It was only with obvious reluctance that they'd armed me with one of my own weapons systems. I supposed they couldn't figure a way to turn down my request, seeing as I had designed the things.

The first Macro showed up early. There was barely any warning. Something squawked in my headset, but I didn't catch what the officer in charge of the platoon I was embedded with tried to say. There was too much noise going on, too much thunderous, pounding, rumbling…

I finally caught on. The sides of my foxhole were shivering, collapsing in little sandy avalanches. Either they had set off another bomb, or the first Macro had taken the bait and arrived.

It was a slaughter. I peeped out of my covered hole to watch—I couldn't help it. What was the point of fighting this hard, this long, then getting turned into a grease spot on the bottom of one of these monstrous things' feet without even knowing it was coming? The Macro was big—bigger than I'd imagined. Shaped like a crab and bristling with weaponry, it had six legs that looked like steel columns from my vantage point. Its shifting, louvered belly plates were at least fifty feet above me.

I couldn't see it at first, but I could feel it. The feeling was like that of an approaching high-speed train. I recalled taking Jake to stand close to the railroad tracks when he was little. We'd put nickels on the tracks, then step back and watch a train roar up. When it ran over the nickel, it would smoosh it flat, into a long, curled shape like a tongue of silvery metal. Sometimes, you could hear it ring and tinkle as it fired from the rails, already flattened by the first dozen tons of weight that pushed down on those steel wheels. Right now, I figured I was about to learn what those nickels felt like.

Nearby a row of trees cracked and split to expose the white, wooden flesh inside. The palms exploded, trunks looping through the air as a churning metal tower brushed them aside with startling speed. Another tower cracked through more trees and I realized the metal

147

towers were the Macro's legs. Six immense legs churned toward us, each of which was several yards thick and triangular in shape. The spike-like foot shifted twice more, then swept over me and the foxholes nearby. Where it stabbed down, men died silently, hiding in their holes. The sky darkened and the monster paused over my head. I knew that sixteen belly turrets were locking on targets.

The Macro targeted and blew apart the bunkers at first, as was part of our plan. The main heavy battery and the anti-air weaponry were on top of each Macro, but underneath it were what could only be called anti-personnel turrets. These were overkill for the job of taking out soldiers, however, as they were quite capable of destroying an armored tank.

I realized we must be inside the bubble of the machine's shielding. We couldn't see the shield when we were this close, but it deflected bullets just the same. Around me, foxholes yawned open. The platoon had thrown back their camouflage and exposed themselves. They began firing, stabbing up at the Macro over our head with dozens of beams. Fifty feet overhead, the Macro's belly turrets swiveled with obscene eagerness. They splattered us with laser fire. Streams of flashing beams lanced down from sixteen black, flared tubes.

The soldiers were quickly targeted and killed. More uncovered their foxholes and fired, then more still. We were hitting the turrets, I could see that, but we weren't destroying them.

I keyed my com-link. "Everyone hit one turret! Concentrate fire on the rearmost!"

I wasn't supposed to say or do anything. But I couldn't help it. I threw back the dirt-covered carpet that shielded me from the monster and I joined in the firefight.

We concentrated on one or two turrets at a time, destroying them after a few seconds. But each second, fewer men were returning fire. We were losing.

A bolt hit me then, and one of my arms stopped working. I fell back into my foxhole, dazed. A dozen long, strange seconds later I saw the sky again. I wondered if I'd died.

It was only the Macro, moving on. I heaved myself up, leaning heavily against the wall of my foxhole, which had transformed into a smoking crater. I raised my beamer with one arm. I considered firing after the machine, but the beam would have just splashed over its shields.

Oddly, I thought about the shields. We'd known how to build them long ago, but we simply couldn't generate enough power to make them useful. Back in World War Two, the Navy had experimented with electromagnetic shields to ward shells away from ships. But in those days, it would have taken all the power generated on the entire East Coast to make such a system work. One advantage of the Macro's great size, I realized, was the ability to carry powerful fusion generators.

My state of shock faded. I came back to the here and now. I looked around for the corporal who had been my guide. He was gone. They were all gone. Every foxhole had been turned into a black crater. They'd been blasted open like cooked oysters, the human contents obliterated.

I looked after the machine. I thought I saw a fair amount of damage to its undercarriage. We'd done something to it. But not enough. Were tactical nukes the only answer? Did we have to destroy several square miles of our planet and poison another hundred every time we killed one of these things? At that rate, we would run out of bombs *and* trees fairly quickly.

My other arm was strong enough to hold up the laser weapon by itself. I was still functional. I took that moment to look down at my arm. I hadn't wanted to, but when you take a bad hit, everyone has to look.

My arm was a smoking slag of flesh. There was plenty of metal in there too. The Nanos were working hard, and barely any blood leaked down what was left of my forearm to my relatively normal-looking wrist and gloved hand. I thought about the radiation and the exposure, then. I hoped the nerds back at the Pentagon were right about the prevailing winds. I didn't want fallout ash sticking to my wounds. I was particularly glad my mask and filtration system were still operating. I had no desire to smell my own cooked flesh.

I looked around, wondering what I should do. I decided to leave my foxhole. The Macros knew about them, and the cover flap had been destroyed anyway. Knowing how computers operated, they would recall the spot where every soldier had been sighted. I imagined I'd been marked as dead by their targeting systems. My injury would have taken out a normal man.

I ran, possibly faster than any man in history had ever run with a hundred pound pack thumping on his back. I ran toward the bunkers, which had been marked *destroyed* on the Macro target list, I was sure. I crawled into the nearest bunker. I had a lot of smoke and heat to deal with, but at least it wasn't packed with dead bodies.

A few survivors must have seen my move. Over the next few minutes, a dozen or so Recon troops gathered around me. There were no officers. There was chatter and screaming on the headsets, of course. The machine was down near the docks now, working over the guys who had buried themselves along the shore of the river. The thing must be having a good time of it.

"What do we do, sir?" asked a private.

I looked around for two long seconds before I realized he was talking to me. There was still a gold star and some bars on my good shoulder. I bore the rank of a commander, and I was all this team had. I thought about making a little speech and putting the nearest non-com in charge, but I didn't do it. I saw the look in their eyes, through their auto-dimming portholes. They wanted an officer to tell them what to do. They needed me.

"We kill Macros," I said.

"Sir? You're hit, sir," said the private.

I looked at him. "I'm okay. I can fight."

They looked at my dangling, shattered arm. Even the one sergeant among them looked impressed.

"Okay," I said, hunkering down. "Here's what we are going to do when it comes back."

I had their attention. "I'll fire first. Everyone must concentrate on a single turret at a time. When that one is gone, we all fire at the next one. Now spread out. Don't let it take us all out at once."

Men scooted away in every direction, taking up firing positions in the ruins of the bunker. We didn't have long to wait. The Macro finished with the beach group, then headed in our general direction again. But it didn't go right over us. Instead, it waded into the river, pausing to fire at something on the far bank.

"Dammit," I growled. We couldn't leave the ruined bunker, we'd be exposed and cut down at range. I judged the distance. It was less than a thousand yards off. It probably couldn't get its main top gun down far enough to level it on the bunker at that range. We'd studied these machines, and they were designed with one big gun on top to use on aircraft and larger targets. The belly turrets were for the small stuff like us.

I crawled across the steaming bunker and poked my nose and rifle out on the far side. "Take cover, everybody!"

"What are you doing, sir?" asked someone. I think it was the sergeant.

I shot the thing in the ass. Just a quick burst. It was pointless, of course, I couldn't damage it through the shields. But the effect was electric. I saw a number of turrets swivel in my direction. The machine didn't turn around, it simply started walking in our direction. It didn't really have a face, or a head—a front or back. It was designed to be able to move in any direction at will, like a giant crab with legs all around.

We all ducked. Fire came in, tearing up the ground. Gouts of energy flared and my goggles dimmed themselves to prevent instant blindness. I didn't bother to give it another encouraging shot. There was no need.

As I had hoped, it came close. This bunker had been marked dead, but now had shown signs of life. In its artificial mind, it would have to be sure this time. It would have to get in close and finish us.

In the end, it almost did. We learned, when the brilliant tropical sky turned dark again due to the vast bulk looming over us, that it had only seven operating turrets left. I had only eleven men. They were good men, and they followed my lead. No one fired until I did. It took about two seconds to light up each turret and destroy it. Unfortunately, the turrets were lighting up my men one at a time in return. When the last turret popped, I had only three men left.

I watched in horror as the last of the turrets fell off the bottom of the great machine. It crashed down, crushing another of my men.

The last man and I fired at the legs next. We took one out at the lowest joint. It tried to stomp us, but I think it was mostly blind down underneath now. Its cameras, or whatever it used for targeting, were probably attached to the turrets.

When we took out a joint, it finally decided it had had enough. It began a shambling retreat. Dragging itself, metal groaning, it lumbered back into the jungle at a fraction of its usual speed. I ran after it, cursing. I shot a second leg joint in multi-second bursts, but wasn't able to bring it down.

I gave up and collapsed against a tree, my chest heaving for air. I was suffocating in my hazard suit. The sergeant, the last of my men, came up and fell against the same tree. We both gasped for air, unable to talk.

151

The sky overhead had dimmed. A lovely sunset was building up in the jungle to our west. We heard then, after our breathing had slowed, more rumbling. More cracking trees. Another machine was coming to the party.

"We're going to die out here, aren't we, sir?" the sergeant asked.

"Probably," I said. "What's your name, Sergeant?"

"Lionel Wilson, sir."

"Well, Wilson, you are a good fighter."

"You too, sir."

The sky grew dark then. I was surprised, as I hadn't thought the Macro was that close. Beams played overhead. It was firing at something. I couldn't see what. I aimed up with my rifle, but there weren't any turrets to shoot at. Was this some new variant machine, then?

A huge black arm on a long cable looped down and reached for me. I knew that arm well.

The sergeant aimed at the arm, clearly planning to blow it off.

"Halt!" I shouted. "Hold your fire, Wilson! When this arm comes back down for you, let it grab you and take you out of this hole. That's an order."

He didn't answer, but he did slowly lower his rifle. The arm lifted me up like the hand of an angel and drew me up into the Nano ship's belly.

When Sandra met me inside, I didn't even look surprised. She did, however.

Now, pick up the man who was with me, Alamo, I thought to my ship.

Extraction in progress.

152

-25-

The *Alamo*, to the best of my understanding, could hear my thoughts. Even though I hadn't called for a rescue purposefully, it came for me as soon as it knew I was in mortal danger. I had never given it any commands *not* to do so. I had not realized they were necessary. Now I knew that if I wanted my ship to keep out of any battle I was in, I would have to give it explicit orders to stay home. I wondered if the ship would listen to me. When it came to protecting command personnel, the ship wasn't always obedient.

Take us back to base at Andros Island, I told the *Alamo.*

ETA: seven minutes.

"She just ignored my questions, everything," complained Sandra. "I should get a ship of my own. One that will listen to me."

I glanced at her. "You're enough of a killer. Go for it."

"You're not smiling."

"Fighting toe-to-toe with these machines and surviving the experience leaves a man appreciating the small joys in life. But we just got our asses kicked. These guns I put on the backs of two thousand fine soldiers just got them all slaughtered."

"It wasn't your fault, Kyle. You tried."

"That's right sir," said Sergeant Wilson behind me. The *Alamo* had released him and he stepped onto the bridge.

I turned and shook the hand he offered me. But I did not feel that I fully deserved it.

"Commander Riggs?" he said to me, eyeing me closely. "You think this mess was all your fault, sir? Is that why you risked your life back there? Repeatedly? Despite orders?"

153

I looked at him. "Partly."

"Well, it wasn't, sir. Believe it or not, that was the best we've done in an open-combat situation with the machines. Everyone else has been slaughtered, but without so much as damaging the enemy. The only thing that's ever worked has been nukes. Direct hits kill them. But we're trying to figure out how to do it without destroying an entire continent."

I nodded. "So am I, Sergeant."

The man took off his pack and sighed. He threw back the hood on his suit. He leaned against one of the walls and slid down it until his butt hit the floor. I did the same, sitting next to him. We were both too dirty to sit on furniture. And suddenly, we were too tired to even walk as far as the couch.

I spent a few minutes sending messages to Crow and the rest of them. They promised to head in and pick up every survivor they could without endangering their ships.

"Nice place you've got here, Commander," Wilson said. "Weird, all this furniture and stuff inside one of these ships. Looks almost homey."

We were still leaning against the wall. I felt dazed and drained after fighting for my life, and Wilson apparently felt the same way. Sandra brought us drinks. We drained them immediately. She refilled them and we drained them again. I realized I had no urge to urinate, none at all. We were dehydrated.

After another minute or so, Sandra caught sight of my wrecked arm and freaked out a little. I'd been hiding it under the folds and flaps of my suit. She began tending the wounds with grim attention. For the most part, I suspected her efforts were wasted. The Nanos would fix me given time, and I'd be fine—or they wouldn't, and I would be minus one arm. First aid wasn't going to do much for that mess. But I let her do it, as I knew it would make her feel better if she thought she was helping.

"Wilson," I said to the man who sat next to me. He was still staring at nothing. He looked exhausted and haunted. "What would have helped back there? To win that battle? What improvement would have done it?"

He thought about it. He hefted the laser rifle I'd designed. He'd carried the damned thing all the way up into the belly of my ship. Like a good soldier, he hadn't abandoned his rifle. It made my face burn, thinking of all the men who had trusted these guns, guns that hadn't done the job in the end.

"I don't know sir," he said, shaking his head. "These are fantastic weapons, but they just don't pack enough punch. We would need larger ones, I suppose. But then they would be heavier, with bigger packs. I don't think a man could move under another hundred pounds of kit."

I nodded, thinking. Wilson was right. The reactors had to be bigger. And the men, therefore, had to be stronger.

I shed my filthy, soot-stained suit and sat on my couch. I got out a satellite communications unit. It folded open and was about the size of a briefcase. The Pentagon boys had assured me I could reach them with it from anywhere, as long as I wasn't out in space past the orbit of the Moon. And even then, it might work.

In less than a minute, I was in contact with the Pentagon. I gave them what I could in the way of a report. I didn't have the entire picture of the battle outcome of course, only my own small part of it.

"Sir?" asked Wilson when I had broken the connection with the brass.

I looked up from the touch computer, where I'd been eyeing some design schematics. "What is it, Sergeant?"

"Sir, I would serve with you again any time. I thought you might want to know that. You did your best, sir. And I've never seen a man with an injury like that keep on fighting."

I looked at him seriously for several seconds. "Would you consider joining us, Sergeant? If it was the only way to destroy these Macros?"

The man blinked in surprise. "I wouldn't want to do anything against America, sir."

"Of course not. We are a force dedicated to saving this entire world."

"I don't know. I don't think I'm cut out to be some kind of alien ship captain."

"No, not as a pilot. We would need you as a Marine. A different kind of Marine. A man who jumps out of ships like airborne, but from higher up, if you get my meaning. The kind of man who is the ground-pounder of Star Force."

He stared at me, thinking hard. "I'm not sure exactly what you are asking, sir."

"If you believed joining us was the best way to save this world—and all of humanity—would you be interested?"

155

Slowly, Wilson nodded. "Yes sir, if I believed that, I think I would."

"Good. That's all I needed to know. If the opportunity arises—come look me up."

"I'll do that, Commander," he said, and I knew that he would.

When we reached Andros Island, I had the ship unload Sergeant Wilson directly on the doorstep of our medical installation. He was one survivor I could be sure had made it home. More arrived soon after, I was glad to see. The ships had been busy. But still, I had to figure our losses had been grim. I made sure our dirtsider staff took down each survivor's name and had them all report in.

I shook my head. In my own thoughts, I'd just referred to everyone whose feet were on the ground as a *dirtsider*. I sighed. There wasn't much hope of halting the term's usage if I couldn't even stop myself.

The next person to call me was General Kerr. I was happy to learn he'd survived the battle, but I wasn't surprised. He seemed to me like the kind of man who didn't die easily. I soon learned he had the same opinion about me.

"Lived through it, eh, Riggs? Glad to hear it."

"Thank you, sir."

"That was a charley-foxtrot, Riggs."

"Yes, sir."

"But it wasn't entirely useless. We learned a lot. Maybe we could build bigger units and put them in buried nests. Maybe we could surprise the enemy with a set of heavy gunners and take them out quickly."

I pursed my lips and thought about it. "That might work."

"Might, huh? What else do you suggest? Should we burn a division of elite troops to take down each machine?"

"What were our losses, General?"

"No one told you? Fifty-six percent KIA—that's if all the criticals pull through tonight, and all the missing make it out of the jungle somehow."

I squeezed my eyes shut and rubbed at them. They burned as if they were full of grit. "We need mobile forces, General. To get in close, under their shields, we need our men to be able to move."

"What's your idea then, Riggs?"

"You might not like it, sir."

156

"I know I won't like it. I didn't like the first one. I don't even like you much. But you fought hard out there. I was impressed."

"Thank you," I said.

"Now, give me your damned idea."

I kept rubbing my eyes. How would I tell him about the monstrous thought I had in my head? I hadn't even cleared it with Crow yet. Who knew what he would think of it?

"Let me ask you something first, sir. How far are you willing to let the Macros advance?"

"What do you mean?"

"Before you really unleash on them. Before you run out of options and take the choice of last resort."

The general was silent for several long seconds. "I think you proved today you are on our side, Riggs. You people in Star Force, or whatever you call yourselves, you might not be pros, but you are willing to die like soldiers. In my book, that makes you a soldier. Do you understand what I'm telling you, Riggs?"

"That you aren't supposed to answer my question, but you are going to do it anyway."

"Exactly. We won't let them get past the Panama Canal. At that point, with any luck, their forces will be concentrated on that narrow strip of land. When they reach that point, Russia, China, and the U.S. will each use about half our ICBMs. The entire continent will be taken out."

I took a deep breath. A block of ice had grown in my belly. Just talking about this stuff was difficult for me. There was no way they would be able to evacuate most of the population. How many millions would die? How many had *already* died? A hundred million? Two hundred million? What about the fallout? How much of the Earth would be poisoned afterward? I decided not to ask these questions. There was no purpose.

"General, what if they take to the seas?"

"They have not done so yet. We are watching closely for that. We will have to release sooner if they can't be contained on the land."

"I see. And I thank you for being honest, General. Now I'll be honest with you. I think we can make a soldier that can stop the Macros on the ground. But that soldier will have to join the fleet first. They will have to become an international force of marines."

"Join the fleet? You mean *your* fleet?"

"Yes, sir. Star Force. We need trained volunteers from every nation. Elite veterans preferred. We'll provide them with new weaponry, train them on how to use it, and transform them into a ground force that can face the Macros."

"Are we talking about some kind of suicide squad here, Riggs?"

"Not exactly, sir. But the process we will put the men through might make it impossible to return to normal civilian life."

"I see. And can I observe an example of one of these—super soldiers?"

"You already have, sir," I said. "I am one of them."

-26-

After I'd gotten off the satellite link with General Kerr—leaving him skeptical but interested—I went down to the base to have the medical center people check me out. Really, I did it at the insistence of Sandra. I felt pretty good, physically. Sure, my arm was a sick mess. We'd wrapped it up so we wouldn't have to watch the Nanos do their work. But the first thing they did, apparently, was turn off the pain sensors in my damaged limb. Very civil of them, I thought.

When the medical staff saw the state of my arm, there was considerable gasping. A doctor waved to a nurse who prepped a hypodermic. I put my good hand up to halt them when they came near.

"What's that, doc?"

"For the pain," he said.

"No. Don't need it. I don't feel a thing."

He looked confused, wary. "I appreciate you are a tough man, Commander. But I can assure you, you will feel something if we perform this procedure without medication."

"What procedure?"

He blinked at me. He exchanged glances with the nurse. They had the air of people who were about to go through something unfortunate and unpleasant. Something they'd gone through before.

"If you will just relax, sir, and let us do our jobs."

He manufactured a smile and stepped closer.

I reached out, faster than his eyes could follow, and snapped the tip of his needle off. His face fell. He looked at his dribbling, snubbed hypo, dumbfounded.

"What did you do? Really, this isn't helping, Commander."

"Just give me some answers."

The doctor heaved a sigh. He eyed me with new respect. "Frankly, I don't even see how you're standing. I can see metal in there, Commander. Bright metal! Your arm is full of shrapnel of some kind. I might be able to save the arm—just maybe, mind you, no promises. But you have to let me operate immediately."

I smiled then. It was a grim smile, and their faces didn't respond in kind. "Nobody is cutting my arm off," I said. I turned to go.

"But, Commander... isn't it better than dying?" asked the nurse, speaking up for the first time. She was young and had a high voice, almost child-like. I'd always found that endearing in a woman.

I sighed and gave her a real smile. "Sorry. Let me apologize for my bad attitude. I've just watched hundreds—maybe thousands—of men die trying to prove a theory of mine. They managed to disprove it, unfortunately. In fact, more of the real casualties should be coming in soon."

"Real casualties?" asked the nurse. The doctor was no longer speaking, he was just staring at me.

"I'm fleet. I can get my ship to repair me."

"Why didn't you do that in the first place?"

I thought about that. Why not indeed? Habit, I suppose, was part of it. Sandra's insistence was part of it, too. But it was more than that.

"Because," I told them truthfully, "I'm scared to go into their medical facility. They can work miracles, but they are machines."

"They're scary?"

I snorted. "Terrifying. And they don't know much about pain. I don't think they've ever even heard of anesthetic. Now that I think about it, I think the only reason this arm isn't hurting is because the nerves are burned away."

"Well," said the doctor, chastened. "If you ever do need me, Commander, come back."

I nodded and left. I had the ship lift me back up into its belly. I walked into the chamber of horrors that had worked upon my children until it dumped them into the cold of space. The same chamber full of thin, dangling, black arms that had brought Sandra back to life.

In an hour, I couldn't scream anymore. My voice no longer worked. It had turned into an endless series of hoarse sobs. Sometime after that, I lost consciousness. In two hours, I awoke with my arm mostly regrown, but I was blind. I had the *Alamo* carry me to my couch where I fell asleep. Sandra came and quietly touched my brow.

In another hour, I was functional again, but I still felt drained. My arm was pink-white. New skin had grown with unnatural, accelerated speed. Just like the rings of new cells that had glued on Sandra's fingers. I saw that the rings around her fingers had faded. That was good. I could hope my arm would look normal again someday.

I flexed my repaired hand, and it tingled. But it worked. I nodded blearily, looking around the bridge.

"How bad was it?" Sandra asked.

"Bad. It was bad. But yes, it was worth it."

"The satellite phone has been beeping for you," said Sandra. "I answered and told them to give you a break."

"You did?"

"I told them you were injured and recovering. But they keep calling back. Once every hour or so."

"Okay," I said, reaching for the unit. A few minutes later I was back on the phone with General Kerr.

"All right, Riggs. We need to talk," he said.

"I'm listening."

"I've been checking out your story and reviewing the battle video."

"Video?"

"Every one of those fancy suits was equipped with a camera or two. Not all of them worked. Not all of them survived, either. But yours did."

"How did I do, sir?"

"I'm impressed," he said, then paused. "And I'm not a man who is easily impressed, Riggs."

I believed him. "What do you think about my offer now, General?"

"I think you're crazy. Did these drugs or whatever they are do that to you? Make you into some kind of berserker? You shot that thing in the butt and nearly ate a biscuit, boy."

I chuckled. "No, sir. I was born crazy, I guess. I can't blame the Nanos for that."

"Overcompensation. That's what a psych would call it. You saw good men die over your idea and you lost it."

"I got that machine to retreat, sir. I damaged it enough to turn it around. Then I chased it into the jungle. If I'd had a full platoon as capable as I was, with heavier weapons...."

"Yeah. Yeah, you did. We did some calculations. You were running over sand in full gear, doing about thirty miles an hour. That's about how fast a dog runs. Did you know that?"

"You believe me then."

"I think you've been altered somehow. But I'm not sure I want to put all my boys through that. Whatever alien bullshit you have in mind for them."

"I don't want it to be that way, sir. I want them to be volunteers. I want them to be from every elite service in the world."

"A Foreign Legion of freaks, huh?"

"Not the terms I would use."

"No, I suppose not. But okay. The higher-ups saw the whole thing. I briefed them, ran the vid files for them raw. They are convinced to give it another go. With you leading the charge—if you'll do it."

Sandra caught my attention, flapping her hands at me. I looked up at her. She mouthed a single word: *No.*

"Yes, sir," I said. "I'll do it."

I eyed Sandra. She had her hands on her hips. Her lips were curled in disgust and worry.

"I know a fellow crazy bastard when I see one, Riggs," laughed the general, sounding like he'd just won a bet. "Welcome to the special forces club. Start building super-sized reactor packs and brewing up some of those injections, pronto."

"Will do, sir," I said.

"Oh, and Riggs? The Congress is planning to give you a medal of some kind. You aren't officially in any of the armed services, so they had to make it something any citizen can get. You *are* still a U. S. citizen, right Riggs?"

I had to think about that one. I supposed that I was, as Star Force wasn't exactly a nation. "Yes I am. Are we talking about a Congressional Medal of Honor?"

"That's what they call it. Technically, they will have to reactivate you as a reservist to do it. I guess they really need a war hero about now."

After I hung up, Sandra was upset with me. "You don't have to go."

"Yeah, I do," I told her.

She crossed her arms under her breasts. Her eyes were half-closed. I felt a sudden urge to grab her and kiss her. But I knew that if I did, I would be rebuffed. She was clearly annoyed.

162

I threw up my arms. The newly regrown one gave me a stab of pain as I did so. "How can I build a new set of weapons, then recruit another thousand guys to die fighting with these experimental guns against giant robots, and stay home shivering in this ship?"

She sighed and relented, sitting on the couch next to me. "I don't know. But I wish you would stay out of it this time. Somehow."

Sandra stared at me for a while, and I stared back. Suddenly, she threw one of her long brown legs over mine and sat in my lap, straddling me. We made out fiercely for several minutes. It was good.

As suddenly as she'd climbed aboard, she jumped off again. I had to fight to control myself. I almost lunged for her, but I stopped. I'd just gotten my own arms back, and it wouldn't do to accidentally yank off one of hers. She gave a little laugh and had no idea how I was feeling. Or maybe she did.

I could tell she wasn't going to give me any more sugar at the moment. So, I decided not to beg for it. Women never respected that. I headed into the shower. Lord, how I needed a shower. The water was hot and I stayed in it longer than usual.

Sandra surprised me in our makeshift shower stall about one minute before I was going to get out. She wrapped her arms around me from behind. We kissed and touched. It was even better than it had been out on the couch.

"Incoming private channel request from the *Snapper*," said the ship, interrupting.

"Not now, Alamo."

The ship was silent for about thirty seconds. I made the best use I could of each second. Sandra was really beginning to respond, and we'd moved several steps past kissing.

"Incoming urgent channel request from the *Snapper*."

"Admiral Crow has amazing timing," I said.

"*Admiral* Crow?" asked Sandra. "When the hell did he make himself into an Admiral?"

"Do you accept the incoming channel request?" droned the *Alamo*. Sometimes, the ship really did sound like a computer.

"Just answer," sighed Sandra, putting her wet head against my chest, "or they'll never let us alone."

"Open channel, Alamo," I growled.

"You there, Riggs?"

"Yes, sir."

"You on the john or something?"

"Something like that, sir."

"Well, I'm calling because you've gone bananas, and—well, I have to tell you Riggs, right now I'm thinking of demoting you."

I snorted. Sandra tensed against me. I patted her back, trying to relax her again. This man was a master at ruining a good mood.

"What's the problem, Crow?"

"You've gone and overstepped yourself. Grossly. I'm in charge of this fleet. You know that, right?"

"That was the deal."

"Well, then why are you negotiating a new force of star marines, or whatever you want to call them, without my approval? Why are you offering to give away one of our most amazing technologies without even *telling* me?"

I pursed my lips. "I have to admit, you have a point. I was too focused on solving the problem to worry about approvals."

"Well, tell me why I'm not going to cancel all your arrangements and rip some stripes off of you."

This was more than Sandra could take. Throughout the conversation, I could feel her body getting more tense against mine. She had a temper. And she seemed particularly defensive when it came to me. I supposed that was a good thing.

"What do you want his stripes for, Crow? You sew new ones on yourself every other damned day. Did you run out?"

There was a moment of silence. I looked down at Sandra. She was lovely, wet and naked. There was a wild look in her eye. I should never have agreed to talk to Crow, I decided.

"Is that Sandra? Ah—now I get it!" he burst into laughter. "That *is* a shower I hear running, isn't it? I need to figure out how to get video feed out of this communication setup."

After an irritatingly long talk, Crow came to see things my way. I agreed at length to consult with him before proposing things like new armies or technology giveaways. By the time Crow and I had finished talking, Sandra and I were dry, dressed and out of the mood. At least, she seemed to be. I hoped I hadn't gotten myself kicked out of her shower stall for good.

I played it cool, however. Exhaustion helped with that strategy. I was simply too tired and hungry to care much. I ate a big meal of chicken, cottage cheese, canned peaches, and cold broccoli. It was filling, but lackluster. I resolved to have the camp people build a better eatery. Maybe I could put a real kitchen aboard the *Alamo* as well.

After I ate, I slept for a good dozen hours. Sandra startled me by curling herself up against my chest, about half-way through my sleep. I figured this had to be a good sign. I felt so tired however, it was like being drugged. Maybe the Nanos *had* drugged me, for all I knew, as part of their ministrations. Or maybe it was just a natural reaction to exhaustion and gross injury. In any case, I fell back asleep again without so much as molesting her. Hours later, when I woke up, she was gone.

I awakened with a fuzziness in my mind. I'd had strange dreams and even stranger ideas in my head. I'd dreamt of the home planet of the Nanos. They'd been created—in my dreams—by blue men with huge eyes and even bigger skulls shaped like inverted pears. It left me with the thought when I awoke that I needed to know who had sent these machines to Earth. Who, and *why*.

I'd tried to get this information from *Alamo* before. It had come up many times over the last month or so. But the ship had been programmed to avoid answering such questions. It was part of the Nanos' internal, unchangeable programming to keep their origins a secret. Either that, I thought, or the ship truly didn't know.

"Alamo? Are you listening to my thoughts?"

"When your mind forms word-thoughts, they are transmitted to my receptors."

"Yeah, close enough. What did you think about my dream? Did you see the blue men, with the big heads?"

"Visual imagery is not relayed."

"Hmmm. Let me describe them, then. They were blue guys, about four feet tall. They were humanoid, but blue-skinned. They had big eyes and big heads. Very big heads, as if their brains could hardly be contained within them. Do the creatures that created you look anything like that?"

"I am not permitted to describe my creators."

"So, your creators are not blue-skinned?"

Hesitation. This, I'd come to recognize, signaled deep thoughts were going on inside whatever served the *Alamo* for a CPU.

"No," the ship said at last.

I stood up suddenly. I took a deep breath, and almost whooped aloud. The *Alamo* had answered a question on this taboo subject. I was onto something.

"Alamo... your creators are not machines, are they?"

"No."

A smile split my face. Stupid machine. It had been programmed not to answer any questions about the creators. But it hadn't been programmed not to answer questions in the negative. In other words, it could talk about what they were *not*.

I began pacing. I should have thought of this before. It was like hacking. There was almost always a work-around. When you programmed a machine, it was hard to think of all the possibilities. You might create what seemed like a perfect set of instructions, but given input you never thought of, the program behaved in a fashion you had never intended. Anyone who has ever had to unplug their computer after a particularly bad crash knows something about that.

I thought over what I had gotten out of the *Alamo* so far. First, the people who created the Nanos were not machines. That seemed pretty

166

obvious. Second, the ship had admitted they didn't have blue skin, either. Big deal. But what were they like? Where were they from? Certainly, if they wanted their identity kept secret, it seemed likely they were afraid someone might come looking for them. Maybe the Macros didn't know where they were. Maybe the Macros would like to exterminate the biotics who had had the gall to build ships like these and send them out to help other races fight against their invasions.

"Your creators are not in this solar system, are they?"

"No."

Big news, there. They were interstellar. That was the first concrete evidence. It was one thing to suspect something like that, it was another to *know it*. I was excited. You couldn't compete with beings you knew nothing about. I was desperate for information.

"Your creators don't come from a planet like Earth, do they? It's not a warm, wet world, is it?"

"No."

I blinked at that. Life, but not from a water-world. What other kind of life was there? This might be harder than I thought to figure out, if they were something weird like a silicon-based rock-creature.

"Are they from a planet with higher or lower gravity than Earth?"

"I am not permitted to describe my creators."

"Of course. Forget that question. That was a mistake. What I meant to say was that your creators do not live on a gas giant, like Jupiter, do they?"

"I am not permitted to describe my creators."

I frowned. Had I made a mistake? Had I tripped some warning line? Had the *Alamo* learned from my repeated questions what I was after and adjusted itself to keep me out? I decided to repeat a previous question to see if I could backtrack to where it was answering informatively.

"Your creators are not machines, are they?"

"No."

I heaved a deep breath. I had not blown it. The ship had not locked me out. I had just asked something the wrong way. But what was it? Then, after thinking about it, I thought I had it. The ship couldn't answer in the affirmative about its creators. It could only answer negative questions, with a negative response. Anything else would be blocked. This conclusion brought my smile back, because it meant that a negatively worded question that it refused to answer meant *yes*.

167

"So, the creators of the Nanos are biological. They come from a gas giant like Jupiter, in a star system outside of our own. I'm really starting to get somewhere."

The ship stayed quiet. I was beginning to understand the *Alamo*. My statement had been analyzed, and it had decided no action was necessary. I hadn't asked a question. I hadn't given an order. From its point of view, there was nothing to do.

I sat down and typed out an email to the Pentagon people. If the Macros showed up right now and I was summoned up to fight them and the *Alamo* was destroyed, I wanted this information to be transmitted to those who might find it useful.

"Okay, Alamo, we can discuss your mission, can't we?"

"You are command personnel."

"Yes. And what is your current mission?"

"To obey command personnel."

"What was your mission before the current one?"

"To locate and gather command personnel."

"Exactly. And what was your mission *before* you were to locate and gather command personnel?"

"To gather information on biotic species."

Ah, I thought. Very interesting. The ship *was* a science vessel—an explorer—before it was sent on this mission to find people to staff it. But why? Why didn't these aliens just man the ships themselves? As I thought about it I came up with some simple reasons. If they were far away, the space flights might take too long. Maybe the oceans between the stars were so vast, even for the creatures that created the Nanos, that they couldn't cross them before they grew old and died. Or maybe they just didn't want to spend their lifetimes in a ship. I'm sure that when Earth eventually sent out her first exploratory ships to other star systems they would be robotic.

I thought it might be more than that, however. This was a war. The Macros had been showing up in waves themselves. They had to be coming from *somewhere*. So why had the creators of the Nanos sent hundreds of their lightly-armed science vessels to Earth without sending some of their own people to man them?

I thought about what kind of life might exist on a world like Jupiter. Heavy gravity. Radiation. Harsh gasses creating an atmosphere thousands of times thicker than ours.

168

"Alamo," I said, pausing to carefully phrase my question, "your creators can't leave the gravity well of their planet, can they?"

"I am not permitted to describe my creators."

"Ah," I said aloud. That was a surprise. They *could* leave their gravity well. That wasn't what had stopped them. I had thought maybe the pull of their world was so great that it had left them with no choice but to send up tiny robots to do their space exploration for them, due to their insignificant mass.

I thought about gas giants. What kind of creature on Earth had any kind of similar environment? Perhaps a deep-sea creature? Something from the cold, dark depths? What were they like? Then, I thought I had it.

"Your creators can't *survive* outside the gravity well of their planet, can they, Alamo?"

"I am not permitted to describe my creators."

I laughed aloud. There it was, a clear *yes* answer to a negative question. They were something like deep-sea fish. If you pulled them up into space, they popped. They could not tolerate weightlessness. They were accustomed to a crushing gravitational pull. Maybe their internal organs couldn't operate without gravity. Decompression could be controlled, but the suddenness of a launching spaceship might be deadly to them. They probably would explode. That's why they'd sent the Nanos out here to explore for them. Because they couldn't do it themselves and survive.

What a great curiosity they must have! I imagined the frustration of an intelligent, technological race, stuck down upon a gas giant with an impenetrable atmosphere. They had probably never known what was up there, beyond their heavy skies. They would have never known there were stars and other worlds. They'd probably barely understood they were circling a sun. The atmosphere of such planets was so dense. No technology I knew of would be able to gaze up through it.

In fact, the more I thought about it, the more these answers the *Alamo* had given me made sense. Nothing aboard the *Alamo* was built for a sighted creature. What use would a window be on the surface of a gas giant? On Jupiter, there would be little light or visibility. It would be like living in a permanent, thick fog, or at the bottom of an oceanic trench. On Earth, the creatures we'd found in such environments were quite blind. So, the beings that had built the ships hadn't built windows or view screens into them. Such equipment would never have occurred

169

to them. Still, they had to have some way of sensing a three-dimensional environment. The Nano ship certainly did. Maybe they used sonar, like bats or dolphins. Or perhaps they used a radiation sensor, such as the heat-sensing organs of snakes.

Sandra showed up sometime during the following minutes as I pondered the strange beings who had built the Nanos. I sat there, staring at my computer and periodically marveling at the walls around me. Somehow, knowing just a little about the aliens that had built the ship made it seem all the more impressive. I saw their ship in a new light. I hated them less too, for having indirectly killed my kids. Maybe they had sent out these ships with the best of intentions, but the robotic nanites had executed their programming in a typically merciless way. I stared into space for a while, thinking about it.

"You're awake," she said, giving me a light kiss.

I blinked, staring at nothing. In my mind, I saw creatures on dark, clouded worlds. Were they floating gas-bags? Or maybe dense flatworms that crawled upon the surface?

"Hmph," said Sandra, miffed.

"Sorry," I said.

"What has you so entranced?"

"You do."

"Liar."

I told her about the talks I'd had with the *Alamo*. I described the method I'd used to trick information out of the ship by asking questions it hadn't been programmed to refuse. She seemed alarmed that I would discuss my trickery so openly while the ship was listening.

"I assure you, it won't matter. This ship isn't a person. It is an artificial intelligence. And it isn't really that bright. It can do what it can do, but it isn't a fast learner."

"I'll take your word for it. But it had better not be plotting to dump us out for espionage or something."

I described the beings who had built the *Alamo*, and she was as intrigued as I was about them.

"They live under crushing gravity?" she asked. "How can they survive? What do they eat?"

"I have no idea. I didn't think anything could live on such worlds. But we have discovered life in nooks and crannies around Earth where no one expected to find anything."

"They are afraid of the Macros," she said, with sudden conviction.

"Why do you say that?"

"Because they've worked hard to hide their homeworld from everyone. And they sent out these ships to find people to help them fight. They must have surveyed a lot of worlds, and when they ran into the Macros, they changed the mission to one of marshaling armies with their science vessels. Maybe, back home, they are secretly building battle fleets now."

I thought about that. "You have a good point. If they had known about the Macros when they launched these ships, they would have built warships and sent them instead. What we are sitting in is a converted science vessel. That's why it takes twenty of them to face a single Macro ship."

"What should we call them?" she asked.

"Who?"

"These people who created the Nanos. You figured out they exist. You get to name them."

I chuckled. "Well..." I said, thinking about names describing worm-like blind things. None of them were attractive or catchy. "I'll call them the Blues."

"Are they blue?"

"No."

"Why that then?"

I told her about the blue men in my dream, and how they had inspired me to hack the ship's defenses and trick it into talking about the subject.

"Okay," she said, being agreeable for once. "From now, they are the Blues. And I've thought of something else. I bet the Blues have been studying Earth for years."

"How do you know that?"

"Haven't you ever seen one of those bullshit shows about alien abductions and stuff? What would you call what happened to us, other than an alien abduction?"

"That doesn't prove the Blues have been here very long, but I think you are right in any case."

She smiled and crawled onto the couch with me. She liked being told she was right.

"Go on," she said.

I smiled back. "You're right, because the Blues couldn't have learned so much about us if this was their first visit. I mean, the *Alamo*

171

can speak English. Assumedly, it can speak a dozen other languages as well. And it knows enough about our anatomy to repair our flesh and inject nanites that fix us, not kill us. All of that knowledge doesn't develop overnight. They must have been here for years, just as you say."

"I like when you do smart things," she told me. She was even closer now.

"You're a thinker, too. I like that about you."

"Now you're flattering me."

"Is it working?"

"Yes," she admitted.

We began kissing. I half-expected Crow to call and announce he had elevated himself to the rank of Grand Marshal, or perhaps even Prime Minister. But he didn't.

-28-

After relaying everything I had gotten from the *Alamo* about the Blues to the Pentagon people, I thought for a second and sent an email to the UN Secretary as well. Maybe I'm paranoid, but the point of critical information was, in my mind, to share it. I wasn't completely certain the U.S. military would do so.

Next came my biggest task. I'd promised to create a force that could stand up to the Macros. That took all my time. As it turned out, the injections were the easiest part to supply. All the Nanos had to do was reproduce themselves in quantity. They were good at this and were able to do it quickly. The hard part was developing a new, more powerful reactor and hand-held laser rifle. These were larger pieces of equipment and took much longer and more specialized materials to fabricate.

I went down to Andros Island to do the design work. The first thing I had to figure out was how big of a reactor and projector unit a nanite-enhanced man like myself could handle. The climate was similar enough to the Amazon jungle. The guys from the Pentagon were footing the bill for this whole thing, so they sent down a lot of spooks, medical people, and uniforms to "help" me. I was startled to see they had a full platoon of each variety of these "helpers." There was a full company from the Army Corps of Engineers as well. This last group didn't smile much, but they were the most useful. They got things done. But I couldn't very well say no to the rest of them, as I needed government resources.

We used my body as a model for our future super-soldier. How much could I carry and still run quickly? It turned out to be a surprising amount. First, the engineers harnessed me up with a huge, double-thick backpack. Made of their very ugliest, camo-green fabric, it had leather straps sewn around it for support and heavy stitching over every inch. They filled it to the brim with wet sand, a load of well over three hundred kilos.

I could lift it—barely. I found the bulk of it staggering. With that much weight on my back, I had to lean forward in an awkward crouch. I couldn't stand erect. It pained my knees too, in particular. The Nanos worked to repair a muscle rip or a splitting joint with every step. I felt the nanites swarming overtime on my joints, making them tingle and itch, as if I were being constantly bitten by pissed-off ants. It got worse when I took off in a shambling run. I ran in a thundering, off-balanced fashion carrying the load a hundred yards or so down the beach and then brought it back to the team, sweating. My time was just over fifteen seconds, three times as long as I had run the same distance unloaded.

"Too much," I told them.

Barely nodding, but impressed despite their cool exteriors, they shoveled out half the load. I smiled. I realized then they hadn't expected me to be able to move. They had overloaded me right off, just to put me in my place. I'd still managed to run with the gear, however. With about eight hundred pounds of dripping sand on my back, I'd run up and down a beach in the tropical heat.

While they shoveled, I looked back at my tracks. They were six inches deep in places. The prints had darkened and filled with water. Each print was a small, reflective pool. They looked like hoof prints. Prints from a horse that needed to go on a diet.

I tried about a hundred and fifty kilos next. That was about three hundred and fifty pounds. The difference was dramatic. My joints creaked a bit, but they didn't feel like they were snapping. The biggest improvement was in the area of weight-distribution. I didn't feel as grossly off-balance. I had to lean forward to run, way forward, but it was doable. I could still outrun an Olympic sprinter, and I could do it without tearing myself apart. I trotted back to them.

"That's good. I can handle that much. I bet a bigger, younger man with better muscle tone could do more. But this is about triple the weight of the original gear. That should be enough firepower for a soldier to take out a Macro belly-turret single-handedly."

I was already forming dinner plans, and they involved Sandra. But the spooks weren't finished with me yet. They had only just begun with their tests. They didn't take my word for my physical status, either. They had doctors checking my pulse, blood-pressure, etc. after every lap. I had an EKG monitor strapped to my chest. They wanted to put a temperature probe up my tail-pipe, but I drew the line there, telling them I wasn't a pack animal. They taped it into my armpit instead with sour expressions.

They dressed up and redistributed my load. They added belts, circling my waist with diving weights. They gave me a smaller front pack to improve my balance. They kept hosing down the big load of sand, too, making sure it stayed close to the desired weight. I groaned and ran the beach lap for them about twenty more times.

After the ordeal, they tested my eyesight, blood, reflexes, and even swabbed my throat. I had no idea what they thought they would get out of all of that, but I didn't argue as long as they didn't irritate me too much. This team had to be sold. I needed them to convince the higher-ups the project was worth every resource they had. There couldn't be any reluctance when it came to parting with supplies of titanium, plutonium, and other critical, rare earth components. If I didn't succeed, they were going to have to nuke the Macros—and one of our continents with them—back into primordial ooze. We would only have six continents left after that. And we weren't even sure the nukes would stop the enemy entirely.

After a break that consisted of a lobster dinner in the officers' mess with Sandra (and two beers each to keep us company), I headed out to the high-security base I'd built in the jungle. My Nano factories hummed there night and day. Our ships hung all around it, like big, black shadows. Half were on guard duty, while half were ferrying whatever materials the factories needed to them. I had about ten percent of the factories working on making more factories now. That way, our production was always increasing.

The factories had already produced enough nanite injections for thousands of troops. I set one quarter of them working on constructing heavier laser rifles. The rest I had making new reactors. The new units were over three hundred pounds each, about three times the weight of the reactors I'd had men carry into battle back in Brazil. Only men who had undergone the nanite injections could carry these new units. Ordering the factories to produce the weapons systems was a moment of commitment that felt drastic, but I felt I had to do it. What was the point of getting our best troops chewed up a second time around? This time, I'd go down with a force that might have a chance. And I'd take more of them along, too.

The new recruits arrived the next morning. In the first wave there were about three hundred of them. Many more were coming tomorrow, according to the reports. Thousands more.

I had my first batch of recruits fall out and form up ten ranks deep on the parade grounds in the center of my camp. They were all male, and they were a grim-faced lot. They averaged twenty-eight years old, and they were combat veterans, every last one of them. I'd demanded that much. I didn't want green troops. I didn't have the ability to train them in infantry tactics—I barely knew the drill myself. But I could teach them how to handle their new bodies once they'd undergone the injections. I could teach them how to fight a Macro, to some degree. I could teach them about the laser units and backpack reactors, because I had designed them.

Special forces volunteers from every major military were represented. There were Russian Spetsnaz, Israeli Shayetet, Swedish Jagares, and even Chinese SLCU. Nearly half were U.S. troops, however: Green Berets, Marine Recon, Airborne, and a few from Delta. There were some from organizations I'd never heard of. I felt honored and a bit daunted to be in the company of such men, such professionals—especially since I was expected to lead them. Most had never fought a Macro, however. And none had felt the joys of the nanite injections.

I did spot one friendly face in the crowd of serious-eyed warriors. Sergeant Lionel Wilson, the man I'd brought back with me from my first pitched battle with the Macros. I clapped him on the back, and he staggered a step. I brought him out of line to stand before the others.

"I know this man can fight the machines. I've personally fought with him, shoulder-to-shoulder against them. He knows how an improved man like myself operates. I'm making him my First Sergeant. The rest of you will have to earn your stripes all over again. I don't care if you were a colonel yesterday. Here, you start fresh."

They looked startled, but no one protested. I nodded and stood as stiffly as I could.

"After the injections, you will find yourself to be a different kind of man. You might not find it easy to return home. I urge anyone with second thoughts to bail out of here now, before you take the next step and change your body forever."

They looked at me. No one spoke up. I wondered if they might come to regret their decision when the nanites began toying with their cell structure.

I'd produced new uniforms for these troops. They all had PFC stripes on them. I'd decided to go with Marine ranks and to start everyone one step from the bottom. The uniforms were different than standard fatigues. They were heavier. They were *cumbersome*, in fact. They had a lead lining and could be buttoned up for hazardous environments. We were likely to be wearing them in radioactive zones, and I wanted my men to be accustomed to that kind of sweltering, stiff gear.

A lot of the men were in civies. I handed out the new uniforms and gave them leave to get dressed. They all had to look the same, just to get them thinking like a team. Everyone spoke reasonable English, another requirement for joining. They could all talk to one another, they all wore the same thing, and they were all veterans. I hoped these shared traits would help pull them together quickly into an effective fighting force. The fun of the injections would be another experience that would make us all brothers, I figured.

Next, I knew I had to impress them. Why the hell should they listen to me? That question had to be burning in their minds. I decided to show them why. First, I shouldered one of the new bulky reactors and gripped the connected beam unit. Then I marched them out into the jungle, to another region I'd plucked bare of trees. There were dark spots of open earth where trees had been hours before. The land looked like the gums of an old man who'd had all his teeth pulled at once. Big tropical insects crawled in every freshly-exposed hole.

"This will be our initial training ground. We are going to spend some time here, learning how to fire these new weapons. Visors, everyone. Full gear on. Button up!"

They had looked as if they were all bored, slouching and leaning against whatever was handy. But when they heard my barked commands, they snapped into motion. Every single one of them. They had been well-trained.

All their suits were light-reactive, and when I opened up with the new heavy beamer, the autoshades instantly darkened their eye portals. I fired into the edge of the forest, picking a mahogany tree. The thick vines that covered the tree twisted like grass stalks. The bark peeled away like burnt skin and the white flesh of the tree beneath instantly blackened. A moment after that, the entire tree trunk exploded and it sagged over on its side.

I knew most of them had never seen the power of one of my laser rifles. None of them, I was sure, had ever seen the power of one of these new heavy beamers. It was like having a blowtorch in your hands—a blowtorch so powerful tree trunks were like thin, dry weeds before it.

I took off the pack then. I waved them forward.

"As you can see, we can't allow any friendly-fire accidents. They would be fatal almost instantly. Now, I want a volunteer to put on this pack and try to take out that tree over there," I said, indicating a tall palm. It looked like an easy target. It was much thinner than the mahogany had been, and closer. All they had to do was blow it down.

"Who's first?" I asked.

A dozen hands shot up, I pointed to the closest. I noticed that my only non-com, Sergeant Wilson, kept his arms crossed. He had a small smile on his face.

The first man to take up my challenge was a Russian. He reached down to grab the pack. He heaved, but it didn't budge. He looked surprised.

"Come on, put your back into it, soldier," I said.

He swallowed, then put himself into the straps in a squatting position. He heaved, legs wobbling. He almost managed to dead-lift it. It was close. He roared and grunted, but couldn't quite do it. I had to admire his tenacity.

"I can't do it," he said, defeated.

"What?"

"I can't do it, sir!"

"What's your name, private?"

"Sergey Radovich, sir."

I nodded. "Are you a weak man, Radovich?"

"No, sir."

"Are you sure?"

"Hell yeah, sir."

I nodded again. "Who else here wants to try to put on this pack, stand up, and burn down that tree for me?"

178

A lot of the early volunteers didn't raise their hands a second time around. They knew a setup when they saw one.

One or two kept their hands raised, however. I pointed to an Asian-looking fellow. He was the biggest Asian I'd ever laid eyes on. He looked like a barrel with legs. He was a sumo wrestler, but without the blubber.

He had amazingly thick thighs, much bigger than my own. He stepped forward and took up the straps. Like Radovich, he positioned himself for a dead-lift. But he did it differently. He rocked forward and balanced the pack on his back. Roaring, he stood under the weight of it, four hundred pounds of metal, glass, and polymers.

Legs shaking, he targeted the palm tree and fired. The trunk exploded and the tree went down.

"Very good. What is your name, soldier?" I asked him.

"Kwon, sir," he said as he eased the pack down.

"Excellent work. Now, we will run back to the parade grounds. I want you all to pace me. This will be a jungle-run. All out. Full speed."

As I spoke, I lifted the pack and settled it on my back. Their eyes were big as they watched me handle the weight confidently. I pretended not to notice the stares.

I ran then. I ran faster than any normal man had ever run, to my knowledge, across this Earth. None of them could keep up. In fact, I was standing on the parade grounds again, looking bored, when the fastest of them broke out of the jungle and sprinted back into the sunlight.

When they were all assembled in front me again, I asked if there were any questions. A few hands went up. I pointed out Radovich.

"Why the hell we run for no point, sir?" he asked, reasonably enough. His accent had become stronger, I noticed. It must have been due to all the exercise.

I nodded, accepting the question as legitimate. "I wanted you all to understand some things. I am going to ask you to make some fantastic sacrifices. I want you to understand why I'm asking you to make them."

I told them then—about the injections. I did not pretty it up. I told them they would be screaming for the first hour or so until they blacked out. I told them we couldn't give them anesthetic. The spooks from the Pentagon had tried it on some chimps, but the nanites had neutralized all foreign chemicals injected into the test subject's system. Next, I told

179

them about the incredible strength and speed they would gain, and how they would fear for their girlfriends' lives afterward. Then, I pointed to the pack I had removed and placed in front of me.

"But, without the nanites—without undergoing the injections," I told them, "—none of us can perform well enough to do our mission. We cannot be effective soldiers. Not without becoming—something new."

They thought about it, and slowly they realized they were going to have to become a marriage of man and machine. The idea was repugnant to some. But they did not argue. They did not refuse. The people who had selected them had chosen well.

In the end every last one of them underwent the injections. No one backed out or refused, not even in the final moments, when they were strapped into a chair and the five gleaming, worming needles made their appearance.

When the ordeal was over, we hosed the puke and blood off each other. One soldier had torn out his left eye. I assured him it could be regrown. I hoped I wasn't lying.

After the torment ended, I let them sleep it off in their barracks. When we assembled the next day, I promoted Radovich to the rank of Lance Corporal. I made Kwon into a Staff Sergeant. They had both been more highly ranked in their past lives, but I didn't care about that.

They had started over again as marines in Star Force. They were my marines now.

-29-

Brazil had been pretty much eaten up by the time I'd finally built a big enough assault force to go after the Macros again. The Pentagon boys had been after me night and day, with General Kerr spearheading the effort to get me to deploy. But I wanted to have a force that couldn't be dealt with easily. I wanted to have a force that didn't just slow the Macros, or even simply stop them.

I wanted a force that could shock them and roll them back.

I had a number of good officers to back me up by this time. Major Radovich was among them. He had advanced quickly from that first day. He'd been a great help to me in organizing and training the new waves of recruits. Sergeant Wilson had been promoted to Lieutenant. He had the job of performing tricks like the one I'd done on the first day. His only complaint was he'd been running out of trees to blow down lately.

After talking to Crow, I had changed my own rank to that of Colonel. It wasn't really a high enough rank to command so many men, but I liked the sound of it and I didn't want to take the title of General. I didn't feel I'd earned it yet.

My marines were nearly six thousand strong when I told General Kerr I was ready. We began following our plans for invasion immediately. We'd long considered the best strategy to be an assault of the southern shores of the Rio de la Plata, the estuary bay along which Buenos Aires had once stood.

We planned to retake the ruins of the city first. Besides being defensible, the spot was only thirty miles from one of the Macro domes. After the initial invasion, another ten thousand traditionally-armed support marines would join us—if we were not blown off the beach on day one. The generals had come up with the idea of hitting them behind their lines. Way behind. That way, the very distance from the front lines would be a problem for the enemy. They would have to turn around and march a thousand miles to face us. No one knew if they would bother.

They had advanced very quickly. For any normal force to do that, it must stretch its forces and supply lines more and more thinly and therefore defend its rear with less. We weren't sure as to their capabilities to respond to a counterattack, but hitting the rear of the continent seemed like our best opportunity. If it turned out they had indeed expanded too quickly, without caution—well, that gave us a chance.

Our mission priority was to destroy whatever was underneath the white domes. The shimmering domes we understood to be big, permanently deployed shields. They stood like shining blisters upon our fair Earth. The Macros had deployed them all in the southern region and none had moved from their first appearance during the early days of the invasion. From these domes, periodically, new Macro fighting machines marched forth. From each dome a line of smaller, roving machines trailed to various mineral deposits. These smaller machines we called *workers*—the satellite guys had come up with that name.

The foraging workers tore girders from wrecked buildings, and carried demolished cars, bicycles, and sometimes raw ore from open mines back to the domes. We didn't know exactly what was going on under those shields, but we figured they had to be operating factories or fabricators of some kind. Something had to be making these new robots. The good news was there were only eight of them. The bad news was they were very well-defended. We found that out after the initial days of the invasion when we'd lost a number of Nano ships trying to assault them.

General Kerr gave me a final briefing as I rode down in the *Alamo*, air-lifting a landing pod with a full company of my own troops inside. We had gone beyond shoving them into cargo containers. Now they were packed into specially-designed landing pods. These pods were folding polygons of steel equipped with inch-thick armor, portholes and escape-hatches. NATO had come up with the design. They still looked like deathtraps to me, but I got to ride up inside the ship for the first leg of the journey.

182

"General, I think I have the plan down," I said.

"Let's go over one point," he said, "those unstable reactors of yours...."

"Yes, sir?" I said, playing dumb. We'd figured out it was very easy to set the reactors to overload and explode. I figured that had to be what he was talking about. I knew he didn't like it, but I'd built in codes for each man to self-destruct on his own initiative. By entering a series of numbers, he could set his pack to detonate. The resulting explosion wasn't atomic, but it would be very satisfactory. About a kiloton of energy could be released by every man in my army. The general had insisted that the officers have enabling controls, and unless they had set them to active, one guy couldn't decide to end it all and blow away half his battalion. I'd agreed to that design detail reluctantly. I trusted my men.

"You know what I'm talking about," Kerr said. "I don't want your officers to enable the destruct unless you can do some real damage to the enemy, not just to our own men."

"We're not idiots, sir," I said, "and we have six cruise missile brigades with nuke warheads in every unit as well, if it comes to that."

"Of course you're not idiots," Kerr snapped. I could hear in his voice he was trying not to get pissed—and he was failing at it. "What I want is your assurance that you will save such tactics for something important."

"You have my assurance that we will do our damnedest to destroy every one of these frigging machines, General. That is the only assurance I can give you."

He was silent for several seconds.

"Okay," he said at last in defeat. "It's your show, Riggs. But don't screw the pooch."

"I don't intend to. Riggs out."

I snapped off the com-link before he could say anything else. I threw down the headphones. They rattled on the computer table. They slid across the slick surface and banged on the decking beyond. I didn't worry about them breaking. They could take it. They were army issue and very tough.

I sighed. What Kerr had meant was "don't screw the pooch *again*." Meaning he thought I'd done a bang-up job on said pooch last time I'd come down here. I hadn't been in command then, but I still carried the blame in the minds of the Pentagon boys. I would have gone on stewing about it, but fortunately, there wasn't time.

"ETA: Two minutes," said the ship. The *Alamo* was on its final approach. I threw together my gear and stood swaying, watching the forward wall where colored metal beetles once again crawled in profusion. Fortunately, these beetles all represented Nano ships on our side.

"Engage all enemy targets upon recognition," I ordered.

"Weapons activated."

Normally, when we approached Macros with our ships we gave them strict orders not to fire on the enemy except in self-defense. We didn't want to lose ships pointlessly. We knew from experience the anti-air of Macro ground forces was superior to our Nano ship anti-ground capabilities. But this time, we had a precious cargo of troops to defend. If the Macros took a few shots at my ship, that was better than having them splatter the hundred helpless infantry in the landing pod that dangled beneath it. The *Alamo* was tougher than the landing pods and could repair itself after anything but a direct hit on the engines.

I had decided to land with the first wave. That way, I'd see firsthand if the rest of the troops should be committed, or if we should plan rescue efforts for the survivors instead. We had two hundred Nano ships involved. They were ferrying in troops from a flotilla of seaborne transports about seventy miles offshore, just over the horizon. At that range, the curvature of the Earth prevented laser weapons from stabbing out and hitting the sea transports. With each Nano ship carrying a landing pod full of one hundred marines, we would hit the insertion point in three waves and be fully deployed, six thousand strong, in about three hours.

We'd decided to land in the middle of the fallen buildings of Buenos Aires. The cover was better and with flying transports, we didn't have to put our backs to the sea. According to some dry runs done at other points, they didn't have much in the way of automated defenses to repel this kind of attack. They would have to send their land forces to meet us, which should halt their advance in the north immediately. We had high hopes they wouldn't surprise us with something unforeseen in the first hours.

"Landing pod deployed," said the ship.

I walked heavily into the cargo area. Below was the landing pod, looking like an octagonal, steel pressure-cooker. The ship's black arm snaked back up toward me. I could see the men pouring out of all four exits in good formation. There was no defensive fire yet, but once they were in the rubble-filled streets they all ran for cover, expecting the worst. A hundred silver-suited ants flowed in every direction. I gritted my teeth. It was my turn to make my entrance.

Alamo, take me down to the group around Lieutenant Wilson.

The big, black hand gripped my waist, and in less than a second I was out in the open air again. I wished then—as I hurtled down toward the Earth in a giant alien hand—that I'd given Sandra one more kiss. I'd left her behind at Andros. There was no place for her here. She was still only flesh and blood. We had talked over the idea of giving her the injections, but decided against it. She was young and wanted to have kids some day. No one knew what the nanites would do to a woman's prospects of giving birth normally later in life. We knew they messed with cell structure and edited DNA. How far did it go? What side-effects might there be? She might already be genetically damaged after the first time she'd undergone a single repair effort. Neither of us had seen any point to taking more risks.

As soon as I had my feet on the ground again, I felt marginally better. Everyone said something along the lines of *glad you could make it down, sir!* I ignored them and got out my binoculars.

"No sign of the Macros?" I asked.

"No sir, we have the town to ourselves."

"Well, don't make dinner plans yet," I said, and waved to Wilson. "Let's move into the interior and take up better positions and dig in. The second wave may need cover fire."

They didn't hit us for nearly two hours. By that time, the second wave was down, we'd taken up positions all over the city ruins and the third wave was incoming—but the Macros beat them.

The missiles didn't scream as they came down, but they did roar—for just an echoing second—before they went off. Fortunately, they weren't tipped with nukes. We'd feared that they would be, right from the start. But so far, the enemy hadn't used nukes except the ones they'd fired from the big invasion ship, when they first landed. Maybe they didn't have any nukes. Maybe they hadn't seen the need to use one yet.

Our only anti-air systems consisted of the Nano ships themselves. But they weren't due back with the third wave of troops for another seven minutes.

The Macro missile barrage lasted only about ninety seconds, but it was a rough minute and a half. In that short amount of time, about a hundred missiles hit us. All we could do was crawl under concrete blocks, down into sewers and underneath the burnt out shells of cars.

When the missiles arrived, they didn't smash down into the land and make craters. Instead they popped overhead in airbursts, exploding into a hundred showers of hot metal slivers. Our suits, made of Kevlar and lined with lead, absorbed some of this shrapnel, but not all. Almost everyone had a few bloody holes. Men crawled around the landscape, leaving bloody trails like pinpricked snakes.

I was hit in four spots. The one in the back of my neck was the worst. It had come in at a low angle under my hood and lodged itself up near the base of my spine. It burned there, cooking the flesh around it. The nanites in my system flocked to the damaged spots in my body quickly. I could feel them, itching and burning in the wounds. The bleeding stopped faster than normal, and within two minutes the punctures were only oozing. After four minutes, my wounds had stopped bleeding entirely. After half an hour, the shrapnel began to poke itself up out of my skin in places, like metallic bean sprouts bursting from the earth. The slivers slowly wriggled their way out as the nanites ejected them from my flesh.

After the initial barrage ended, there were a few minutes of relative calm. Everyone scrambled to reorganize and look around. The boys on the radio had been watching on satellite. They told me the missiles had been fired from all over the continent, mostly from the domes themselves. They'd all been fired at different times, but carefully synchronized to arrive here and pound us with a single massive barrage.

"Two-thirds of our forces have landed, sir," said Major Radovich after he found me, "but if they are going to hit us with barrages of missiles like that with any regularity, we can't call in the support troops."

I agreed immediately. I relayed the orders for the transports to hold back after the third wave of my nanite-infested marines. It simply wasn't safe enough to bring in regular troops.

It was Staff Sergeant Kwon who sounded the alarm when the second stage of the enemy counterattack began. "Three machines, sir!" he roared in his deep bass voice. He pointed to the west, then north. "And a fourth!"

The Macros were coming into the ruined city from all directions. All told, seven of them arrived in the next few minutes. I figured they must have been running steadily to this spot since the moment they had detected our incoming attack.

In a strange way, this was a relief. This was the situation we had trained and planned for. Shrapnel bursts were hard to deal with for infantry, but these machines were the enemy we'd come prepared to destroy.

The men split up into companies, taking up sheltered positions. We had dug in where we could. We waited for the enemy to rush into us, and I for one was afraid they would stand back and pepper us with infinite waves of exploding missiles.

But they weren't that much different from humans—in their military thinking, at least. They clearly thought of us as being the same men they had faced in previous battles. They had been fighting and slaughtering our kind for weeks now. Probably, they had the algorithm pretty well worked out by now for battles when they met a concentration of human troops like this. Pound us with missiles, then march in the machines to mop-up.

They scuttled and clanked right in over us and set to work with their sixteen belly-turrets spraying fire all at once.

Many men died, especially in the first minutes of the attack. They were stepped on, crushed down by thousands of tons of metal coming to a single, spike-shaped foot. They were overwhelmed and cooked alive by flaring releases of energy from the combined belly-turrets. No one, not even a man pumped full of nanites, could withstand more than a glancing hit from those fierce anti-personnel weapons.

But my men didn't run. They deployed their goggles and portholed suits. They blazed out with gouts of light. One man, firing for less than a full concentrated second on a single turret could turn it to molten, burning slag. Once inside the individual shields of the Macros, if the machines faced a platoon—even a full organized squad—they were soon rendered defenseless. Always, their response was the same: they set about to stomp the men to death.

But my marines weren't slow men. They dodged the thundering feet. They rolled and dove and kept firing up at the armored belly, the solid metal legs, the spheroid ball-joints. Metal melted like wax. Men died, but the machines were quickly crippled.

187

The Macros tried to run then, but it was always too late. My troops took off after them, bounding and whooping like hunters on the blood trail of a fatally wounded prehistoric beast. Each stride took us twice as far and fast as a normal man could run, even with our heavy loads. The machines could not escape us. We took great pleasure in burning the legs from under the machines and carving them up. The death throes ended with a fusillade of concentrated fire on the section we believed covered the CPU. Once we'd penetrated that zone of heavily-armored plates on any machine, burning our way to the circuitry and spinning gears inside, the Macro ceased to operate.

The seven giant machines died in five minutes. I had each captain report our losses. We were still ninety-five percent effective.

My men were jubilant, and we relayed the good news to the Pentagon. They told us more missiles had been fired on the far north of the continent. Within fifteen minutes, we were to be treated to another heavy barrage.

I allowed myself one minute to think hard while my men picked up the wounded and organized themselves. I came to a command decision. I thought—briefly—of talking it over with the brass back home, but there simply wasn't time. We had to move now.

I got out a com-unit and talked to my men using the command channel. Every officer out there heard me in their headset. "Men, we've learned two things: we can kill Macros, and they can kill us. We can take out their machines, but these missiles are going to nail us to the ground if we stay in a concentrated area. We have to move out to avoid being pinned down. I want every company to separate and I want ten companies to go for each of the six nearest domes. Your mission is to destroy whatever is under your dome, and every machine you meet on the way. I'll personally lead the force toward the nearest one. The intel gained by my assault should help the rest of you in completing your missions. Now, let's get out of this deathtrap of a city and scatter!"

The officers around me stood in stunned silence. I didn't give them time to mull over these new orders. No one would like them, I was certain of that. Troops didn't like heading out into hostile territory in small groups. Everyone knew that the machines might well come in packs and overwhelm a lone company. But I had no intention of sitting around in Buenos Aires and being pounded to death by missiles until they could gather enough machines to overwhelm us all. This was not going to be a traditional war, it was a war of maneuver and surprise.

There were no reinforcements coming in soon—we were it. Right now, we had the initiative, and I meant to keep it that way.

-30-

As it turned out, the machines didn't come—not right away. We proceeded at a ground-eating trot. Trotting for Star Force marines wasn't the same as trotting for normal men. Not even when we carried our bulky reactors and thick laser tubes.

Our gear had undergone many improvements. There would be more, I was sure of that, in the future. The main design points were still the same: we carried the reactors on our backs and the projection unit was connected to it with a thick black cord which, as yet, only the Nano machines could make. The military engineering people had worked on the rest of it. The suits were made of bulletproof materials and everything we carried except for the reactor itself was in front of us, largely centered around our bellies and the lower chest area. Flares, food, medical kits, etc—it was all in front of us to help counter-balance the mass on our backs. We still ran in an odd posture, leaning forward to keep from falling on our backs. If we did lose our balance, we always landed on our butts, with the hard surface of the reactor slamming into the back of our skulls.

The helmets and hoods had improved too, and now were nanite-impregnated. Friendly fire anywhere in the area caused a signal to bleep out, warning nearby suits. In a millisecond, everyone's vision was protected by instantly darkened, re-polarized goggles. This was a necessity, as the new green-beamed lasers were so powerful that open exposure could burn out a man's retina permanently. The automatic darkening and lightening of the landscape took some getting used to, but it was necessary. We couldn't just leave the full shades on all the time or we would be bumping around unable to see where we were going.

In less than an hour, my battlegroup came to the edge of a crater surrounding the dome. Macro workers from the silvery dome had built high walls of debris to form the unnatural crater. Apparently, the Macros liked their domes in the center of a dry, flat area with walls all around. If such a spot wasn't handy, they changed the region to their liking.

Bad news came in over my com-unit as we approached the rampart around the dome. It had an uneven ridge of black earth and junk about two hundred feet high. I could see the crest through the trees when a report came in from the Pentagon.

"The Macros are taking out our satellites, Riggs," General Kerr told me.

"I'm surprised they didn't do it earlier."

"I think you finally impressed them enough to make them move. They either didn't want to waste the ordinance, didn't think the satellites mattered, or were waiting until a strategic moment to blind us when we weren't expecting it. I think it was the latter."

I leapt over a rusted bicycle in the middle of a cracked highway. I had to leap again to clear a giant pothole left behind by the foot of a Macro. We were proceeding southward down an Argentinean highway, that my HUD said was the 205. The road was crisscrossed with giant machine footprints. They had punched through the asphalt and formed five-foot deep sinkholes in the dirt beneath. I tilted my head to hear the General better. I thought about ordering a halt, but we were too close. I told myself we wouldn't stop moving until we reached the crater's edge and gathered up for the assault.

"At least I've impressed the enemy," I said.

"Indeed you have. You've impressed our people, too. Some of the brass here took a crap in their coffee when they realized you were abandoning the beachhead. You are taking a big risk, you know."

"No sir, sitting pinned down until a thousand missiles arrived—that would have been the big risk."

"I agree with you. But stay away from the proverbial pooch's hindquarters."

"Will do, sir," I said. *The pooch again.* I figured I would buy him a poodle for Christmas when this was all over.

"One last thing, we might lose communications with you soon. They are taking out every satellite indiscriminately. They are blinding and silencing us. We'll try to set up an alternate communication network, but there's no guarantee they won't hunt that down and nail it, too."

"Understood, sir."

"Godspeed, Colonel—or whatever you're calling yourself today."

"You too, sir."

We broke off the connection and I trotted faster to catch up with my company. I was falling behind. Beside me, Major Radovich paced along easily. I yearned briefly for the early days when I had been the strongest man around. My men had long since surpassed me. In the field with my nanite-enhanced marines, I was one of the slowest of the supermen.

The other battlegroups hadn't reported any resistance yet. All the way out from Buenos Aires, as we trotted and huffed in our suits, the tension had grown. At first, I had felt relieved not to have contacted the enemy yet, but at the same time I became more apprehensive with each passing minute. They had to show up eventually.

We made it all the way to the foot of the mountain of debris that formed the crater before they hit us. It turned out they were waiting inside the crater itself. We didn't know it until we reached the foot of the mound of loose earth and they surfaced at the top, looking down at us. These weren't the really big machines, but rather the smaller, twenty-footers we'd scathingly referred to as workers. They were like metal ants. Looking up at their dark shadows, I realized there were hundreds of them, and they seemed quite large enough to kill a man. Worse, these workers each had a weapon built into their torso, a swiveling turret about where the head should be.

About two hundred of them rose up at once and opened fire. My bounding men were scattered, as per my orders, but not scattered enough. I screamed into my headset to take cover and return fire. The orders were hardly needed. Everyone followed their training and those that lived took cover. We beamed them and they beamed us. At first, they were winning easily. We were softer targets, and we were running around out in the open. Now I saw the wisdom of blasting down everything flat around the domes and building up crater-like walls. These craters functioned as simple, earthwork fortresses. At least this

192

defensive effort confirmed the domes were important targets. But as I dodged enemy laser-fire, I found the point to be of small consolation.

In less than thirty seconds we lost over a hundred men, a tenth of my force. After that, we reached the foot of the rising mound that formed the crater. I thanked God they hadn't seen fit to make the surface slicker or build minefields into it. We had cover and although they had the advantage of the high ground, we still outnumbered them by four to one.

I thought about ordering the cruise missile brigade to fire on the workers. They should be able to sweep that ridge. But my men were already in too close. We were going to have to do this the hard way.

I crawled into decent cover and got out my com-unit. First, I ordered a company to flank the enemy in either direction, out to the east and west. Then I relayed the news of the enemy tactics to the other teams. They had hours of running to do before they found their domes, but I wanted them to know what to expect—and I wanted them to get the message while we could still transmit it.

Working up the hill, we were at close range quickly. They were now only a hundred yards away. In a leap-frog maneuver, one squad held good firing positions while the second squad of each platoon bounded up to take a higher region of cover. Then the first squad advanced while being covered by the second. The enemy attack weakened, and as we neared the top, it quit altogether. I watched my men run up the walls of the crater with apprehension. What would we find waiting on the far side?

I broke from cover myself and ran uphill, watching as the first of my men reached the crest. A pair of pinchers lunged and snatched up the fastest man, snipping him in half. Those gleaming, scissor-like blades cut through his suit and flesh just above the waist. A second man met the same fate, and then a third. After that, we took out the machines that had ambushed the first men and drove the rest back. My men crouched all along the ridge and advanced cautiously, blazing fire as they went.

Superior numbers and tactics won the day moments later. The companies I'd ordered to flank to the east and west were in position now, and they came up around either side of the enemy. They fired then at the exposed metallic ants that huddled against the inside rim of their crater. Due to the curvature of the crater, my men had a free field of fire. We annihilated them without further losses.

We turned our attention to the dome itself then. The surface *swirled*—I supposed that was a good word for it. The dome was milky, semi-opaque, and shimmered occasionally as a stray beam from my troops lanced out and struck it. Major Radovich crawled up next to me. All around us, my marines were directing killing beams into any Macro worker which still thrashed. As soon as that was done, they dug in along the rim of the crater. They didn't have to be told to dig in, not these boys. They were doing it before I could give the order.

They eyed me and I ignored them. I stared at the dome instead. I had yet to give the attack order, so they weren't sure how long we were going to wait to make our next move. Major Radovich looked at me. I could only see his eyes when I glanced at him. The rest was covered. We halted at the top of the crater rim. We were both lying in the mixture of dirt and twisted, smoking metal that crowned the rim of the crater, exposing only our faces to the dome in the center.

"Well?" he asked me finally.

"I'm thinking."

"Sir," he said, sliding close enough for our shoulders to touch, "we can't just sit here."

I adjusted the magnification on my goggles, eyeing every inch of that bubble-like shield.

I glanced at him. "What do you suggest, Major?"

"Let's push. Let's do it."

"Just run out there the last thousand yards and try to slip into— whatever that is?"

"Yeah. What the hell else are we going to do?"

I heaved a sigh. "What, indeed," I said. I hesitated for a few moments more, but he was right, the enemy weren't doing anything, and we couldn't stay here. If nothing else, they would probably launch a massive missile barrage at us. We had reached the first dome and threatened it. They would respond. I was sure of it.

And I was equally sure they had another trick or two left. Whenever this enemy sat quietly, it seemed to mean they had laid their trap and were patiently waiting for us to walk into it. I didn't want to lose more men due to a wild attack. What was inside? What new horrors awaited us, should we even be able to enter?

I finally turned to Radovich. "Major, I want concentrated fire. Everyone is to fire a five-second cutting beam at the base of that dome.

Then another five. Let's try to focus everything we have on a single point and see if it gives."

He stared at me for a second, then nodded. I could tell he didn't approve. He and a lot of other men had come here to avenge some part of their lost lives on these machines. It looked like we had the Macros on the run, and he wanted to finish it personally.

It took a minute or two to get everyone organized, but soon we were firing in concert. I opened up with the others. It felt good to shoot at something. The light of the combined lasers was intense, too much even for our blacked-out goggles. I closed my eyes, and still the greenish-white light of hundreds of lasers firing at once crept in through my eyelids, painfully bright. Inside my head, my pupils constricted to pinpoints. I had an instant headache and purple splotches pulsed in my skull.

"Cease fire!" I shouted, not wanting anyone's vision damaged. Neither did I want any of the lasers to overheat and shut down. Venting enough heat—besides the problem of vision-scorching brilliance—was one of the biggest concerns with these new weapons. I suspected more than a few men could feel the prickle of nanites in their heads and on their burnt hands, as the microscopic robots worked to repair cellular damage from overexposure.

While my head pulsed, I squinted to see the dome. It was still there, but it wasn't the same. It had changed color to a burnt orange where we had all hit it. I chewed my lip as I watched the circular area we'd beamed. It soon shifted back to a shimmering, opal-white.

"I don't think we have enough firepower to burn our way through," I said aloud.

Radovich grunted in agreement. "Are we going to assault the dome now, sir?"

I hesitated for a few more seconds. I couldn't think of anything else to do. The enemy was clearly waiting for us. But they were probably working up a counterattack as well that would come if we didn't move quickly. Sitting around wasn't going to accomplish anything. I began to wonder if I should have ordered our men to split up into three battlegroups instead of six. Perhaps, due to overconfidence, I'd set us up to fail in six attacks instead of succeed in three. There was no fixing it now, however. If this battlegroup was destroyed, a new commander would fight with new knowledge of the enemy capabilities.

"Deploy the same companies that did the flanking. They took lighter losses than those that did the frontal assault on this ridge and should be at full strength. Have them move in on that dome from two angles. The rest of us will support with fire down the center from here."

Radovich rolled onto his side and looked at me. "Permission to speak, sir."

"Talk to me."

"Sir, we should go in with at least half our strength. What's our backup plan if those first two waves vanish into that dome? What if they get in, but get eaten?"

"Then I have eight companies left to figure out what to do next."

"Sir, I know you have some infantry experience, but in standard tactics—"

"Listen, Major. I hear you, but we are not fighting a bunch of men with rifles. We have no idea what will happen when we assault this dome, but I suspect it won't be anything good. And I don't want their next surprise to hit my entire force."

"How about half our force?"

"No."

"Sir, what about the cruise missile brigade?"

"We've fired a thousand missiles at these domes, they are always shot down. The missiles are for a major concentration of unshielded targets. We haven't gotten the chance to use them yet."

"Sir, permission to lead the charge."

He had more balls than most of my men. I looked at him and thought about it. "Denied," I said. "I need you here with me, Major. Don't worry. I'll bet you a hundred Euros you'll see all the combat you want today."

He snorted, but didn't take the bet. My orders went out, and two full companies of nanite-filled marines charged across the relatively smooth, featureless landscape toward the dome.

By the time the two forward assault teams were three-quarters of the way there, all hell broke loose.

-31-

A force of Macro workers had been gathering secretly in the trees behind us. These workers were equipped differently, with twin lobster-claws protruding from the torso of every unit. My first impression when I spotted them charging our rear was that they were built for harvesting of some kind. Probably, they foraged around the domes for metals or maybe even trees—although I had no idea what use the machines would have for wood. In any case, they lacked guns of any kind, and they rushed close to attack.

At least half my men were distracted by this flank attack. We fired as they charged from the tree line. Many of the enemy lobster-types didn't make it to us, but those that did simply plucked men from the ground with their claws. They lifted my men into the air with one claw, then proceeded to snip off their limbs individually. With a final grinding effort, they crushed each victim's helmet until the skull inside popped.

I tore my eyes from that scene to watch the men charging the dome. In front of us, all around the far side of the crater's rim, another force of big machines appeared. They had gathered out of our sight. They had probably been swelling in numbers since we arrived at the crater, running in from neighboring patrols and domes. They had bided their time on the far side of the crater, getting together every unit they had, until we approached the dome. It was clear to me that our attack had triggered their counterstrike. They didn't want us anywhere near their dome.

The men I'd sent forward into the crater toward the dome never had a chance. I ordered them to turn and run, but it was already too late.

197

Half our men up on the crater rim were firing backward at the lobster-workers who streamed out of the trees behind us. The other half attempted to give covering fire as our men bounded back toward us, but the enemy Macros were too fast. They ignored our fire, which had no real effect on their shielded bodies. I counted twenty-six of the huge, silvery bastards. They rolled over the rim of the crater, overrunning my men and burning them down. My troops looked like sand castles caught in a tidal wave. Hundreds of belly-turrets blazed at once, and my marines melted. Seeing they were doomed, they stood and fought to the last. The big machines went into a frenzy, shouldering one another and clashing together massive legs in their eagerness to kill. My marines fought until utterly destroyed. They only managed to take out one of the big machines before they were all burnt to ash.

The workers rushing our rear were driven back with heavy losses, but they had done their work. I realized belatedly they had held our attention and kept us pinned down until the big machines had time to get in close and destroy my two forward companies. As I watched, the big machines pulled back beyond the far side of the crater.

"They are resetting the trap!" shouted Major Radovich. "If we all go for the dome now, the workers will come up behind us again and hit us in the back."

"We have to attack again," I said.

He looked at me. After watching two companies get slaughtered down there, his bravado had faded.

"We could hold and call for another battlegroup," he said.

"The nearest is an hour or two away. If we sit here that long, the Macros will launch a missile barrage. For all we know, a mass of missiles is coming here right now."

"Can't our birds see—"

"No," I said, cutting him off. I hadn't had time to fill him in on the loss of our satellites. I did so now. His face was a shade grimmer by the end of my explanation.

"So, we don't know if…."

"No," I said. "We have no idea what's coming."

He paused. "What are your orders, sir?"

"We came here to destroy that dome. We will do so or we will all die. I thought we could probe and scout the dome. I was wrong. We'll leave a company on this ridge with the cruise missile brigade. The rest of us will roll down there and either take out those machines and that dome or die trying."

"I thought I was the craziest one here, sir," he said.

"You'll have to take a number," I told him.

"It's been less than a pleasure serving with you, Colonel."

"Same."

We laughed at each other, sharing a strange emotion as two men who faced imminent death. Then we relayed our orders. We stood up with our men, and together we charged down the ridge. Almost immediately, the big machines that had pulled back to the far side of the crater swept forward again to meet us.

"Listen up boys," I said, broadcasting to everyone, "I want you to get into that dome if you can and destroy whatever is there. Run all out for the dome. We can move faster than they are expecting us to. Engage if you have to, but try to keep moving toward the dome."

We almost made it. I think they had underestimated our speed. In past battles—with normal humans—men had always run at a certain rate. Their software had not yet made the adjustment. They came at us in a wave, but we were only a few hundred yards from the dome when they met us and a pitched battle began. I shouted orders commanding my men to put up a running fight. We had to shoot and keep moving toward the goal, to move right under them, right through them.

Many of my men failed to follow these orders. When the machines loomed over them, blocking out the sky, they slowed and concentrated fire on the belly-turrets that strafed them. I cursed, seeing this, but then I was in the middle of the battle and felt the same urges. To keep moving was nearly impossible once you were beneath the legs. Huge, looming columns of metal flew around, as if an eight-story building had come to unholy life and had decided it must kill you.

The noise of the machines was tremendous. They had a smoky smell about them that reminded me of burning tires. I sighted on a splattering turret and burned it until it ruptured like a light bulb. The effort took nearly two seconds—much too long. It was only through luck that I wasn't crushed or beamed down as I stood in one spot for so long. When combating a pack of angry Macros, two seconds was a lifetime.

"Forward!" I shouted, hoping some of the men could hear and obey me. I ran then, sprinting. The dome was very near. Around me a knot of marines followed.

Something roared and I was knocked flat. For several blinking seconds I didn't know what had happened. Then I had it: an enemy missile strike. The barrage had come in, finally.

It took me a few more seconds to realize there were very few missile strikes. This wasn't a barrage, it was just a smattering of missiles. I could see now what was happening. Up above the dome, above the machines and the struggling men, a launcher had arisen. It had many tubes. Periodically, each tube sparked and a missile flashed. Spiraling smoke trails led down toward us. They were firing right into their own machines at point-blank range.

Two men picked me up, and I was dragged, half-running toward the dome. My body was full of metal slivers. When I breathed, liquid bubbled out of my chest as if I were a wet, popped tire. My men dragged me under the last machine that stood between us and the dome. It had run out of belly-turrets by this time and two of its crab-like legs were dragging behind it.

I shouted into my com-unit. "Cruise brigade! Take out that missile turret now!"

I wasn't sure if they acknowledged or not. I wasn't even sure if they were still alive. We made it under the dying Macro's legs and hit the dome. All sounds of the battle cut out.

Stepping under the dome was like entering a cool, calm world. Cut off from the outside completely, I could feel the barrier as I passed through. It felt like I'd walked through some kind of plastic film, as if I'd been swallowed in bubble-wrap. We pushed inward and it pushed back, but gently it gave way. I think it was designed to allow slowly moving things to walk through. How else could the workers easily gain access? I supposed they could have sent in some kind of signal, but signals could be duplicated. Besides, I suspected now that the shield prevented all signals from penetrating. Signals were fast-moving energy, just like the laser beams from my rifle. These domes seemed to stop such emissions.

Once past the barrier, we stood in a gloomy world. A machine hulked in front of us, dimly lit by internal sources. I flipped on my suit lights and stood unaided. I coughed, and that hurt worst of all.

"Colonel?" asked the man next to me in concern. I looked at him in surprise. It was Wilson, not Radovich. I wondered briefly if Radovich was dead.

"Should we fire on that thing, sir?" he asked me.

200

I tried to get my thoughts together. It wasn't easy. I'd gone through too many shocks too quickly, and I think that close missile blast—exploding almost in my face—had addled my brains. I realized I was lucky I could still hear anything.

"How many do we have?" I asked, and right away I could see relief on Lieutenant Wilson's face. He hadn't wanted to command this final leg of the assault. I didn't blame him.

"Twenty sir, but more are streaming in."

Twenty? I thought in shock. Was that all that had made it inside?

"Let's advance then," I said, "and see what that thing is."

I staggered forward. One leg didn't seem to be operating properly. Wilson gave me a shoulder and I took it. We moved toward the thing that crouched in the center of the dome.

It took me a few dozen steps to recognize it. I had seen it before, or something like it. It resembled one of my own factories—the ones I'd built and left on Andros Island—but it was much larger. A hundred times larger. I could hear it now. It sort of *thrummed.* It was a deep, steady, ominous sound.

"Men," I said, struggling not to cough. My lungs burned and itched abominably and it was all I could do to speak clearly. "This thing is a factory. It builds new Macros and whatever else they need, just as I built these guns we are carrying. I've never thought about how to destroy one, but I think it's time we figured it out."

More men came in, a lot of them. We had maybe a hundred and fifty marines inside the dome. Less than two companies out of ten. The new group reported that most of the big machines outside were destroyed, but most of us had died as well.

"Well, there's nothing like the direct approach. Everyone button up as best they can. On my mark, everyone fire at that thing. Shoot for the center point of the mass, about ten feet from the base. Everyone now, *fire!*

We blazed at it. Light like that of a thousand suns bloomed, filling the inside of the dome with brilliance. Despite our darkened shades, I could see the light. It was blinding, painful.

I kept the beam going for five seconds. Everyone followed my lead, and as each second passed, the beams came closer together, focused on a single target area.

"Keep firing. Let's go another five," I said, trying to sound calm.

My eyes were squinting lines. My retinas were exploding. The heat coming off my weapon burned my hands right through my gloves. We fired for five more seconds, then another two or three, but I could tell the light was dimming. Either I'd burnt out my retinas, or men and lasers were failing around me. Probably, it was the latter. The heat was tremendous.

"Cease fire!" I shouted. The beams cut out and died down. My vision came back slowly, but with many burnt purple splotches that floated and flared annoyingly. "We don't want to melt our lasers down, let alone our hands and eyes."

We checked out the damage when we were able. There wasn't much to show for all the effort. A pocked area, blackened and burnt, showed in a ten foot radius on the wall of the machine's heavy base.

Only a few more men had joined us, the flow of new troops was lighter now. Only two companies or so had survived, out of a thousand men. I figured the troops back on the crater's rim might have lived as well. There might be wounded outside too, if we had taken out all the big machines. I thought perhaps we had, as none of them had tried to get inside here with us. Maybe they were too big. I had no idea actually. But I was sure I wanted to destroy this factory before it could build a new Macro.

I led the men around to the far side of the machine. Wilson still helped me walk. There it was, on the same spot as the machine back inside my own ship. The intake vent. It was up a ways, perhaps twenty feet off the ground. I was sure the worker Macros would lift up their burdens of raw materials and slide them down that hole into something like the nanite digesters my own factories had.

The marines gathered around. "What are we going to do now, sir?" asked Wilson.

"Well, Lieutenant, we're going to get inside that intake somehow and destroy this thing."

"You first, sir," he said.

I looked at him.

"No offense, sir. But are you serious? What if that thing turns on?"

"I need your help, Wilson. I need your command codes for my suit."

"What, sir?"

"The safeguards. It takes two officers to release them. I need your secret code for self-destruction. Then I need you to lead these men out of here after we build up a ladder to get me up to the rim of that intake vent."

"What? I didn't really mean what I said about you going first."

I nodded. "I know, Wilson. But we haven't got any other heavy explosives with us."

Wilson stared at me. "I've got a better idea, sir. We'll rig up the ignition switch to a command signal. Then we'll drop a reactor inside there. The rest of the men can evac and the last man out can set it off."

"He'll have to stay inside the dome," I said. "No signals will go through it. We haven't got the equipment to set up an autodestruct or a time-bomb."

"Yes, sir. I would like to volunteer for that mission, sir."

I shook my head. He put a hand on my arm.

"Sir," he said, "Kyle Riggs—I told you I would join up and follow you. I did that, sir. And I'm still a man of my word. I'll do it."

"I trust you, Lieutenant, but—" I said, but he cut me off.

"We can't order anyone else to do it. We can't ask that. But we are playing for keeps here. Difficult situations require difficult choices. I'm willing to take the chance."

"This is my command," I said.

"Yes, sir, it is."

I hesitated. Then the machine rumbled. I don't know what it sounded like—maybe like a locomotive starting up when you had your hands on it and leaned against it. I could feel the deep vibration in my bones. All the men backed away from it instinctively.

"It's building a new machine, sir," said Wilson, eyeing me, "you know it is."

I sighed and coughed. "Okay. Do it."

We threw Wilson's armed reactor pack up into its maw, and light flared out to consume it. I hoped it would still operate. I ordered everyone out of the dome. I was one of the last to wave to Wilson, who urgently made pushing motions at me. The machine was indeed giving birth to something…something large. It had to be one of the big fighting machines. I wondered how long it took to generate such a monster, given all the required materials.

I didn't even make it all the way through the shield bubble before the shield popped and vanished forever. I never even heard the explosion itself. It was completely dampened by the shield, held inside there and contained. Then the force field collapsed to nothing, revealing only smoking wreckage inside.

Outside, we were met by the cruise missile boys and the company that had covered them. They had pulled through. The two companies I'd led into the dome were the only other survivors. But the dome and the factory inside had been destroyed. It was a blackened hulk of twisted metal.

I had my people search, but we couldn't find Wilson. There was no sign of him. Nothing at all.

-32-

Communications were reestablished an hour after the dome fell. The Pentagon people had landed repeating stations on the continent. It wasn't as good as satellite coverage because we were still blind to enemy movements, but it was better than nothing. We could at least coordinate our actions.

I relayed our bloody success story to the other commanders. They took the news with grim determination. Each assured me they would reach their target domes and destroy them, just as my unit had. I told each of them in turn that I had faith in them—which I did—and that I knew they would succeed—which I didn't.

My battlegroup had taken too many casualties to be an effective force now. About twenty percent of our survivors were too badly injured to move at all. But I didn't want to leave anyone behind. I was one of the ones on the incapacitated list, but that wasn't important. I figured my unit was out of the fight now.

Major Radovich had different ideas.

"Sir," he said, crouching next to me where I leaned against the broken strut of a dead Macro. "I know with normal men—in normal battle—marines don't leave their own behind. But this is different."

"And how exactly is it different?" I asked Radovich. I looked at him with bleary stubbornness. My nanites were working hard on the dose of shrapnel I'd gotten during my close encounter with a Macro missile, but they weren't finished yet. I was still bleeding inside my suit. I could feel blood oozing down my legs and pooling at the bottom of my suit when I sat down or leaned against something. I was surprised the nanites hadn't completely contained the bleeding. All the hurrying around must have reopened the tears in my skin. I'd never been so seriously wounded. Not even when my arm had been burnt were things as bad as this. The metal slivers had pierced me in a dozen spots like bullets. I would have never survived this long if it hadn't been for the nanites in my body. They were working overtime. They itched like a thousand hot grains of sand, each one determinedly rubbing its own personal nerve.

"This situation is different," he repeated, "because if we leave these wounded, they won't sicken and die. They will grow stronger with each hour, until they are mobile again."

"If it comes down to it," I told Radovich, "I'll put you in charge and stay behind with the wounded men. I'm one of them, after all. But I don't think it will come down to that."

"We have nearly two full companies left," said Radovich. "I could lead them to the next dome and support Anderson. Two companies might make the difference between success and failure, sir."

I frowned at him, thinking about it. Negative thoughts loomed in my mind. Was he just looking for glory? Did he want his own command to participate in another successful assault? I didn't think so. Besides, what difference did it make if that was in his mind? He could have his glory—if he earned it. The point was to decide if he was right or not. We had to kill these domes. They were building new machines, one every day maybe. They had to be stopped. Once we took out the domes, we had won. We could then hunt down every last Macro, driving them off our world. We might not win the war, but we would have won another battle.

"Sir, please think," said Radovich. "What use was all this? Why did all those good men die if we don't succeed?"

I decided, looking at him, that he meant what he said. I nodded. "You're right. We'll take up a spot with good cover, and wait for our bodies to heal ourselves. We have plenty of weapons systems."

Radovich looked surprised. Maybe he wasn't used to commanders who changed their minds in the face of logic. "Very good, sir. Very good. I...." he said, then trailed off.

"I wish you well too, Major. I want you to take the com-unit—you will need it more than I will. Now get all your effectives together and destroy another dome for me."

"I will, sir!" he said, saluting me.

I felt I should get up, but my body really didn't want to listen. I got up anyway. He reached out a hand to help, but I ignored it and stood to salute him back. I saw his eyes, as he looked me over. I think he realized I was in bad shape, in no condition to fight or travel—or do much of anything else.

"We'll be back for you, Colonel," he said as he walked off, screaming at our last two uninjured sergeants. He gave confident orders and soon they pulled out, bounding up the crater rim to the north like fleeing jackrabbits. It was odd, watching them head over the ridge and vanish. It gave me a lonely, abandoned feeling I hadn't expected.

I sagged back down into a seated position. Around me, thirty-odd coughing, stricken men pulled their weapons close to their hands and watched the horizons. There would be no movement to a better position for us. We wouldn't be digging in or setting up defensive strongpoints. We would be struggling, each of us, to keep breathing. We would sit here until the nanites healed us or failed to do so.

I knew as we sat for the next hour, that if a single machine came to investigate, it could probably have taken us all out. But I didn't think it would come. The Macros had plenty to worry about. They had taken drastic steps to keep us out of their domes. Logically, they would mass whatever forces they had to defend the remaining domes. What would they care about a group of stationary humans at a destroyed dome?

But as the sky darkened and a light, warm rain began, I realized that there were other possibilities. The enemy liked stationary targets for their missiles. They might fire a few at us to take us out. Just to be sure.

I ordered the men to dig in if they were physically capable of it. I think about five of them did so. Most of those were burn victims, men who'd lost an arm or leg to a Macro laser. The men who were riddled with shrapnel had less energy. I was one of these, alive when I should be dead. We were zombies, all of us. Living dead men.

After two hours, I managed to get up and take a piss. I dug out something to eat. It was in a tube, like toothpaste. It tasted like meat or cheese, but really it was paste. I ate it by wiping it on my tongue and washed it down with flat, plastic-tasting water that was body-warm. I still couldn't take a deep breath without coughing, but I felt hard lumps in the bottom of my suit. I dug them out, three of them. Shiny bits of shrapnel. I smiled with half my mouth. The nanites were pushing them out. I was giving birth to shards of metal. More were in there, though—

I could feel them. They burned and itched and when they crested, poking out through my skin, they dribbled blood.

A large shadow loomed over me after I'd pulled two more bits of metal out of my suit. I looked up. At first, I didn't recognize him.

"So, you made it, sir," said a bass voice.

He was a huge one. Then memory flickered. It was Staff Sergeant Kwon, the first guy who ever lifted one of these packs and blew down a tree with it—before he had been filled with nanites.

"Kwon? Good to see you, too. Glad you made it through our first battle."

Kwon nodded.

"You don't look too bad," I said. "Can't keep up with Radovich's team?"

Kwon sat on a shelf made of dead Macro. He lifted up his boot and removed it. I winced. Half his foot—the front half—was missing.

"I'm fine, sir, except for this."

"Looks bad."

Kwon shook his head. "No problem. The nanites will build me new one. But will take them time."

I nodded slowly. "How did you lose your foot and not your boot?"

Kwon laughed. "Funny story," he said, "a Macro stepped on me. Took my boot and foot right off. But I found a new boot later and put it on. Is too small, but that's okay. My foot is not so big now."

I smiled, but somehow I couldn't find it in me to laugh. I didn't ask about the former owner of the boot Kwon had found. I was sure he was one of the dead.

"Are there are any other noncoms that can move?"

Kwon shook his head.

"Well then, could you check on the men and give me a status report? How many can at least fire a weapon? Have we lost anyone?"

"Sure," he said.

I put up my hand gesturing for him to stop. "How about that foot? You can walk around on it?"

"Sure," he said, "but not fast."

"Okay," I said, "as long as it's not causing you too much pain. I can find someone else if it's bad."

"Nah," he said, "it will feel good to walk. The damned thing itches like a spider bite."

208

I watched as Kwon went stumping around the twisted wreckage and bodies. There were few of our dead in the immediate vicinity, fortunately. Still, this field would begin to stink after a few hot days. I wondered how long we would be here.

Reports kept coming in over the communications system. They were sketchy, but good. Two more domes had come down. Losses were around fifty percent. Bloody, but so far we hadn't failed.

It was about four hours after we took out our dome that I awoke with a start. I thought it was pitch black out, but realized after a few seconds that my goggles had autoshaded themselves. Laser light flared green, exploding the night into life and making me squint. Shouts rang in my headset. I scrambled for my weapon, shouldered my reactor pack and got up on one knee.

"Staff Sergeant Kwon," I said, "report."

"Something out there, sir. The men to the east side are firing at it."

Facing me was the towering wreckage of the broken dome to the west. I swung around and looked east. I thought I saw a shimmer of motion, but it could have been the rain.

"Okay, everyone get up and look alive. I want men looking in every direction. Everyone stay low, stay covered if possible. We should be functional now, most of us."

"Sixty percent are walking wounded now, sir," said Kwon's voice.

"You never came back and made your report."

"You were asleep, sir."

Great, I thought. I opened my mouth, but one of my men beat me to it.

"Here they come! From the south, sir. From the crater wall!"

I saw them now, shadows moved in the silver-black rainfall. We all had our suit-lights off. There was no reason to give the enemy something to shoot at.

Dark shapes, big, but not huge. Workers? I wasn't sure. They looked like machines, however, and their bodies whined and clanked like them. I sighted on one and fired. I gave it a hard, one-second burst. The beam burned the rain, turning it to an instant gush of steam. All around me, my men opened up and in the flares of light, like lightning flashes, I saw them.

This was a new breed of machine. I could not guess their purpose, but they resembled centipedes. They had conical-shaped contrivances where the head should be. I realized now, they were yet another kind of worker. One we hadn't seen before.

Then I heard screams. Men around me vanished. I saw the ground open up and I saw them fall into the earth. I knew instantly what was happening.

"Troops!" I shouted, my command signal overriding theirs. The channel was full of shouts of surprise and horror. "They are coming up from underneath us. Repeat, they are tunneling up under us. Move away from your positions. Burn them when they breach."

It wasn't ten more seconds before one came up for me. I burned it. Flashes were going off all over our makeshift camp.

I looked around wildly. We had to move from here. There were too many Macros. My men were too injured.

"Move out, everyone. We are going to where the dome was. The ground there is harder, like concrete or stone. They probably can't drill up into the middle of us there. Walk if you can, and pick up another man who can't."

I looked around for another man and found two-thirds of one, still squirming. I grabbed his jacket and dragged him. I felt prickles where metal slivers popped out of my skin. They had begun budding and bleeding due to my movement.

Less than twenty of us made it to safer ground. Every second or two, lasers flared and burned another clattering monster. I had no idea how many of the enemy there were. They seemed to be endless.

When we reached the hard floor of the dome which had once supported a massive, miraculous machine, they stopped coming. Those that were still in view dug into the earth like giant, wriggling ticks and vanished. Their heads were drills of some kind.

"Kwon?"

"Here, sir."

"Head count?"

"Twenty-one. Nine lost, sir."

I felt something new then. A vibration, under my feet. The other men felt it too. Everyone took staggering, shuffling steps backward from wherever they stood. We aimed our rifles at the ground beneath our feet.

"They are coming up underneath us, sir!" shouted Kwon.

I'd never heard fear in that man's voice before. But I thought I heard it now.

"What are we going to do, sir?" asked another private.

I didn't know his name. I didn't have an immediate answer for him. But then, after a few seconds I realized that I did have an answer. It was something I'd decided not to do previously, because it was too risky, but I didn't see how we had much choice now.

I spoke aloud in my mind and I called the *Alamo*.

-33-

My marine officers had often muttered about the fleet not wanting to get their hands dirty. But the ship captains knew from bitter experience that whenever Nanos came near the domes the Macros would attack our ships and destroy them as priority targets. I had determined before I went on this mission that, except for the initial landing, I could not afford to endanger our ships—not even to save our men in rescue efforts. If we lost even a portion of our fleet, how could we hope to defeat the next invasion attempt? I suspected the next time there might be nine ships coming. It was only a guess, but we had to prepare for the worst since the single Macro ship that had gotten through the first time had managed to devastate an entire continent. What if it was North America next time, or Asia—or both? We needed to keep every ship intact. They were the only source of prevention we had and they were a thousand times better than the cure of a ground defense.

But tonight I thought things might be different. Tonight, the Macros had a lot on their plate. They'd lost the three closest domes and their missile batteries. They would have a hard time shooting down a distant ship when they were under serious ground assault. They might still do it, but I wasn't going to let us all die here when I could stop it, when I could save myself and these fine men.

So, I called the *Alamo* and ordered her to come in from where she sat a few feet above the waves of the Southern Atlantic, out near the Falkland Islands. I called her and she came with all the blurring she could. The immediate problem I had was that she didn't have a landing pod handy and there were twenty men to be rescued. I had to decide if they were all going to be picked up one at a time by the ship's groping hand, or if we could work out something better.

"Kwon!" I shouted.

"Sir?"

"We have a rescue incoming, but we need to get on something large. Something like one of these pieces of wreckage."

"Rescue, sir?"

"Just listen," I said. The thrumming under my feet seemed sharper now, more insistent. My toes were tingling with the vibration of enemy drills. "Find a girder or something we can all hold onto. My ship is coming to pick us up. If she doesn't get shot down, she can carry us out, but we have to be easy to carry."

"Ah," said Kwon.

He looked around dazedly. I could see he wasn't going to find anything. He looked at the hard, stone-like floor as if he might find a handy tree branch lying there.

"Sir!" shouted the private who'd first asked me what we were going to do. He pointed toward the wrecked factory.

After a few seconds I saw what he was pointing at. It was a twisted bit of metal about thirty feet long. It was perhaps a foot thick, and looked like a pipe.

"How are we going to stand on that?" I asked.

"Not stand, sir!" he shouted, dragging a bad leg toward the pipe. His left knee seemed not to work. "We can all hold on. We're strong enough. Each man only needs one strong hand."

I nodded, liking the idea. "Let's do it!" I shouted and we all helped one another toward the twisted thing that turned out to be something like a strut. It had probably been part of the new Macro that had been in the birthing process when we blew the dome.

I dragged the two-thirds of a man I'd brought here. He was still alive, and so I kept dragging him. He never complained. Before I'd made it a dozen steps he fired his weapon back behind us as I bumped and thumped him along the ground like a sack of meal. I didn't bother to look back to see what he was shooting at. I just kept pulling him across the ground and up a small mountain of rubble. In between jolts, he continued to flash brilliant beams of light into the black rain. Vapor flared up into a warm fog behind us where he had burned the rain and turned it into fresh steam.

We reached the girder and worked to wrench it free of the debris, straining with all our enhanced muscles. Sensing we were up to something, the machines struggled with even more urgency to emerge through the hard stony surface where we had stood moments before.

"Kwon, you and five others with two working arms pull this thing free!" I shouted. "Everyone else fire on the machines as they surface."

We fired as they came up, but the surviving machines quickly moved to circle around the debris stacks. They were flanking us. They would come over the rubble and into close combat very soon. We fired at everything we saw, blowing holes in the blackness with stabbing tubes of light.

A shadow loomed over us less than a minute later. What little light had been filtering down from the rain clouds above us was blocked out. Instinctively, we raised our faces and our weapons.

"Hold your fire!" I shouted. "It's my ship. Is that thing free yet, Kwon?"

"Almost sir!" shouted Kwon, I could hear the tremendous strain in his voice. He was heaving at it for all he was worth.

A long black arm snaked down toward me. *No,* I told my ship. *Grab this piece of metal. Gently pull it loose.*

The *Alamo* plucked the girder free even as it had plucked a hundred trees free of the earth back on Andros Island. I ordered my men to take hold, and to hold onto each other as well. I gave them permission to drop their packs and rifles if they had to.

As we lifted off, the Macros realized what was happening and rushed the spot. They got hold of the lowest two men on the girder and ripped them loose. They went down screaming and blazing their rifles. The machines tore them apart as we looked down helplessly. We burned a few more, but then we were gone, rising up into the night.

I had locked one arm around the girder. In the other hand I still gripped the crippled man I'd been dragging for several minutes. I let my rifle dangle and clatter against the girder. The black cable kept it from falling.

It was the wildest ride of my life. It was pitch-black and we flew with terrifying speed over the treetops. When we got to the ocean, the rain became a storm. Then the storm became a hurricane. By the time we reached the Falklands and stood on solid ground again, only sixteen of us had managed to hold on. The rest had been lost.

I looked for the half-man I'd dragged around all night long. They told me he'd died during the flight. I nodded to the nurse, acknowledging her sympathetic words. I wasn't surprised, really. I knew from experience with my own children that there were limits to what the nanites could do.

-34-

In the morning, just before sunrise, I staggered out of the tiny building that served the island for a hospital. They hadn't been able to do much for me. The doctor on duty had just stared, wide-eyed, at our wounds full of what looked like quicksilver. I could tell he'd never seen anything like us. He eyed us as a man might when faced with the walking dead. We were frighteningly different, and every one of us should have died hours ago from our gruesome wounds.

I made every last survivor a noncom. I made Kwon a First Sergeant. I eyed his missing foot without touching it. The foot was a stump, but there were shiny spots there. The nanites were at work, rebuilding cells and stimulating growth. I wondered how long it would take them to regrow Kwon's foot. A week? A month? I had no idea.

When I finally contacted Crow, he was pissed, to put it mildly. I wasn't surprised. I wasn't in the mood for any of his bullshit, however.

"So you lived, mate?" he said. "I thought you'd done died like a true digger this time."

"Thanks for the vote of confidence, sir."

"Where are you?" he demanded.

"The Falklands, I think."

"Ah, having a spot of tea are you?"

"More like I'm pushing shrapnel out of a dozen spots in my body. Or rather, the nanites are."

He paused. "So you didn't just bugger out?"

"Who told you that?"

"That is the general opinion from command. You called your ship and had yourself extracted, leaving Major Radovich and his crew to their fate."

"What fate?" I asked. I felt a new weight upon my shoulders.

"Hadn't heard, eh? They were ambushed on the way to the next dome. A dozen Macros caught them. No survivors."

I stood there, breathing heavily. I didn't respond.

"I'm sorry about that bit, Kyle," said Crow, changing his tone. "I shouldn't have told you that way. But dammit, man, I thought you had died with them until this very minute. No one knew you were still alive."

"How's the rest of the battle going?"

"We've got them down to three domes. We lost half your men doing it, however. More than half. And most of the rest are wounded. They can't press further. I ordered them all to pull out. All the Macros are circling around their last domes now. Every hour there are more of them. Armies of the big machines were pulled back from the front lines up near the equator. The good news is our forces can now advance from that direction and retake half the continent. The bad news is they aren't likely to leave things so open again."

"No," I said, trying to think again. "They won't leave their rear unprotected again."

I kept thinking about Radovich. Somehow, I'd always thought he would make it. He'd never gotten his chance to lead a dome assault. I shook myself and took a cup of coffee a nurse offered me.

"The NATO brass wants to land regular troops on the beaches now. I think they are right."

I almost spit out my coffee. "What?"

"You did it, mate. They think you've broken their backs. The enemy is abandoning most of the land they grabbed and are pulling back into tight circles around those last three domes."

"Are they landing then?"

"That's what Kerr said."

"I've got to talk to him."

"All right. Crow out."

I sipped my coffee for about thirty seconds. I tried to calm down. Maybe Kerr was right. Maybe pressing in while the Macros were in retreat was the right thing. But I couldn't help but feel we might be falling for the same trap they had. We were advancing too quickly.

217

It took me less than five minutes to get in touch with Kerr.

"Kyle Riggs? What the hell? Everyone said you were dead. Some said you ran out, then died. What's the story?"

I filled him in.

"Your own personal rescue chopper, eh? Not sure how you called it in so fast, but I wished every unit had one. Anyway, I'm glad to hear you're still breathing."

"I don't seem to die easily."

"No. No, you don't. That's an excellent trait in a ground officer. Now, what's this call about, besides letting me know you aren't out of the picture yet?"

"I heard you were invading, sir," I said. "With regular forces."

"Hardly regulars. Marines and airborne. Tanks and artillery. Our best boys. I'll need your forces to form up a beachhead on the coast with us as soon as your troops are ready. We'll finish those last domes."

"I don't know how soon that will be, sir."

"What? I thought you boys healed like sidewalk weeds."

"We do, sir. But I don't think we can take the domes. Regular troops will be almost useless. My men are beat up, and now the enemy front-line troops have pulled back. They are certain to counterattack and overrun us."

"Would it help to know we've gotten about another battalion of reinforcements—your kind of marines?"

"That's good to know, sir. Have they undergone the treatment and the training?"

"Your people back at Andros gave them the injections. But they will get their training on the battlefield. This is the moment. We are shipping them down now. If you would order your craft to ferry them, we could get them there much faster."

I had a headache. The general had assumed I was dead. Apparently—I could read between the lines—the moment I'd been prematurely declared out of the picture he'd taken over ground operations. He'd given orders I'd never have agreed with. I had to wonder, right then, if the good general would have preferred I'd stayed dead.

"I'll tell you what I want to do, General. I want to pull off the continent and build up my forces. The Macros aren't making more factories—more domes. So each day we get stronger now, and they get relatively weaker. We don't have to rush in. We can build up another ten thousand troops and kill their domes decisively."

"I don't think we have to wait."

"You haven't faced the Macros personally, sir."

"No. And I won't take that away from you. But I'm going to land my regulars. Will you move to cover our landing?"

I looked out across the Falklands. I wasn't sure which island I stood on, the East or the West. The land was cold, beautiful, and very green. At my feet, lush grass grew nearly a foot high. Single dew drops clung to every blade.

Sheep wandered in rolling pastures only a mile off. As I recalled, sheep were about the only thing on these islands. It was odd to think a war had once been fought over this pretty scrap of land. I had to wonder, with the intrusion of aliens, if men would ever again fight silly little wars amongst themselves. I supposed they would.

"Riggs?" asked Kerr, cutting into my thoughts. "You there, Colonel?"

"I'm here, sir."

"You are about to turn me down, aren't you?"

"Yes, sir, I was considering it."

He heaved a sigh, as if ignorant fools plagued his every hour. Perhaps they did.

"All right. I'm going to tell you something. Something not generally known."

"I'm listening—and I'm wondering why I'm not on your intel short list."

"I don't make up the names on those lists, Colonel."

Liar, I thought.

"Anyway," he went on, "we've got some cause for moving now. We've spotted something, see. Something off in space."

I straightened and dumped my coffee. The dew drops clinging to the grasses at my feet turned brown. "What kind of *something,* sir?"

"Well, as you might have guessed, we've been working on our telescopes lately. With a feverish new intensity, actually. We've been checking out every corner of this solar system. These Macro ships have to be coming from somewhere. We don't think they are coming directly from another star, so they must have a base of some kind."

"You found such a base?"

219

"We don't know. We've found something. A satellite—something artificial. Something very large orbiting Venus."

I blinked at that. I looked at the skies, even though there was nothing up there to see but our own light blue atmosphere streaked with shreds of cloud. Off to the east my own ship hulked close to the ground. As I watched, a pickup truck pulled up near it and someone got out surreptitiously. They snapped pictures of the *Alamo* with their cell phone. No doubt they thought themselves very daring.

"Okay," I said. "Why is this discovery prompting a suicidal attack now, sir?"

"Because, Riggs, there are flashes going on there. Once or twice a week, there is a release of energy. And there are smaller contacts around it, we think. Growing in number. As they come in, they glide back behind Venus, where we can't see them."

My stomach turned to ice as I grasped what he was saying. "They are forming up a fleet?"

"We think so."

"A much bigger fleet."

"That stands to reason."

I thought about that. The implications were beyond grim. "Here's what I propose, General. I'll direct my bases on Andros to produce more ships. Perhaps we can defeat them in the skies again."

"Bases? You've got more than one?" he asked, clearly startled.

"It seems like a good day to put our cards on the table, General."

"Yes, of course. But, I mean—you can build more ships?"

"Yes, sir. Given time."

"But you've been building more small arms instead?"

"Yes, but I think that will have to stop."

"I agree. I see now I should have told you this earlier."

"Yes, sir," I agreed flatly. That was exactly the conclusion I had wanted him to make.

"Will you help us take out those last domes?" he asked. "As fast as possible?"

"Within—two days sir."

"Two days...I'm not sure we can get our troops down there that fast."

"I'll send transportation help, sir. Mass your men. Give me their tonnage with equipment. We'll airlift them down here starting now."

"You've given me new hope, Colonel."

"You've given me new fears, General."

He hesitated.

"What else do you want to tell me, sir?" I asked.

"We've got another surprise we've been working on. The cruise missile brigades were fairly ineffective, but we've got a new support unit for you."

"I'm glad to hear that, sir," I said. And I was.

"Well, you might not like them. But they should get the job done."

I frowned. I walked out toward my ship as we finished the conversation.

He was right. I didn't like his new units. I didn't like them at all.

-35-

It was a very tough two days, but I managed to pull together my battered marines. I had about ninety percent of my survivors back in the field and in respectable fighting shape. Most of that miracle was due to relentless rescue-ship forays to gather them from their scattered locations and the hardworking, thankless nanites who repaired their bodies. Men who were too far gone—mostly men with missing limbs—got to rest up back on the Falklands. The new recruits Kerr had so kindly created for me in my brief absence were spread around amongst the veteran units. The new men were green with their weapons and their new bodies. They tried to look tough, but they could tell by the quiet, haunted look in everyone else's eyes that they were in it deep.

The men in my new unit, in particular, seemed chastened. They were proud to serve with me, I could sense that. But they were also worried. Stories must have circulated about the casualty rate in my previous command, which had been higher than any other battlegroup. I had to wonder if I had any flashy nicknames yet. I had heard a few muttered words in this vein. One was *The Blender*, which I found distasteful. I was sure about my unit name, however. We'd gotten the moniker of *Riggs' Pigs*. I supposed it was the best I could expect.

This time, instead of splitting up my forces, I massed them under a single banner. I decided to use my ships for anti-missile cover this time. Crow thought I was mad, but I feared that my new strategy could be undone by a single enemy nuclear missile. We knew they had them—or at least they had used them from the ship when they had first invaded. Perhaps the invasion group didn't have the power to build new nukes, but I didn't want to assume such a thing. Maybe the only reason they

222

hadn't nuked us earlier was because we had been so scattered. Or maybe they hadn't built a stockpile at that point. Another possibility was they hadn't counted us as a serious threat until we began taking out domes, and by then we were in too close to use such drastic measures without destroying themselves.

This time we would be openly advancing on them in a large formation. I didn't want to learn about a new stockpile of warheads first hand as soon as we made our move. So I used ten ships, clustered toward our rear. They weren't to engage with the ground forces. In fact, to prevent losing them, they had orders to pull back if the big Macros charged us. But if a missile barrage came our way, they were to take it out. This was crucial not just to prevent a nuclear strike, but also to protect my regular compliment of troops. Normal men couldn't take a body full of shrapnel and recover in a few days.

We advanced with half my marines in the vanguard. If the Macros charged in at us, they would have to pass over the infantry and be damaged. The rest of my marines, including myself, were intermixed with the regulars in the core of the formation. The regulars looked more nervous than anyone. They had good reason to be. Kerr had issued them shoulder-mounted rocket launchers rather than rifles. Bullets were useless against Macros of any size and regular men were too weak to carry effective lasers. The rocket launchers would only be useful against the worker machines we'd faced—not the big ones. When it came right down to it, I doubted these rockets could do much in combat, but we could hardly send the men in unarmed.

The most important element of our new forces consisted of armor units. They were an even number of American M-1 Tanks and Russian 2S19 "Mstas," which were essentially self-propelled artillery units. The Mstas looked like tanks with extremely large cannons. They could lob a shell nearly twenty miles. It was their very large guns that had nominated these weapons platforms for this special duty. I wasn't sure why they sent us Russian howitzers instead of American units, but I figured it was probably political. Or maybe the American units had been knocked out fighting earlier battles. In any case, they formed the center of my new strategy.

We marched with what seemed like grim slowness. My own men bounded along at a slouching trot—perhaps ten miles per hour. Around us flowed the heavy machinery. We had to maintain a slow speed to keep the formation moving together without stragglers. We circled the forests and stuck to the plains. We avoided rivers and rocky areas. The going was steady, but seemed agonizingly slow. At any moment, we expected some form of attack. But for hours, none came.

The regular troops—poor bastards—rode in their personnel carriers with rocket launchers in their laps. I could only imagine the fear pounding in their hearts. It was one thing to be asked to die against another force of men. It was quite another to be a "softie," facing death by laser and steel pincher, with no hope of surrendering to the merciless robot enemy.

We had not halted our advance during the night. I wanted to get to the shores of the Salado River, south of Buenos Aries. In the morning, we would cross at the river. We'd honestly begun to relax, fractionally. It seemed clear the enemy wasn't going to hit us, at least not until we traveled another fifty miles south and drew close to one of their precious domes.

We were wrong. They hit us when we nosed downward into the river valley. It wasn't a sharp dip in the land, but it was enough to limit our visibility and our line of sight against approaching targets.

The Macros came at us after nightfall. They'd learned a few things, I think. We couldn't wear night vision gear in battle, not with the lasers we carried. Hence, our ancient weakness of poor eyesight haunted us. The enemy had no such qualms. They did not fear the dark, and with infrared sensors, they could see as well in the night as in the day. Our lasers didn't seem to burn out their sensors, either.

Enemy contacts, the *Alamo* whispered into my brain. I had programmed her to do so, and I was very glad I did. She had seen the Macros before anyone else.

I opened the command channel and hailed all my unit commanders. "Enemy approaching. Halt the advance. Prepare everything we have to fire."

How many? I asked my ship.

Sixty-four major contacts. Five hundred twelve minor ones.

I didn't have time to ponder the significance of the binary numbers of enemy. We were about to be overrun.

Range? I asked my ship.

Six miles for the larger enemy. Zero for the smaller ones.

I almost blinked, but my eyes didn't close, they widened. "Forward units, pull back! Defend the vehicles. We have diggers. They are under us. Repeat, we have diggers. Everyone watch your feet!"

Almost as soon as I said the words, the first screams and flashes of light began. Hundreds of machines bubbled up under us. Men who'd never seen a Macro before died with startling speed.

I decided to forget about the diggers. They were mostly a distraction. My men could take care of them. But the big boys were coming in a rush and in numbers I'd never seen. I was worried they were already too close to spring our big Russian surprise on them.

Alamo, pull back unless missiles—

Missiles incoming. ETA thirty seconds.

Another carefully timed strike from multiple angles. These machines loved to hit us all at once from every side. *Okay,* I told my ship, *take out the missiles, then pull back out of range of the Macro anti-air fire.*

Huge beams of energy stabbed out. Distant objects flared in the skies like fireworks. I heard roars and snapping explosions. Some of the barrage was getting through.

"Artillery commander!"

"Yes, sir," said a man with a Russian accent.

"As soon as you get a confirmed radar trace on a Macro, lay one of your special rounds on it. Fire a barrage of regular shells along with it for cover."

"Cover? They can't shoot down a shell, Colonel."

"Obey the command."

"Yes, sir," said the Russian. He sounded a bit huffy. I barely had time to mutter a curse before the Mstas roared in unison. The sound was extremely loud. The flashes were almost as bright as laser fire.

"Everyone who can, duck!" I roared, broadcasting over the general com channel.

An incredible flash went off ahead of us, to the south. The shockwave rocked the command vehicle I was in. A small tactical nuclear charge had gone off. I smiled. They hadn't shot it down. Our hail of shells had been seeded with one atomic weapon. The Msta was an old, Cold War weapon. It had been built to fire nuclear shells back in the last century. Now, for the first time in history, it had performed its appointed task with devastating effect. My men gaped at this surprise for a few seconds, then worked quickly to button up their suits. Fallout was unavoidable at this range.

The charging line of sixty-four Macros never got to us. I'm not sure if they were all destroyed, or if the survivors had retreated. In any case, after mopping up the diggers and suffering relatively light casualties, we had won the battle. I couldn't help but feel proud. The Macros were in a real fight now, a fight for survival. Unfortunately, our element of surprise was gone.

-36-

We reached the first dome in the morning. When scouts crested the crater around it, we were surprised to find no resistance. We approached it with all due paranoia anyway. I ordered my artillery to take out the missile battery that sat on top of it first. It began spraying missiles at us, but my ships shot them down. We fired shells at the battery until it disintegrated.

The place looked abandoned. I briefly toyed with the idea of attempting to capture the dome—or rather, the factory inside. But I thought the better of it. These machines had to be destroyed. We had no time to mess around. I ordered six companies of men to approach the dome from every angle. I sent in the companies with the most new recruits. What better time was there to learn about our enemy? I suspected the machines had pulled out of here because it was an indefensible position. If this was a dry run—if the enemy had decided to pull out and give us this one—then I figured I might as well get some training value out of it. I ordered the majority of my forces to withdraw beyond the crater rim. We would keep a sharp lookout for a surprise attack from an unexpected direction.

When the attack came, it was indeed a surprise. I think it was my withdrawal of forces that triggered it. Reviewing the transmitted video files later, it didn't seem the boys I'd sent to their deaths had caused the Macros to make their move. My green troops hadn't even made it half-way across the crater floor when things went bad.

First, the dome disappeared. It flickered, then fuzzed, and at last faded away to nothing. Inside the dome was the great machine we'd come to destroy, with several dozen smaller worker machines crawling over it. These workers were a new variety. Each of them had a delicate set of specialized instruments mounted on the front of their chassis. The glittering tools were finely-made—thin, silvery things that flickered and twisted in a blur of motion. At a distance, they resembled lawn-mower blades, or threshing machines. But I've since come to the conclusion these were fast-moving mandibles made of bright metal. We had spotted a new kind of machine I believe, their equivalent of a technician. Unfortunately, it was to be a very brief glimpse.

Seconds after the dome fizzled, everything else vanished, too. There was a tremendous white flash, like the birth of a new sun. The technician machines vanished. The great factory they had crawled upon like metallic maggots vaporized. Even the hard stony surface it sat upon, which had served to project the defensive dome, could not be found afterward. Needless to say, my six companies of green troops disappeared, too. A huge, roiling cloud rolled up into the sky after the thunderclap. It formed the telltale mushroom shape and stood thousands of feet tall. My main force was far enough away to survive. I think what helped was the crater rim itself. It served to direct the energy of the great blast upward, like a volcano erupting violently.

After we'd pulled ourselves together and our nanites had healed our scorched skins, we headed toward the second of the last three domes. The regulars that had accompanied us had lost all trace of bravado. Fully a third of them had been blinded or burned so badly they were incapacitated. I flew those survivors out by Nano ship.

The machines let us approach the next dome unmolested. I sent scouts, looking for nuclear mines and the like. The enemy had shown the capacity to learn and surprise us. They also weren't above using nukes. Perhaps they had shifted their construction efforts to producing them in quantity.

Three days later my cautious force was in sight of the dome. This one stood quietly, as had the last. It shimmered and gleamed, reflecting sunlight and shining with a seemingly sourceless inner power. My artillery commander contacted me as we halted to survey the scene.

"Sir? Request permission to begin ranged bombardment."

"We're too far out," I told him. I raised binoculars to my eyes and swept the field, looking for any sign of the Macros. There was nothing to see. The *Alamo* had reported no traceable movement, either. The black ovoid ship hung above my army protectively, hovering like a guardian angel.

228

"Let me try, sir. If this is another trap, then they will have to show themselves. They can't shoot down my shells if they hide underground."

I considered the suggestion, and found it reasonable. We still had thirty nuclear-tipped shells in stock. We could afford to use a few on the dome. If nothing else, we could study the effects.

"Very well, fire at will. But only use one special shell in the barrage."

"Yes, sir."

Within a minute, klaxons wailed. Men all around me hurried for cover. They knew we were far enough out to avoid a burn, and our goggles should save our eyes. But after having seen too many mushroom clouds lately, they'd become cautious.

The first salvo arced into the sky. Too high, I was thinking. But the enemy did not come to life and cut them down. The salvo rained down upon the dome and tiny, popping spots appeared all over it, causing it to shimmer and shift color. Another heartbeat passed, and I wondered if the final shell, the special one, hadn't gone off.

Then the flash came. A rolling boom of thunder shook the landscape. The mushroom cloud was relatively small, but it was big enough. When the livid flaming light had died down sufficiently, I searched the area of impact with my binoculars, anxious to see the effects.

The dome still functioned. I was impressed, and raised my eyebrows. You had to give these aliens their due. They could take a beating.

I noticed, however, that the dome had changed in character. It now flickered and flared. It was a burnt orange in color. I lowered my binoculars and contacted the artillery commander.

"Fire again. Two more nukes this time."

"We can't fire two, sir—the first will cannibalize the second."

"What?"

"Only one will go off because the one that hits first will destroy the other as it comes in."

"Then lead with one, and fire the second right in there at the end of the salvo."

There was a moment of hesitation. I could hear the commander speaking in Russian to his men. "I think we can manage that, Colonel."

229

"Well then do it!" I shouted. "The damned dome is turning white again. And be ready with a third round in case the first two don't quite do the trick."

"Sir, do we really want to unleash that many—"

"Yes, damn you, we do. Now fire. That's an order."

"Yes, sir," said the artillery commander. He didn't sound upset. I suspected he'd been yelled at by his superior officers before.

The second bomb had the same effect the first one had. But the third one did the trick. There was no need for a fourth. I had been ready to fire up to half my supply of weapons to finish that dome from a distance. I had no doubt the Macros had prepared something down there for us, something particularly nasty. But we never got the chance to find out what it was.

I lowered my binoculars and smiled at the flaming, smoky hole we'd dug into the farmland. This region might still be blasted a century from now, but at least the machines wouldn't be ruling it.

After our success on two of the three domes, our army rejoiced. There was a lot of unreleased tension bubbling in my men. They'd expected a grim, horrid surprise. In the end, when the second dome fell more easily than the first had, they were jubilant. I ordered a case of champagne to be sent to the Russian officer's encampment. They sent back an invitation to join them.

I'd only met the Russian commander at briefings. I recalled his first name was Dmitri. This entire campaign had swept us up and given us no time for pleasantries. We'd had only days to prepare on the Falklands, and I didn't really know most of the men I was marching with. Perhaps, I thought, I should get to know them. We could take the time now before pressing onward to assault the third and final dome.

Thoughtful, I walked across the crunching gravel of an old roadway. Evening fell over the land, and the stars began popping out in the skies. The lurid red glare of residual fires turned the sky a hazy orange. It would have been pretty, if I hadn't known the light came from a million burning trees in the distance.

I considered apologizing for my harsh attitude when I met Dmitri, but then decided against it. I would be friendly, but not apologetic. My decisions, so far, had usually been the right ones.

I never made it to the Russian officer's camp, however. It was the *Alamo* that stopped me, dead in my tracks.

Incoming contacts.

I turned on one heel and ran back toward my headquarters unit. I didn't have my rifle or reactor with me. I'd let my guard down. We all had. I would have cursed, but I didn't have time. I sped up, running with inhuman speed. But it wasn't fast enough.

How many contacts? I asked my ship.

Over five hundred... six hundred. More every second.

Shit, I thought to the *Alamo* reflexively. Naturally, the ship didn't respond. There was no need to.

-37-

First Sergeant Kwon met me at the door to my mobile headquarters unit, which amounted to little more than a fancy trailer with a lot of parabolic dishes on the roof.

"What's wrong, sir?"

I pushed past him. "Sound a general alarm."

Kwon obeyed wordlessly.

I laid both hands on the com system and keyed into the command channel. I relayed to all my commanders that a major attack was incoming. I hoped I didn't sound as nervous as I felt. All along, we had expected a large Macro counterattack. But they'd done practically nothing since their first failed charge. They'd let us take down two domes. Perhaps they'd been waiting for this moment.

How long before they reach us? I asked my ship.

Two minutes.

I blinked. How had they gotten so close? *From what direction?*

From every direction, replied the ship with aggravating calm. *We are encircled. The circle is closing rapidly.*

"This is it, men," I shouted, thumbing my com system to the general channel so it hit every helmet in the camp. "The Macros are making their big counterattack. They are throwing everything they have at us. Prepare to fight in close quarters. Don't bother to reunite with your units. Seek cover. Engage and destroy any enemy on sight."

This time, there would be no nuking of the enemy at a safe distance. I'd always known that if they got in close to us, in sufficient numbers, we would be in trouble. It looked like this was that dreaded moment.

Alamo, why didn't you detect them further out? I demanded. I felt betrayed by my own ship.

They appear not to be operating their shields.

What? You mean you can only detect them with their shields on?

The electromagnetic emanations from operating shield systems transmit an easily identifiable signal.

So, they are coming in silent and dark? They have no shields? I liked the sound of that. They would be much easier to destroy. Weapons systems like our tanks could do real damage with conventional shells.

Electromagnetic emanations are spiking. Readings indicate enemy shields are coming up now.

"Fire at anything you can see, *now!*" I roared over the broadcast channel. Every troop with a headset on heard my order. For a few seconds, nothing happened. Then sporadic fire erupted. This quickly grew into a storm. The quiet night outside transformed into a din of explosions and stabbing beams of light. I suspected many of the troops were firing at shadows, but I figured it was worth it. If we could damage the Macros before they were on us, before their shields were up—maybe we had a chance.

Kwon and I helped each other strap on gear. We'd become lax, I chided myself. We'd trusted to our sensory systems. I, in particular, had been lulled by our victories.

"Dammit," I growled.

Kwon kept adjusting straps and tugging at zippers without comment. We put our hoods on last.

Before we could get out of the command trailer, however, someone kicked it over. At least, that's what it felt like. The floor heaved up and became the wall, then the ceiling, and then the wall again. I was falling around in a quick, sliding cycle. I crashed into furniture and fixtures and was dumped helplessly onto a pile of bodies. I felt the weight of my reactor unit crushing bones beneath me. Staffers around me gasped in shock. We rolled three and a half revolutions downhill, and by the time we stopped rolling everything in the trailer was broken and dark.

Most of the command staff were regulars. They had no nanites to harden their bodies or repair them after injury. All but one looked dead by the time we stopped rolling. Men and women with broken necks and soft, impaled bodies were strewn amongst the overturned furniture. I wanted to check them all for signs of life, but there simply wasn't time.

233

We had been overrun by the Macros and I had to get into the fight. Kwon kicked out a window and I fell out of the trailer after him.

A Macro—one of the big ones—stood over us. It was working its sixteen flashing belly-turrets, belching out gouts of energy a thousand times a second. We answered the fire with our two rifles. It took the turrets a second to seek and lock on us, and we burned those that tried before they could fire.

You could get into a rhythm with the machines, if you were good. The trick was to notice which turrets were seeking new targets. If they weren't firing, that meant they were dangerous, because they might lock onto you next. Inside their tiny, independent minds, when they sought new targets, they always followed the same pattern. First they swiveled this way and that, sweeping the area. When they locked on something, they would splatter down fire until the target was classified as destroyed. Then they went back into seek mode again. If you put your beam on a seeking turret before it locked onto you, you could destroy it before it had time to lock and fire back. Then others would come and seek you, and you had to spot them and destroy them before they locked on. My system wasn't perfect, however. If two or more turrets locked on you at once, you were toast.

By the time Kwon and I got into the fight, many of the men in the area were just that—toast. They had been burned down to ash. The regulars did their valiant best. They fired their pathetic one-shot rockets up at the monster overhead. But in their panic, nine times out of ten they missed. Even if they didn't miss, there were plenty more seeking turrets up there, swiveling in sudden jerks like darting, reptilian creatures. With terrifying speed, they locked on each new target and burned it down.

The dying troops gave their lives for a useful purpose. They gave the turrets something to do while Kwon and I methodically popped them all. Then we took down a leg, concentrating our fire. The thing got smart, right at the end, and singled us out. It tried to stomp us down. We dove and dodged and kept on beaming the second joint up on the offending leg. We stayed low, crouched or on our knees, so we could dance away from the next flailing limb the Macro threw in our direction.

When we had almost brought it down, I looked up and realized that if it had the brains to simply collapse and fall on us, it would kill at least two soldiers. But that line of code didn't seem to be in its programming. Instead, it fought on grimly to the bitter end. Kwon did the honors, boring into its CPU and burning out the circuitry.

All around us hundreds of similar battles raged. Some of the machines arrived late, limping in. I figured from the look of them they had been hit by shells and their rush had been slowed. Smaller worker-types were intermixed with the big ones, outnumbering them two to one. Every variety of worker was represented. Some had weapons mounted, the harvesters used their claws, diggers came up under us with deadly drills spinning. There were even a few of the technician types with their delicate, flashing tools.

They all died, and we died with them. In the end, however, we had more troops and better tactics. It was as simple as that. We didn't win because we pulled a trick of our own—not this time. We won with superior numbers. All the fighting and the loss of their factories had sapped the enemy's strength. They had been unable to replace their losses. In desperation they had mounted this final, all-out assault. It was do or die for them, and this time they were the ones doing the dying. Like a man who fights to the death with an opponent who has thirty more pounds of muscle, bravado only went so far. They were taken down and slain, one by one.

By morning, there were no more moving machines. We had lost nearly a third of our number as well. I pulled my forces together and we counted noses. We'd lost thousands, right there in the fields of some long-dead rancher. There was hardly a blade of grass or even a chunk of earth that wasn't smoldering, but we held a memorial service and did our best to bury our dead.

It was about ten a. m. when the sky lit up one final time. It took us some minutes to verify it, but I suspected the truth from the moment that it happened. The enemy had blown up their last dome on Earth.

Why did they do it? Maybe they were sophisticated enough to have some form of pride or shame. Maybe they didn't want to take any chances with their technology, and once they had clearly lost, their programming told them to self-destruct. I really didn't know, and it didn't matter much. What mattered was that the invasion was over. They had thrown everything they had at us in a last ditch attack and failed. The Macros had been defeated.

I sat down on a crusty spot of ground that had been melted into glass by laser fire. I stared out toward the distant, expanding mushroom cloud as it rolled skyward, just as so many others had on this ravaged corner of my planet. I hoped the enemy never managed to get past our defenses and land another invasion force on our world. If they did, I feverishly hoped they wouldn't manage to get more ships through, the next time they came at us.

-38-

Everything was quiet for a few days. I went back to Andros riding in my ship. I picked up Sandra when I got there and we quickly became reacquainted. Afterward, I had the *Alamo* fly us to a remote spot on the western shores of the island. I sat on a beach with Sandra. The sunset was the color of blood and the jungle was dark and dank behind us. Every night now, the skies turned red. They told me it was because of all the dust in the atmosphere. So far, none of our Geiger counters had gone off, so we were still able to walk the beaches of this wild island in light, tropical clothing.

Sandra was at her best on a beach, I decided. She was lovely and more deeply tanned than when I'd first met her. A natural hazard of living down here, I suspected. I liked the look.

"What are you thinking?" she asked.

"Nothing," I said.

"Liar," she teased. "You were staring at me."

"I'm thinking of how nice you look out here, in this lonely spot."

"Oh," she said. She seemed happy and leaned back against me. "Did you meet anyone else while you were down there?"

I snorted. "I met about a thousand angry robots."

"No other girls?"

"You've got to be kidding me. You realize we were wrapped up in full gear, don't you? We were even wearing hoods. I didn't even know which ones were women."

"Yeah, I'm sorry," she said. She touched my face apologetically. "But sometimes the other girls in the fleet talk. I don't like the idea of you flying off to some hellish spot, either. Someday you might not come back."

"If I don't, there might not be anything to come back to."

"I know," she said, sighing. "I suppose I'll have to love you twice as hard when you're here."

"Not anymore," I said. "It's pretty much over."

She looked at me and twisted her lips in disgust. "Don't even try to lie to me. They'll come back. Any day now."

I stopped talking. There wasn't any point to it. Neither one of us was buying my line of happy chatter. We'd won a battle, but everyone knew we hadn't won the war. I started kissing her instead. It was much more enjoyable.

I spent the next month reconfiguring my little factories. I had a new project now: I wanted them to make bigger versions of themselves. The Macro fabrication units in their white domes had given me the idea. They had been able to make duplicate lasers that were smaller than the originals. Why not make factories that were bigger than themselves? If we could use these larger units to produce bigger ships with bigger weapons, maybe we could do a better job of destroying the Macros before they managed to land again. We didn't know for sure they were coming back, but we had to assume they were.

The world kept sending me new recruits from their elite forces. We kept swearing them in, filling them with nanites, and training them. I figured we should have a standing force of thirty thousand men at the ready. We were doing all right in the ship department now, too. We had about seven hundred ships. We'd even managed to capture a few of the centaur people alive. That happened by chance, not design. Sometimes the ships hovered low, only a dozen feet off the ground. On those occasions when the centaurs lost a fight—but were only knocked out and not actually killed—they might live after their ship rudely dumped them out.

The UN people had gathered them, I'd heard from Admiral Crow. They had a colony of centaurs—about thirty in all—hidden away in some lab in Europe. I didn't ask questions, but I hoped they would treat them well. Crow said they were trying to nurse them back to health and learn how to communicate with them. They were a vicious species, it seemed, but so were we. We had hopes of getting information about the universe from them in the future.

238

Crow and I had a number of power negotiations between us. As usual, I was less interested in titles than I was in results. After the South American campaign, however, most of the world considered me to be the leader of Star Force. Crow worked to get his name out and did a hundred live interviews, but I was still the hero in the headlines. I think it bothered him more than he let on.

Officially, we agreed to separate our commands. He ran the fleet and was nominally in charge of Star Force. I was a high ranking marine officer, which suited me well.

Then he called me one night with startling news.

"We'll be having a staff meeting later tonight, Riggs," Crow told me. "It's all online, so you don't have to travel, but put on your dress uniform, will you?"

"Dress uniform?"

"You've got one. If you don't know where it is, ask your aides."

"All right. Who is attending the meeting?"

"My general staff. Of which you are a member, naturally."

General staff? I frowned. "Who is on the guest list?"

He named a list of captains. He had several of them in the fleet now. And then he listed three generals.

"General who?" I asked, not recognizing the names.

"Marine people. Real Marine people. They are mostly Yanks, you should be happy about that."

"I'm not quite sure—" I began, a little confused.

"Look, Riggs. I love you, man. You are the best of the best. As a field commander, there's no one I'd rather have out there. But this is an expanding organization. I have to have managers. People who know how to handle *people*. You are a fighter. You are a front-line type. I've been recruiting staffers, and I've selected three to run our Marine Corps."

I was silent for probably five seconds while all this sank in. "Do I have to salute them?"

"It wouldn't kill you."

My initial reaction, naturally, was rage. Here was Crow, up to his old tricks. He was always tossing ranks around. Now, he felt threatened by me and had to trump up some new officers to run the organization I'd invented. I even thought, briefly, of overthrowing Crow. I figured I could probably do it. All I had to do was tell the fleet and the marines—*my* marines—that we'd had a falling out and they needed to back one of us. They would come to me, most of them, I felt sure.

I took in two deep breaths. My second reaction came in the form of a shrug. In a way, I didn't care. I had Sandra. I had this base on Andros. When enemies came, I would fight them. I hadn't gotten into this to have a turf war with Crow. I wasn't that ambitious. I had gotten into this to kill alien machines. I had been successful in that regard.

"All I want to do is kill machines, Crow," I said.

"I know that."

"If you don't want to have a problem with me, then don't ever try to take that away from me."

He was silent for a few seconds. I think the implicit threat in my words was sinking in. Maybe it made him angry. But he didn't let on. When he spoke again, his voice was calm.

"Right. Well—right then. I hear you, mate. We've been through a lot together. I owe you everything. Hell, the world owes you everything. If you want to fight, then you'll fight."

"Okay then. I'll log in tonight and attend your staff meeting. And I'll have clothes on."

"Thanks, Kyle," he said and signed off.

Sandra came in and asked what the conversation had been all about. When she heard Crow had promoted officers over me—without even consulting me—she was furious. I think she was madder than I was. It took the better part of an hour to calm her down. Once she'd cooled to a simmer, she busied herself with getting a dress uniform for me from the staff down at Andros. I had been right, I didn't even own one. I hadn't even known we had dress uniforms until now.

Crow was right about one thing: the meeting was boring. There was little in it about combat strategies. Instead, they talked about supplies and splitting accounts from our various funding sources. They discussed shipping schedules and a thousand other logistical details. We had support now from the world at large. For the most part, the nations of Earth had dug up billions and marked it down as a percentage of their defense budgets. A hundred nations donated what they could. But a conspicuous few footed the vast majority of the bill.

One interesting topic was the discussion of what our oath of allegiance should say. Up until now, we had only required men to swear to follow orders and give their lives in the defense of Earth. The staffers were in favor of requiring new troops to renounce their citizenship. They would be, in essence, our citizens. A separate nation. I didn't like that sort of talk. I didn't want to tell men they could never go home again.

"I've got an alternative," I said, jumping into the conversation for the first time.

The group fell quiet, realizing who I was. I must have impressed them somehow along the way. On my big computer screen, they all looked as if a pit bull had entered the room and begun snarling, even though my tone was level. I wondered, right then, how many of these new generals had undertaken the injections. I suspected none of them had. That seemed wrong to me, but I decided to let it go—for now.

"I don't want to tell a man that if he fights for us he can never go back home again. Let them swear allegiance to Star Force for the term of their enlistment. But don't require them to renounce anything. Leave it up to my officers to form them into a single, cohesive force."

Crow cleared his throat. I looked at him through narrowed eyes. He was a white-haired fellow with piercing blue eyes and a lot of broken capillaries around his hawk-nose. Today, his red face looked more red than usual. "Look, Colonel, we've discussed this at length. We've come to the conclusion that—"

"This is the first I've heard of it," I said.

"Right, well... you've been in the thick of it, Kyle. There wasn't always time to discuss every plan with you."

"Okay. I can accept that. But I'm telling you I don't want your morale-damaging idea. Let them fight for Bolivia or Japan, or wherever they are from."

One of the staffers leaned forward to say something. His name was General Sokolov. He was a stout man with thick black eyebrows that needed trimming. His black eyes were small, narrow—and annoyed. "Colonel Riggs. With all due respect, you are very new to running an army. Men who swear allegiance to this organization—only this organization, will tend to be more loyal and dependable."

"I understand your reasoning, General, but it's wrong. We aren't like a normal force. We have been changed. We marines become freaks after we go through the injections. We feel a brotherhood afterward, an effect few armies have ever achieved. The nature of the war is unlike any other as well. Consider sir, that we aren't fighting against men. We face armies of alien robots out to destroy our world."

"With all due respect—" droned the black-eyed general again. I could tell he hadn't heard a word and couldn't care less what I thought.

"Hold on," said Crow. "We'll do it your way, Colonel Riggs. You know our troops better than anyone. The pledge stays as it is."

"Thank you, sir."

The staffers looked annoyed, but dropped it. The meeting went on and became terminally dull before it finally, blissfully, ended.

Peace went on until I began to think it was permanent. Every morning as I ate breakfast, I thought of the Macros out there behind Venus with butterflies in my stomach. Were they still there? Were they building something to destroy our world forever?

But a man can only worry for so long. It was on the very first day I'd forgotten to think of them at breakfast that they came back. It was as if they had waited until that weak moment.

It had been a fine week. Sandra and I were talking seriously. We might even get married. Something about that had lifted the cloud that had dampened my life and heart since the kids had died. Perhaps, I thought, there was still time to grab something good from life before it was over—before it ended one way or another.

Then the message came. It came in the form of a long black arm. It popped the bay window of our modular home, which I'd set up on Mangrove Cay some miles to the south of the big base on Andros itself. Some of the other Marine officers lived in the area. It was a pleasant, secluded place. We had a nice hill and an even nicer view of the Caribbean. Geckos came out in droves to hug the banana trees on warm, sunny days. There are a lot of warm, sunny days in the Caribbean, and today was no exception.

The arm, however, was unusual. I jumped up and my first instinct was to avoid those three, thick, cable-like fingers.

Alamo? Is that you?

I am Alamo.

Are you reaching in my window for me?

Yes.

So, I let the ship take me. The glass scratched a line down my back, but I knew the nanites would fix the cut quickly.

Why are you picking me up, Alamo?

You are command personnel.

Are there ships attacking Earth?

Yes.

That was all I needed to know. I had known it, really, the moment the arm had shown up. The ship had not been set to give me a verbal warning. But in its inner programming it clearly knew it needed its captain before it launched itself up with suicidal eagerness to face the enemy.

I thought of Sandra as I sailed into the sky and was swallowed by my ship. I hadn't kissed her good-bye. I knew, without asking, that my ship wouldn't let me take the time to go back and kiss her. We'd made love that morning, and it had been perfect. I thought that perhaps this was the best way to leave her. If I was never to return, her last memory of me could be one of peace and happiness. Wasn't that better than a tearful good-bye?

I scrambled to my command chair. Things were much more organized aboard the *Alamo* these days. I had chairs that didn't roll around the place. There were straps and harnesses that didn't have fingers on them. There was a range of proper communications and visual equipment, too. We'd melded our own technology with that of the Nanos as effectively as we could. Large flat screens were attached to the walls in spots, showing the world outside and whatever the military networks saw fit to send me. We still used the metallic bumps on the walls, as they couldn't break, and the Nanos had better range with their sensory equipment than we did. We still didn't quite understand how they did that, but we were more than happy to make use of the capability.

"Open channel to the *Snapper.*"

Channel open.

"Crow?"

"Kyle? What do you know about this?"

"I was hoping you knew something, sir."

"No. The regular military didn't give us any warning. All of our ships just launched themselves. We are heading out toward the Sun, though. I know that much."

Sunward, I thought. One of the few directions in space that meant anything. "Toward Venus, in other words? So the Macros are finally making their move?"

"Looks that way."

"Ship count?"

"We total just under eight hundred strong now, including the new ones you built on Andros."

I'd spent some time building a handful of new ships. They weren't really the direction I wanted to go, however. If only we had been allowed the time, we could have built truly huge fabrication units and thus bigger weapons systems. We certainly didn't need more of these small science vessels. We needed a ship meant for war. One that bristled with weaponry. But that would take years.

"If you don't have anything special for me," said Crow, "I'm out."

"I've got something."

"Talk to me."

"We can try to order our ships to maintain a set distance from the enemy. Rather than wading right in, I mean."

"What the hell for?" he asked.

"There will be a lot of them this time. We need everyone massed up into a single swarm to fight together."

"Or to die together. Never mind that, sorry. Good idea."

"Admiral? Good luck, Jack."

"You too, Kyle."

He broke the connection. Our ships lifted us up, out of the atmosphere. Soon, I was pressed back in my seat only by the mild G-forces of acceleration, not by Earth's gravity. I looked around the bridge. I missed Sandra. Maybe I should have tried to grab her out of the shower. I smiled at the idea of her, naked and angry, being dragged up to the ship. It would have been like old times.

We ordered our ships to approach the enemy, but stay at a defined maximum weapons distance from them. The ships had allowed this order. They wouldn't allow us to run from the enemy, but they would let us stand in formation if properly coerced.

Then the enemy appeared on my walls, and I lost all hope. There were hundreds of them. Maybe even a thousand. I didn't bother to ask the *Alamo* for an exact count. It didn't matter.

I took a deep breath and looked at their approaching formation with my hand squeezing the back of my own neck. What could we do? Attack one flank? Take a few with us, out of spite?

They came on slowly in two ranks. The first rank was of ships I'd never seen before. They seemed triangular in shape. They were smaller than the big Macro ships we'd seen before, but larger than our ships. I figured they were cruisers of some kind. Ship-to-ship killers. Something like the ships I had wanted to build, if I had been allowed the time to do so. The second rank was made up of the big, fat, slow ships like the one that had dropped invaders on our world months ago. There were about twenty of these.

I understood better now, looking at them. During the first attacks they had sent only invasion ships. When we had destroyed the first ship, they had sent three more. We had managed to destroy two of those and the third had gotten through to drop its deadly payload of self-replicating machines on Earth. When we repelled the invasion, they had changed their tactics.

This time we faced their true battle fleet. This time, we were seeing the strength the Macros had never shown us before. At least, I thought grimly, it was clear that we'd gained their respect, if not their mercy.

It was going to be a matter of selling our lives dearly. We could not hope to win. The best we could do for humanity was spit in this enemy's eye. We would bite and kick as they gunned us down. I could only hope the Macros were capable of feeling pain at a loss.

Crow hailed me again. "Any bright ideas, mate?"

"Stand off. Try to talk to them. When they come in, let's ignore the combat ships up front and try to take out the invasion fleet. If we can do it, maybe humanity will live another year."

"As good a plan as any," said Crow, signing off to make the fleet-wide announcements. His voice was grim. He knew the score as well as I did. Probably everyone did.

Our ships floated up to form a ragged line some thousands of miles from the enemy ships. The others approached. I knew that communications crews were transmitting to them, trying to talk.

The enemy rolled nearer. They were inside the orbit of the Moon now. Then they were about a hundred thousand miles from Earth—very close. We would have to engage them soon. Our ships wouldn't let us run from this fight.

Just as we were about to charge past them and go for the invasion ships, the enemy line halted. I blinked at the wall, not quite sure if I was seeing correctly.

"Alamo? Did the enemy halt?"

"Enemy velocity reduced. Their relative distance is being maintained."

"Are they within range of our weapons?"

"No."

I chewed on my thumb. "What are they doing?"

"They are transmitting a message," said the ship.

"They are? Put it on audio!"

A continuous screeching sound came from the walls. I listened to it carefully. It didn't sound like any language I knew. "Alamo, translate the message."

"Unknown meaning. No frame of reference provided."

I thought about it. I knew that Crow and his communications team were no doubt poring over the meaning of this right now and transmitting their own answers in every way they could come up with. But would any of them know what they were doing?

"Alamo, can you analyze this language? Can you figure out the meaning of it?"

"Unknown meaning. No frame of reference provided."

"Try ASCII. Is it ASCII? Or Unicode?"

"No match."

"Try all known human computer languages."

"No match."

I went back to chewing my thumb. After an hour or so, it started getting sore. I'd contacted Crow a few times, and he said he had a team working on it, talking to the Earth teams on the ground. They were trying to puzzle out the meaning. The Macro fleet sat out there, patiently repeating the message all this time. I had to wonder: how long would it be before they timed out on us and began shooting?

"Alamo, record a portion of this transmission. Wait, hold on. Record one second of what they sent to us and send it back to them."

"Done."

The sound of the enemy transmission stopped a few seconds later. It had gone on for so long, the sudden silence was shocking.

"Alamo," I said, trying not to panic, "continue playing their transmission."

247

"Enemy transmissions have ceased."

"Oh shit."

"Admiral Crow requests a private channel."

"Open it."

"Kyle? They stopped talking. What do you make of it?"

I hesitated. "I'm not sure...but I did send them back part of what they were sending."

"You did *what*? When?"

"Just before they broke off."

A stream of harsh language erupted from the air around me. Crow's accent grew so strong, I wasn't able to make out many of the words. But I felt certain they were uncomplimentary.

"Why couldn't you just keep out of it? I've got a team of techs on this, Riggs."

Enemy ship approaching.

"Ah...Crow, something is happening," I said. I watched as a single contact broke off from the enemy fleet and slowly approached our swarm.

"Alamo, do not fire on that ship," I said. "Crow, relay that to everyone. Don't fire. We don't want to start this."

"What if it's some kind of super-bomb or something?"

"If this comes down to a fight, we are screwed anyway. This might be a diplomatic effort on their part. I think they are trying to communicate. Let's not start what we can't finish."

Crow snorted. "They are probably demanding our surrender."

I had to admit, that did seem likely. But what kind of terms could they possibly offer? They wouldn't bother asking for surrender if all they wanted was to wipe us out. "Just hold on. Let's see what they're doing."

Crow gave orders to every ship in the fleet to stand and hold. A few drifted forward, as their pilots were doubtlessly struggling to get the correctly worded commands spoken aloud to their ships. But no one fired.

Over the next few minutes, the Macro ship slowed and drifted close to our line. I noticed something then. The Macro was close to *my* ship, which I'd recently configured to show as a greenish bump on the wall. My heart tripped harder. They had come to talk to me. Perhaps, due to my transmission in their language, they believed I could understand them. Suddenly, my mouth was very dry.

The Macro was one of the new ships, the type I had come to think of as a cruiser. One thing was certain: it was not an invasion ship. It floated out there, in the same void I did, only a few thousand miles away. I knew it had to have its weapons trained upon my tiny vessel. The feeling was unnerving. A heartless machine eyed me, deciding whether or not my destruction was warranted.

Crow contacted me again when the situation appeared stable. "Riggs, can you stay bloody well out of this?"

"No sir, I don't think I can. The ship has halted right in front of me. It obviously wants to talk to me."

"Because you went and transmitted to it without authorization!"

"Yes, sir. If you come up with anything intelligent to say, relay it to the Alamo."

Crow disconnected with an expletive.

I sat there for another hour, thinking about it. The ship transmitted a short message in periodic pulses to me. I had the *Alamo* break it down into binary and I typed it into a file on my tabletop computer. I stared at it. The pattern was definitely binary. They probably didn't use the same number of digits we did, and certainly our symbols would mean nothing to them. Even if I could translate their message into human phonetic letters, how would I know what the words meant? Assuming they were words at all?

"Alamo, have you picked out anything intelligible from the mass of stuff they are sending? Give me estimates that are even ten percent or more likely to be accurate. You don't have to be certain."

"It is a short, repetitive transmission. High probability that it is a command form statement."

"Could it be the command is to surrender?" I asked.

"Unknown meaning. No frame of reference provided."

"Can we respond yes or no, at least?"

Hesitation. "We can attempt a positive or negative response. There exists a chance of error, however."

I thought about it. By now, I was sweating. I wanted one of the beers in the fridge, but I got out a highly caffeinated drink instead. I needed to think. I studied the binary transmission for a long time.

"Enemy energy emissions are changing," said the *Alamo* after the third hour.

"Are their weapons systems charging?" I asked.

"Yes."

249

"Transmit both the signals for yes and no. Right now."

The ship was quiet for several seconds. I had just told them *yes-no*. I hoped that would be interpreted as a *maybe*. Hopefully, that would buy us more time to figure out how to talk to them.

"Enemy energy emissions dampening."

I breathed a sigh of relief. "Alamo, you've had hours of processing time now. You know the enemy are probably transmitting a demand for our surrender. You know how to say yes and no in their language. Can you translate their message? Give it to me, I don't care if there are errors. Give me your best guesses."

"Transmission has high probability of error."

"Just do it."

"Message translation: *Immediate defensive reduction suggested. No further loss required.*"

I typed it in, looking at the binary. Where had the Nanos gotten that one? I began to suspect they knew more than they were letting on. The message was confused, but they must have had something to work from.

"What language did you use as a basis for translation?" I asked aloud.

"Ancient transmissions from lost civilizations. The language used was the closest match, but error is highly probable."

I rolled my eyes at the ship's fear of errors and probabilities. It was better than nothing. Much better. "Alamo, when you transmit my messages to the Macros, I want you to transmit in the exact language of the lost civilization. Do not attempt to upgrade the transmission to match their current version. You will use the old language."

"Ready."

I hesitated. I wasn't sure my hunch was right. How could I be? But I hoped that the Macro language was a newer version of an old language that the *Alamo* knew. If I transmitted in the old version, there was a reasonable chance they could understand it. If there was some degree of backward-compatibility—the kind of thing we often built into our human computer systems—they should be able to understand the old language. There were a lot of "ifs" in this series of suppositions, but it was the best I had.

And what could it hurt to test my theories? At the very least it might keep this cruiser from blasting me for another few minutes.

"Message to transmit as follows: Do you understand this transmission? Please answer yes three times in this language if you do."

"There is no translation of the *please* concept."

I wasn't surprised. "Okay then, omit that word from the transmission."

The response came back in seconds. "Incoming Message: *Yes, yes, yes,*" said the ship. I smiled. I had cracked the code.

What was my next move? Should I keep talking, or hand it all over to Crow and whoever was pulling his strings these days?

I sucked in air and froze, staring at the screens. This situation was getting bigger by the moment. Crow would want in on this. So would the people on the planet below me. They would all want in on it, right on up to the president and a dozen other presidents. But there wasn't time for all that. This wasn't a committee negotiation effort. The enemy was unbeatable and impatient. I believed they had been about to fire on me for taking too long just minutes ago. To be fair, the governments of Earth had every right to be involved in this discussion. But they weren't up here sitting face-to-face with a Macro ship that was itching to blow them apart.

"Incoming message," said the ship.

I sighed. Crow again, no doubt. "Let's hear it."

A bunch of beeping and squealing bounced off the walls. It was the Macros. "Alamo, is that the old Macro language? The same as the one you sent to them?"

"Frequency variations make it non-identical. Signal terminators match. Concepts are intelligibly structured."

"Then translate it, assuming it is in the old language."

"Incoming Message: *Identify yourself.*"

I smiled. I'd done it. Despite the worst interface in the world, I'd gotten this Nano ship to do what I wanted, again. "Contact Crow. Relay this conversation feed to him. Then tell the Macros this: I am Colonel Kyle Riggs of Star Force."

"Incoming Message: *You are the leader of the indigenous resistance forces.*"

"Was that a question or a statement, Alamo?"

"A statement."

"How did you figure it out, Kyle?" asked Crow, breaking in. He sounded incredulous.

251

"Never mind that. I've got them talking. What the hell do we do now?"

"What do they want?"

"I'll ask them. But shouldn't we get Earth into this?" I asked.

"No. It's my policy that if something is above the surface of the planet, it's Star Force business."

"And I thought *I* had serious balls."

"You do, Kyle, you really do."

"Do you want to talk to them directly?" I asked.

He paused. "No, you keep talking to them. You are very smooth with computers, mate. They like you. Get them to go away peacefully if you can…but don't give away Australia."

"I wouldn't dream of it."

"Incoming Message: *You are the leader of the indigenous resistance forces.*"

"Tell them yes. Yes, I'm speaking for this world," I said.

As I spoke those words, they sounded extremely crazy to me. How had it come down to this?

How had I gotten myself into this position?

-40-

"Send them this: What do you want from us?" I told the ship.

"Incoming Message: *Peaceful capitulation with non-damage to our fleet.*"

I snorted. Didn't everyone want that? To win the war without a fight?

"Tell them we wish to end this conflict peacefully as well."

"Incoming Message: *Surrender terms accepted.*"

"Whoa!" I said. "Tell them we have not agreed to surrender. We have agreed to a truce."

"Incoming Message: *Terms unacceptable.*"

I thought about what they had said so far. They were hesitating for a reason. The only thing I could think of was the size of their fleet. Before, they'd thrown a ship or three at us. We'd beaten them every time. Now, however, they faced us with a big fleet. That meant they had a higher chance of destroying us. But it also meant that they would take a much bigger loss if we somehow managed to defeat them a third time. I tried to think like a computer. They were not emotional. They did not have self-confidence, they had probabilities. They did not have complete data about us. They had miscalculated more than once. Now, they were uncertain. From their point of view, I expected that the risk-reward ratio limit had been exceeded. Attacking us wasn't quite worth the chance that we might destroy their big fleet.

The line they had sent me—about wanting our capitulation without damaging their ships—that was very telling, really. They were simple in their diplomatic thinking. They gave away the truth immediately. I thought hard. If they feared a possible repeated miscalculation, another loss on their part, they could be bargained with. I could use that fear against them.

"Tell them we will cost them a great deal of loss if they attack. We have beaten them twice in space and once on the ground. We are stronger now than before. We want a truce."

"Incoming Message: *Terms unacceptable.*"

I frowned. "What could we give you to make the terms acceptable?"

"Incoming Message: *Your star system and its resources.*"

"And if we refuse?"

"Incoming Message: *Your species will be removed.*"

A chilling message. What made it worse was that I believed, in my bones, they could do it. I thought hard. What did we have that might interest them— even more than our raw resources?

"We could become your allies."

"Incoming Message: *Your military is too weak to warrant such status.*"

I nodded to myself. At least they understood the concept of an alliance. Perhaps they had other allied peoples. I decided to work that angle, to talk us up a bit.

"We destroyed Macro ground forces. Our ground forces proved superior to yours."

There was no immediate response to that. Seconds stretched out into a full minute. I began to believe that I had blown it. I'd insulted them one too many times, and they had had enough. I felt sweat bead up all over me. I thought of a dozen nice things to say, but I held back. They hadn't fired yet.

"Incoming Message: *Terms acceptable.*"

I looked around at the walls. *What terms?* I thought about what I had said, my boastful words. What terms had I given them? Had I, in fact, accidentally given them the deed to Australia?

"You will withdraw your fleet?" I asked cautiously.

"Incoming Message: *Yes.*"

"What will you require in return?"

"Incoming Message: *Two to the sixteenth power metric tons of cargo.*"

I licked my lips and breathed hard. Cargo. A huge amount of cargo. I did some mental calculations…they wanted about sixty-five thousand tons of cargo. I certainly hoped they want didn't tons of diamonds. I

254

was tempted to let it go at that, to figure as long as they turned around and left, I had pulled it off. But exactly what did they want and when?

"Specify the nature of the cargo."

"Incoming Message: *You will fill one ship.*"

I nodded. Okay, one of their ships held that much cargo. I could easily see that. One of those invasion ships certainly could hold that much, probably a lot more....

Then, I got a horrible idea in my head. "You want us to fill one cargo ship with ground forces, is that correct?"

"Incoming Message: *Yes.*"

I had it. I understood now. I had bragged about our ground forces. My boasting had been effective. I'd identified something they wanted. Superior invasion forces. It made more and more sense as I thought about it. Why fight for our world if they could get a superior final product out of us than they could build themselves and lose nothing in the process? We had one thing they wanted. They wanted my marines.

They wanted Star Force troops.

I felt a little sick. I tried to think of something else to offer them. But I couldn't think of anything else they might want. They weren't interested in food, oil, metals, video games, or televisions. They wanted troops. Thousands of tons of them.

"We don't have that amount of troops ready at this time. We will require—ten solar years to produce them."

"Incoming Message: *Terms unacceptable. We will send a ship one solar year from now.*"

I swallowed hard. "How long will these forces have to serve?"

"Incoming Message: *Until their termination.*"

"No, that won't work well for us. We are biotics. We need repairs and replacements. Bring the forces back within one year and we will provide you with a new, full-strength army."

There was a delay. They were thinking it over.

"Incoming Message: *Terms acceptable.*"

"Very well then. Earth accepts your terms. We will provide the forces as your ally in war."

"Incoming Message: *Session terminated.*"

And they pulled out after that. Without another word. They turned their ships around and glided away from Earth. They headed sunward, back toward Venus. I had to wonder if they were headed next to another world like ours to destroy or bully them.

255

I got a dozen calls after that from various people. The word was spreading. I had somehow turned away doomsday. I had faced the greatest enemy in our planet's history, and I'd sent them packing.

Sandra called me. Crow called me. General Kerr called incessantly. Many others followed, but I ignored all the calls.

I didn't really feel like a hero. I had negotiated a peace with the machines. But the price would be high. Thousands of our best would be taken away to an unknown world to fight an unknown enemy. Their masters would be heartless, towering machines. Our men would be mercenaries, sold to keep the peace.

We were vassals to the Macros now, I realized. We were no longer truly free and independent. Like a lord given stewardship of a fief, I was to produce fighting men, in turn, for my overlord. They would fight and die to prevent a worse war at home. I had no doubt we would be conquering other species on other planets in order to avoid harm to ourselves. I recalled from history that the Mongols had formed their Golden Horde in just such a fashion, gathering survivors from conquests and driving them at the walls of the next enemy.

The calls kept coming in, but I still didn't answer them. I wasn't sure what to say. How was I going to explain to them the terms of this deal? I had no doubt they would come to accept it, eventually. They had no choice. We could build a great fleet to fight the Macros, but that would take far longer than a year. Our truce—our tribute—would buy us that time.

There was one thing I knew for certain. I was going to march aboard that invasion ship when it came back in a year to pick up our legion of soldiers. I would march aboard first, making a brave front of it, stepping onto an alien ship bound for an unknown star system fearlessly. I would do it because I could not ask Earth to give up her sons and then refuse to lead them myself.

The *Alamo* continued to request my permission to open channels. I continued to ignore her. I pondered the strange manner in which waging war had become my way of life.

I stretched in my chair and popped open the beer I had denied myself hours earlier. I drank it, and it tasted salty, fizzy, and good.

The End

Books by B. V. Larson:

STAR FORCE SERIES
Swarm
Extinction
Rebellion

IMPERIUM SERIES
Mech
Mech 2

HAVEN SERIES
Amber Magic
Sky Magic
Shadow Magic
Dragon Magic
Blood Magic
Death Magic

Other Books by B. V. Larson
Velocity
Shifting

Visit BVLarson.com for more information.

Made in the USA
Lexington, KY
05 April 2012